# Shadows On A Mirror

# Shadows On A Mirror

## ...A Soul To Keep

Edward A. Molnar

Writer's Showcase
presented by *Writer's Digest*
San Jose  New York  Lincoln  Shanghai

Shadows On A Mirror
…A Soul To Keep



Writer's Showcase
presented by *Writer's Digest*
an imprint of iUniverse.com, Inc.

For information address:
iUniverse.com, Inc.
5220 S 16th, Ste. 200
Lincoln, NE 68512
www.iuniverse.com

This is a work of fiction. All the characters and events portrayed in this book
are either products of the author's imagination or are used fictitiously.

ISBN: 0-595-15229-5

For Amanda and Cynthia, my daughters.

Also, special thanks to Mark Flanigan for his sage editorial advice.

# Epigraph

*"In the beginning God created the heaven and the earth…And the Lord God formed man of the dust of the ground, and breathed into his nostrils the breath of life; and man became a living soul…And the Lord God commanded the man, saying, Of every tree of the garden thou mayest freely eat; but of the tree of the knowledge of good and evil, thou shalt not eat of it; for in the day that thou eatest thereof thou shalt surely die."*

*—From the Book of Genesis, The Bible*

# Author's Note

Everyone able to ponder the universe and his existence within it has at one time or another asked the question: *What does it all mean?* The best answer—maybe the only answer (save for *absolutely nothing*)—is that there is some great fabric of which we are all part, a fabric extending across time, from past to future, extending perhaps into other dimensions and beyond the universe we know. The answer is easier to understand and to believe if we also assume that some master craftsman, God if you will, fashioned the fabric. Better still if the craftsman continues to exist and monitors his fabric and, in a benevolent manner, our small involvement within it.

As we become more advanced scientifically, more sophisticated in our knowledge of the universe around us, we also glean more—albeit a very small and probably limited part—of the grand fabric and its design. Of course for us to be us and for God to be God, we could never *fully* know the fabric, and certainly we could never alter it. We could explore the fabric, we could change ourselves and other things *within* it, but we ought not be able to change the fabric itself.

But what if we did? What if, in our sophistication and in our scientific advances, we were to discover—we *did* discover—how to alter the fabric, or even worse, how to destroy the fabric? What would *that* mean?

That question is core to the story that follows, as it should be to every person who believes in God or hopes for an afterlife. Most of the story is fiction, although an intriguing, alarming part is not. The characters are fictional, and the story is set in large part at the National Laboratory in Los Alamos, New Mexico, and at nearby Black Mesa on the San Ildefonsan reservation. Both are real, but the events of this book—as they relate to those places as well as to the American Indians dwelling there now and in the past—are entirely fiction.

# Prologue, Part 1

## Prelude to a Massacre

*Northern New Mexico, near Santa Fe, is a land of intrigue, a land indelibly etched by more than a thousand years of Indian civilization, most of it undocumented. Yet if someone had put that rich history to paper, a single place or a single event would fill but one page of one chapter of a book rife with chapters.*

*But there was an event and there was a place—like the well-thumbed, dog-eared page the book always falls open to when you drop it—that stood out in the stories and the folklore passed across generations by word of mouth. The place was Black Mesa and the event, known as the Black Mesa Massacre, was the last in a series of battles fought between two fiercely competitive Indian tribes, the Hachonee and the Nopeka.*

*Like two rivers born of one source, the Hachonee and Nopeka had the same ancestors, a loosely knit band of nomads called the Pada'ho. The Hachonee retained their nomadic ways, roaming what is today northern New Mexico and southern Colorado. The Nopeka settled in the valley of one of the largest calderas in North America, just a few miles away from what is now Los Alamos. There they farmed the fertile land and hunted the canyons and forests nearby.*

*Despite their differences, the Nopeka and Hachonee retained, for the most part, a common language and a common culture. They ate the same foods, worshipped the same gods, and each believed a man's success or failure in life—synonymous with the destiny of his soul—was determined by two factors time-honored and beyond question or challenge: honor and courage.*

*For many years the two tribes engaged in minor territorial skirmishes, the Hachonee usually the aggressors, but neither side did any real damage to the other—until the Nopeka killed Kiakiali Ahona.*

# Chapter 1

*The full moon and the scrub trees and brush combined to form eerie shadows on top of Black Mesa. The night air was cool and still, and the sound of coyotes howling far away carried easily to the mesa top, but no one was there to hear it. Out of the stillness and among the shadows, eddies of dust formed, and soon long-dead pine needles began to swirl…but it wasn't the wind.*

*    *    *

Alex Feher swatted at something tickling his cheek, then rolled over in his sleep. Morning light, pink on Virginia's Blue Ridge horizon, fought its way through the forest of pines, tall and dense, to Alex's sleeping bag. Reinforcements followed until light and shadows danced gaily on his face like tiny butterflies, black and white. He opened his eyes, bedroom eyes he'd been told, and the other senses followed. Birds chirped in staccato high above, and as he lifted his head, he caught the pungent, bittersweet scent of new pine needles. Only coffee would smell better.

He started a fire, then made his coffee and drank it hot and black, washing down a breakfast of peanut butter granola bars. He packed his gear, tossed it over his shoulder, and started hiking due west. Parked about a mile away, where the road ended and the trail began, was Alex's car, a 1964 Mercedes SL190, maroon and in mint condition, a machine that he loved and pampered like a faithful dog.

He'd needed this break from classes, the way a desert cactus needs rain—not too often but when it does rain, feeling as if it arrived just in time. The school year had finally dragged itself into March, yet in Alex's state of mind the end was still an eternity away. With the end, after he'd graded his last final exam, he'd head for Los Alamos. But he couldn't look forward to Los Alamos—he couldn't look forward to anything. It would probably take Los Alamos to break him of his melancholy.

*　　　　　*　　　　　*

The ravages of death had enveloped Alex like a chilling fog, the kind that dulls the senses, making you feel as if you're somewhere on the outside, watching your own life as it plods along in slow motion.

First his mother. Heart attack. At sixty-five not totally unexpected. But not expected either, not for someone so active and energetic, someone who took so much pride in her weight and fitness. But these things happen, the doctor said.

Bela Feher, Alex's father, held up well enough. But Alex didn't share the devout religious beliefs that sustained his parents, especially as they grew older, and for the first time in his life he had to deal with the death of someone close. He found the administrative details—the arrangements, the funeral, the will—painful and arduous enough to handle, but even tougher were the *big* questions, the hows and the whys. He was having trouble with the answers.

Margaret Feher, Alex's sister, seemed to have an easier time accepting their mother's death. Maybe daughters grieve differently, he thought. Mother-daughter ties are not the same as mother-son. And at twenty-five, she was eight years younger than Alex. He was established in his university career, had already faced many of the ups and downs life had to offer, while her career, her independent adult life, was just beginning.

Maybe she didn't understand everything. Maybe her emotions were only bottled up and ripe for bursting some later time.

They talked for hours before the funeral and even longer after it was over. For the first time Alex truly saw his little sister as an adult. Also, much to Margaret's credit, the positive outlook his mother long ago instilled in him returned.

"Look, Alex," Margaret had said standing on tiptoe to look him squarely in the eyes, "you've got to get over this. You may be older than me, but I knew Mom as well as you did, and instead of grieving, she'd want you to celebrate the life she had—and the life she's given us."

"O.K., Maggie, I agree, life can be great. But I'd also like to be sure there's some reason we're here. What bothers me is thinking that life can end without meaning. What if we live, then we die, and that's it?"

"What kind of meaning do you want? Mom gave us life. Isn't that meaning enough? Someday we'll have kids and do the same for them, and then they'll do it for their kids. And if we never have kids, we'll do it some other way.

"You're a math professor, you're highly regarded by your peers. But even more important you're a teacher. You impact the lives of hundreds of young people each year. And in another year I'll be a full-fledged veterinarian, making the world a better place for beasts of all kinds—and their pets—so I just can't buy your 'where's the meaning' crap."

"Look at it this way, Sis. If we put the earth's entire history onto a calendar, mankind's part of it wouldn't appear until sometime late on December 31st. Doesn't that suggest to you that our lives may have no meaning in the bigger picture, that maybe we're just specks of cosmic dust that come and go?"

"Well, oh highly educated one, what about afterlife? Mom believed in it. And she didn't fear death. Death was a part of life, the part that lets you transition into the eternal afterlife. And eternal is forever, so we *are* part of the bigger picture."

"My soul to keep, forever and ever. Is that it?"

"Sure. Don't you believe in an afterlife, in a soul?"

"I'd like to."

"Don't you believe in God?"

"Again I'd like to, but you know me. I need a little hard evidence."

"All I can say, big brother, is look around you."

She was getting testy and her eyes, large and brown like Alex's, were beginning to well up with tears. Alex smiled resignedly and put his arm around her. "All right, Mags, you win. And for your information, I do believe in God, maybe even an afterlife. But you surprise me. You were pretty liberal in college. I took you for an agnostic."

She pushed him playfully away and with a sexy wink said, "There's a lot you don't know about me, bro."

Two weeks later on a rainy evening, Margaret was dead. A life so full of vitality, so full of promise, had been brutally extinguished by a reckless driver. Now the questions were bigger, harder, more painful, and this time there was no sister to help Alex confront them.

*        *        *

Alex stuffed his camping gear into the small trunk, slammed it shut with a solid, muffled thud, and set out for one more walk. An hour later, mostly uphill, he reached a boulder of smoky white quartz as large as his desk back in the math department at Virginia Tech. A good place to sit for a while. Using his arms for leverage, he hopped backwards up and onto the rock. He gauged the time by the sun, decided he could rest for about five minutes—then he'd head back to the Mercedes.

Before he lost himself in hazy thought he had the feeling, an eerie deja vu feeling, that what was happening had happened to him before. Even more eerie, sending a mild shiver through his numbing body, was the certain knowledge that it would happen to him again. Then his mind drifted away, too easily away, as if the gravity from some massive star, too distant to see, were pulling it.

Suddenly, inexplicably, all his senses came alert. He straightened and stiffened like a hunting dog onto its quarry. He listened first, then looked all around. Nothing at all. Strange, very strange.

A horrifying scream pierced the silence. Alex's hair stood on end. The scream abruptly died, and he jumped off the rock running. The scream had been at least a half-mile away.

Three minutes later Alex reached a jagged cliff, and there in the ravine far below lay the bloody and misshapen body of a boy. The cliff must have given way, leading to a sheer drop of some thirty feet, then a tumble the rest of the way down the rocky mountainside. Alex quickly worked his way down the steep slope. The boy, about thirteen years old, wasn't breathing.

"Shit," Alex said aloud. A badly broken, lifeless body in the middle of nowhere. No one else in sight. Hopeless was the word trying to work its way into his psyche, but he wouldn't let it.

Buoyed by a lifelong credo taught him by his mother—"there's got to be a way"—Alex methodically set to work. He performed CPR and brought the boy back to life. He stopped what bleeding he could, then he made rough splints out of tree limbs for the more seriously broken bones. Finally Alex carried the boy up the ravine and across rugged terrain to the Mercedes. He delicately fitted the injured youngster into the passenger seat. The nearest hospital was fifteen miles away over winding mountain roads. Alex reached it in twenty minutes, holding the boy in place at every turn.

Surgery lasted nine hours. Finally the doctors emerged, declaring the boy would survive. His parents, weekend campers like Alex, had arrived mid-surgery. They proclaimed Alex a hero, as did hospital officials and the sheriff. But Alex gave the credit to his Mercedes for the way it handled at breakneck speeds. His part, he said, was just to do what anybody would have done.

A reporter asked him, as a mathematics professor, how he'd analyzed the situation on the mountain. Alex said he hadn't. He just acted, never giving up hope and refusing to acknowledge the futility that logical analysis might have suggested. What he didn't tell the reporter, because he didn't understand it, was how he knew something was going to happen before it happened.

*     *     *

Alex labored but still took the steps two at a time up to the front door of his townhouse, just a few minutes walking distance from the Virginia Tech campus. Inside he bent to pick up the mail dropped by the mailman through the brass slot in the front door and now scattered on the speckled throw rug that served as a welcome mat. His back ached, scolding him for all the carrying he had done. But at thirty-three he was still in top shape, a lean and muscular 180 pounds on a six-foot-two frame, because he worked to stay that way.

It was two-thirty in the morning, but he wasn't sleepy. He switched on the floor lamp that stood next to his favorite chair, an old blue recliner, and flopped down. Alex raised the recliner's footrest to its highest position and stretched out his legs. He sorted the mail by tossing it onto the floor, bills to his right and junk mail to his left. A single letter remained, the one he'd been expecting from the lab at Los Alamos. He tore it open and tossed the envelope to his left.

"Dear Professor Feher," the letter began, although "Professor Feher" had been lined through and "Alex" penned in above. "Once again I would like to invite your participation in our Summer Program for University Professors, now in its eighteenth year." It was standard form letter and Alex quickly skimmed through the next couple of paragraphs: "...minimum of eight weeks...salary of...travel reimbursement...." Then the personalized paragraph: "You can again expect to be assigned to Strategic Defense Systems," which meant he'd be working on the design of ballistic missile defense systems, part of the Strategic Defense Initiative, more popularly known as "Star Wars." The letter continued, "Amanda and I look forward to seeing you again…. I have spoken with the Andrews…you may occupy their house under the usual arrangement…." Then the form letter resumed, "Please let me know by April 15 of your intentions," and it was signed, "Sincerely, John A. Canaday, Director, Strategic Defense Systems."

The Los Alamos National Laboratory's "Summer Program for University Professors" was supposed to be a way of exchanging knowledge and better acquainting academic institutions with the laboratory's work—at least that's how they advertised it, but Alex knew its real purpose was to attract potential staff to a location regarded by many as remote and isolated. He enjoyed the change of pace, still easy but one gear faster than Virginia Tech and Blacksburg, and the change of scenery, from the lush green of the Blue Ridge Mountains to the sandy, scrub-covered mesas and canyons of northern New Mexico. He liked doing scientific research, and the salary was twice what he could earn by teaching the summer session. He even enjoyed the long drive to New Mexico, grueling torture to some, but for Alex a time for thought and introspection, and it became an annual trek.

And the lab was glad to have him, even just for the summer. He knew he was highly thought of, and he chuckled as he recalled his first summer there. His boss, John Canaday, had given him as busywork a problem thought to be unsolvable, a paradox of sorts, and Alex knew it. But Alex stubbornly refused to give in to impossibility. He searched for higher dimensional settings where a physical paradox in three dimensions might make sense, found it, solved the problem there, then "exported" the solution back to three dimensions. After spending three weeks getting only four hours of sleep at night because he wanted to work on the problem away from the lab and without John knowing it, he nonchalantly delivered his solution, as if the problem had been easy.

John persuaded the lab to offer Alex a permanent job, but Alex said solving the problem had been mostly luck, and no thank you to the job offer, at least not right now.

✻          ✻          ✻

Unbeknownst to Alex, the same day he received his Los Alamos invitation New Mexico papers carried the following story under the headline "Lab Physicist Stricken."

*"Samuel T. Perkins, a physicist at The Los Alamos National Laboratory, died suddenly there early yesterday. According to medical authorities, Mr. Perkins, 37, appears to have suffered a heart attack, although his wife told reporters he recently had a physical exam and had been told he was in excellent health."*

Exactly one week later Alex sent his letter of acceptance back to John Canaday, and the New Mexico newspapers reported "Another Mysterious Lab Death." This time it was a 42-year-old chemist named Francisco Garza who worked—and died—in the same building as Samuel Perkins.

*"Officials said they were uncertain of the cause of death, but once again heart attack was suspected. Like Mr. Perkins, Mr. Garza was reported to be in excellent health."*

Reports this time were more widespread, as most major newspapers and a few television stations in the West reported the second, "coincidental" lab death among their regional items. But no paper or TV station east of the Mississippi carried the story, so once again Alex, in Virginia, did not learn of it.

# Prologue, Part 2

## Kiakiali Ahona Meets Death

*Kiakiali Ahona was Supreme Chief of the Hachonee tribe. The night before he was going to die, Death paid the venerable Indian a visit. Kiakiali Ahona knew Death, for Death had been his ally on the battlefield for many years. Even so, in the morning he would remember the episode as a dream.*

*"My old friend," Death said to him, "we have seen many battles together. You have been a worthy warrior."*

*Proud man that he was, Kiakiali Ahona swelled his chest and jutted out his chin, squinting down his nose at Death. "I did not become Supreme Chief by slaying women and children."*

*"No, you did not."*

*Kiakiali Ahona closed his eyes and nodded once, sternly.*

*"Tell me, old friend," Death said in a voice so gentle as to belie the enormity of his power, "are you afraid of me?"*

*"No," Kiakiali Ahona answered honestly.*

*"Are you afraid for me?"*

*This puzzled the sage old chief. "No," he replied, uneasy with the question.*

*"You should be. Are you afraid for yourself?"*

*"No,"* he said, his mind still struggling with the meaning of the earlier question.

*"You need not be. But fear for your tribe, for they lack your wisdom."*

# Chapter 2

In Los Alamos, Dr. Albert Chen, director of the national laboratory, was as baffled by the deaths as anyone. The autopsies revealed nothing—no cause of death, no reason for dying. The only certainty was a mysterious connection to a new radioactive material. Each worker had been exposed to it.

Chen himself named the material, coining it "G-matter" during one of the early post-mortem meetings. (He had stumbled trying to recall its alphanumeric identification code, which began with the letter "G.") So little was known about G-matter, that despite Chen's request for help from his staff, no better or more descriptive name was offered. Besides, they said, since the substance had a greenish glow, like plutonium in one of its allotropic states, "G" was doubly apt.

The first scientist to die, Samuel Perkins, had been part of an ad hoc team formed by Chen three years earlier. The mission of the team, working part-time since each member already had some other primary project, was to create new fissile materials. They experimented with combinations of atomic particles and plasma-like substances, but had little to show for their effort.

G-matter had been formed early in the project, but the researchers almost immediately discarded it. Although G-matter was highly radioactive, it was not fissile. But the more likely reason for dismissing it was that G-matter had been created very much by accident, a by-product of the experiment, and as such was something of an embarrassment to the team of crack scientists.

But after more than two years, G-matter was the only significant product of hundreds of experiments, so the researchers decided to take another look at what they had created. Dr. Perkins, who had oversight of the subgroup responsible for G-matter and whom the others jokingly had called the "father of whatever it is," took charge of the re-examination. In his effort to speed up the process, Perkins accidentally, carelessly exposed himself to its radioactive rays. He died instantly.

After the second careless exposure and second sudden death without explanation, Dr. Chen had no choice but to suspend all testing on G-matter.

Following the discovery of what seemed to be a super-deadly material, a power struggle ensued for its control. National security became an issue, the White House intervened, and Chen's hands were tied.

Control of the G-matter project was awarded to the military—specifically to one Colonel Billy Hollis the Third.

*         *         *

Colonel Billy Hollis was the archetypal career Army officer. Born and raised in South Carolina, he was the son of a wealthy tobacco farmer and the great-grandson of a local Civil War hero. His home setting was old-style Southern plantation, conservative and disciplined. He was calling his father "sir" soon after he learned to say "daddy," and at age four, with the help of his father, he fired his first rifle. He tried to get into West Point but never made it, so he settled instead for one of the traditional military schools of the Old South.

A highly decorated veteran of Grenada, Desert Storm, and Bosnia, Hollis had entered the Army as an infantry officer. His specialty in combat, however, was demolition and explosives, and after Bosnia he migrated to ordnance research and development. Although Viet Nam was before his time, he insisted that there was only one lesson to be learned from that debacle, and he was never at a loss to explain it to others: "We should have bombed the hell out of them." And while matters of that sort were for policy makers to decide and the Air Force to implement, he was going to do his part by helping the Army build better bombs, which for him meant tactical nuclear weapons.

Hollis had had a long association with the laboratory at Los Alamos, and, being in a position to provide the lab with large contracts to conduct experimental nuclear weapons testing for the Department of Defense, he was a favorite there. He had the run of the facilities, and even before the G-matter project, he was given office space to accommodate his frequent visits.

But Hollis's career was at a make-or-break point. Pentagon brass had already passed him over once for Brigadier General. Chances of being selected were diminishing with time, unless, of course, he could do something monumental and highly visible. G-matter was the ideal opportunity, and he fully expected that the new radioactive material would be his ticket to wearing stars.

Hollis quickly took charge, seizing total control. He confiscated all G-matter notes and materials and personally handpicked his team. Testing then began on what he considered to be a new weapon, his weapon, and he wasn't going to let anything—or anybody—get in his way.

# Prologue, Part 3

# Nopeka Action

*The Nopeka had tired of the Hachonee raids, and the tribe's council of leaders decided on action. Their plan was simple: strike a blow so demoralizing it would force an end to the warring. The Nopeka waited for one of the predictable Hachonee raids, and in a carefully planned ambush, they killed Kiakiali Ahona.*

# Chapter 3

For four days the specter of death competed with the memories of his mother and sister to ride shotgun with Alex Feher from Blacksburg, Virginia, to eastern New Mexico. Alex thought of nothing else. But when the green sign after Tucumcari boldly announced "SANTA FE — 120 MILES," he knew it was time to focus on the future. He said silent farewells to Margaret and to his mother, and then he opened his window to catch the late spring air, downshifted into third, and accelerated until the Mercedes whined its displeasure. He shifted into fourth and when the Mercedes hit one hundred, he shouted aloud to no one in particular, "Enough! Get the hell out of my car!" And with that done, he allowed the car to settle into a comfortable seventy, and headed alone toward Santa Fe.

*       *       *

Los Alamos is located about twenty-five miles from Santa Fe, as the crow flies, just to the west of northwest. You can speed out of Santa Fe, north, along Interstate 285, but you'll slow to glance at Camel Rock, sitting stoically with head erect on your left. You continue on, past the Nambe Indian Reservation where fine pewter-like serving ware is made, then halfway to Los Alamos you leave the Interstate.

The Sangre de Christo (Blood of Christ) Mountains watch from behind as you turn west onto Route 4, and almost immediately you spy Black Mesa sitting by itself, off to the right. The Pojoaque River meanders along the right side of the road as you and it approach, then reach the Rio Grande. A new concrete bridge in its lackluster manner spans the river, while alongside it the old wooden structure, closed off at both ends, preserves the character of a bygone era.

Shortly after crossing the six-to-sixty-foot width of the Rio Grande (depending on the season), the road begins to climb and you continue into Los Alamos along and high above Los Alamos Canyon. The entire drive is about thirty-five miles, which means about forty-five minutes, and singularly the most prominent feature is Black Mesa, which is within sight of you (and you within sight of it), for each of the last eighteen miles.

✳　　　　　✳　　　　　✳

Ten minutes to Los Alamos. Alex's Mercedes, the blood-red hue dampened by darkness, sailed surreptitiously through the New Mexico night and past Black Mesa. The cool mountain air, thinned by elevation, seemed to grip the car and hold it on course, as if ten thousand ghosts lined the narrow mountain highway. Stars looked down like eyes in the nighttime sky, and whatever had been on Alex's weary mind was swept away by a feeling that this countryside, unblemished by modern man, was hiding something. But an aura of mystery was the norm here, for this was Indian country.

Alex downshifted to keep up his speed on the curving, climbing road. The Mercedes responded with a leap, then "Bang!" it backfired loudly. "Damn," he thought, "Carb needs adjusting." He pushed a freckled left hand through his mop of fine light brown hair, then replaced it lightly on the steering wheel. He pursed his lips and crinkled deep-set brown eyes. The car backfired again and this time he said out loud, "Double damn—gonna wake the dead!"

He passed the old guard tower and Los Alamos proper loomed ahead. He could see the lights now—what lights there were at eleven o'clock at night—and the fork in the road that would take him either left to the lab, or right and into the one-street business district. The quickest way to his house, the one he rented each summer, was the road to the right but, for no particular reason, he went left.

"Well, not everybody's asleep," he thought. A bicycle headed toward him, its dim headlight swaying left and right with the slow but steady pedaling of the rider. And a car was coming up fast behind the bicycle— much too fast, and it wasn't giving any room.

The driver blared his horn as he reached the bicycle rider, who swerved in panic to the right. The bicycle hit the curb and the rider flew over the handlebars, somersaulting to land on his back in a patch of weeds.

The attacking car finally veered. Its headlights, like two cannons searching for a target, swept left until they pointed directly at Alex. He reacted purely by instinct, steering the Mercedes sharply right. The car narrowly missed, roared past him, a black Chevy sedan with white government markings on the side. Its two occupants, the driver and a passenger seated erectly in the back seat, seemed unaffected by the incident. Both wore military uniforms—either Army or Air Force, Alex guessed—and they wore the same hats, but on heads quite different. The head in the front was young, oval, and full, while the one in the rear was older and gaunt, like skin stretched over a skull.

Alex straightened his car, then deftly backed it to where the bicycle and bicycle rider lay. The rider, who looked to be about twenty, sprang up and began to dust himself off.

Alex leaned out of his window. "Are you all right?"

"Yeah, I guess so. Just mad. Did you see that?"

"Yeah, what a jerk—he nearly hit us both."

"I didn't get much of a look. Did you see who was in the car?"

"Looked like two guys—the driver and an older one in the back, both military."

"Yeah, that's what I thought."

"Who are they?"

"I don't know their names—they work at the lab. But from what I've heard, they'd just as soon run you down than bother to go around."

"Well, you were pretty lucky, landing like you did."

"My old gymnastics training, I guess." He laughed. "If nothing else, we learned how to fall."

"Can I give you a lift somewhere?"

"No, thanks. I live about a block from here. But thanks for stopping."

"Sure, no problem. Take care the rest of the way."

Alex watched the young man mount the bicycle and make his way down the street on bent and wobbly wheels.

"Yessiree, this was one lucky kid," he said as he pulled away, "and whoever they were in the car were two callous sons-of-bitches."

# Prologue, Part 4

# Wiloloaneha

*Kiakiali Ahona's second-in-command, a young, spirited brave named Wiloloaneha, led the fateful raid. He was at the front, far ahead of Kiakiali Ahona. On horseback and using a lance, Wiloloaneha had already killed two Nopeka when he spotted a group of enemy braves on foot, running for cover in the nearby woods. With a bloodcurdling "Yeeahh!" he kicked his horse and charged the Nopeka from behind. The horse did its part, knocking down one brave and trampling him in the dust, and Wiloloaneha took care of another, impaling him through the back with his lance. While the others fled, a single Nopeka brave stayed to face Wiloloaneha. The resignation on his face turned to determination: better to die fighting than to survive by running.*

*Wiloloaneha extracted his lance from the still-writhing body, reined his horse and turned his attention to the remaining Nopeka warrior. Wiloloaneha warily eyed the small, middle-aged man. In his right hand the Nopeka gripped a mace-like club, a macana. He stood crouched with his left hand lightly supporting the upper handle of his weapon, awaiting Wiloloaneha's charge.*

*Wiloloaneha kicked his horse sharply in the ribs, and with another bloodcurdling war cry, he lunged at the defender. The Nopeka brave dodged to his left and parried the lance's blow. With all the power he could summon, he smashed the macana into Wiloloaneha's right shin. The sickening thud was punctuated by the sharp crack of bone.*

*Wiloloaneha let loose a scream as he rose up in pain, jerking the reins hard to the left. The horse turned and reared up sharply, throwing the already unseated Wiloloaneha completely off in the direction of the Nopeka. Wiloloaneha landed on top of the club-wielding warrior.*

*Wiloloaneha grabbed the shirt collar of the sprawled Nopeka brave, and despite excruciating pain in his leg, pulled himself up, using the body of the stunned Nopeka for leverage. Once upright, he pulled a tomahawk from his waistband and with a sharp blow buried it in the head of the other Indian.*

*Hachonee warriors came to the aid of the crippled Wiloloaneha, helping him back onto his horse and escorting him to safety.*

*After the battle was over, as the Hachonee regrouped, Wiloloaneha learned his mentor and friend, Kiakiali Ahona, was dead. The pain in his leg was nothing compared to the pain he felt in his heart. He cried aloud, vowing revenge upon the Nopeka.*

# Chapter 4

In less than five minutes, driving slowly along the familiar route under the starlit sky, gradually accelerating the closer he got, Alex arrived at the comfortable split-level house he would call home for the summer once again. For the past five years Alex had replaced the owners, Henry and Shirley Andrews, laboratory physicists who were senior enough and wealthy enough to spend the summer traveling. In exchange for the dirt-cheap rent, Alex was expected to take care of the house and perform odd chores, like feeding the cats and tending to Henry's vegetable garden struggling to grow at the rear of the small, sandy back yard.

Alex had been driving for twelve straight hours, and his legs and back were cardboard stiff as he eased his way out of the car. He straightened himself as best he could and half-hobbled from the driveway to the front door of the familiar brick house.

The key, as usual and per the brief conversation he'd had with the Andrews the week before, was under the welcome mat. He unlocked the door and, leaving it open, tossed his suitcases toward the living room couch. Next he located a flashlight and what he could scrounge for supper—two slices of bread and a fist-sized chunk of cheddar cheese. Despite the late hour, with flashlight in one hand and bread and cheese in the other, he headed back out the front door, kicking it shut behind him. He made a right at the sidewalk and another right at the street corner. Deer Trap Mesa was dead ahead.

The Andrews' house sat on the second of three long mesas that came together like fingers on a hand. Although the property line went well beyond the garden, a gentle cliff, extending down into Piñon Canyon, jaggedly truncated the back yard. Beyond the narrow Piñon Canyon was the first, or westernmost mesa finger, Deer Trap Mesa, named for a box-shaped hole carved there by Indians centuries ago.

The hole, or deer trap, was cut into the floor of the middle level of the two-tiered mesa, about twelve feet below the mesa top, and at a small gap connecting Piñon Canyon and the larger canyon to the west of Deer Trap Mesa. The deer trap measured roughly four feet wide, six feet long, and five feet deep: large enough for two Indians to wait in ambush. The Andrews had been fascinated by its history, and had eagerly showed it to Alex the first time he took the house.

Back when the hole was carved out of the soft pumice stone, mule deer abounded in northern New Mexico. Sure-footed animals despite an awkward-looking, stiff-legged gait, mule deer could handle the roughest terrain, making them difficult game to kill.

Indian hunting parties used to drive whole herds into Piñon Canyon, toward the closed end. The easiest escape was through the gap in the mesa, but there the animals had to leap over the trap where the hunters lay in wait with bows and arrows—a convoluted form of shooting fish in a barrel.

A nightly walk along Deer Trap Mesa had become part of Alex's routine. After coming home from the lab, after his chores were done and just before the sun began its final descent, Alex would tour the mesa. Beginning at the closed end, along side of the upper mesa tier, he would walk slowly, inhaling the pleasant fragrances of the piñon and juniper trees, until he reached the deer trap. Then, just as ancient Indians had done, using footholds they had carved in the soft volcanic rock, he'd ascend to the top. Flowering yuccas and Apache plumes dotted his route, and he would either walk or jog to the mesa's far end.

With the oversized orange-red sun setting directly to his left against a sky of gunmetal gray, the view was spectacular. Beyond the sheer drop of Deer Trap Mesa to the western plain below, a vast openness stretched in front of him, finally reaching other mesas far in the distance, with Black Mesa squatting prominently and ominously to the right of center. Further to the right he could see the road into Los Alamos, identified by creamy headlights wending their way high above the canyon floor, much higher even than Deer Trap Mesa. Left of the sunset was a fertile valley that reached to the rim of the caldera remaining from the Jemez volcano, which a million years ago formed the nearby mountain ranges. Stars gradually appeared in the sky overhead, and it was the perfect place to ponder the universe. Soft moonlight usually illuminated the walk home.

This year Alex wolfed down his food as he walked quickly to the deer trap. He was about to scale the mesa when a movement in the hole caught his eye. He froze, startled. He peeked down and the movement had stopped. Then he laughed out loud. It was his shadow, cast by the already present moonlight.

Alex knew why he was jittery around the deer trap. He'd seen a ghost there the first time he went to the mesa alone. Two ghosts actually, crouching in the deer trap, but one was clearer than the other—so clear that Alex could see the fear in his eyes as the Indian waited for the overhead stampede to begin. That night he left more affected by the look of fear than by the ghost itself.

Alex chuckled again as he recalled the incident. He finished scaling the mesa and jogged to the end, guided along the way by the moonlight and his flashlight.

There, unchanged from his last visit, sat a couch-like formation of rock, more than a million years old, flat in the middle and jutting up at each end. Alex could sit and admire the view or lie down and watch the stars multiply overhead. Still tired and cramped from the long drive, he stretched his body the length of the rock.

He began what had become a ritual by tensing every muscle in his body while he slowly counted to ten. Then he reversed the process and relaxed the muscles until he felt completely limp and drained of nervous energy.

The usual routine was to peer upward, waiting, searching for the first star. He always made a wish. Since the stars were already out, he chose the one directly overhead. This time he was selfish, thinking it was about time he settled down. He wished he could find someone to make his life complete. Someone like Lisa Martin. Lisa was the kind of memory that wouldn't fade, a haunting recollection from his adolescent past.

Alex closed his eyes. He tried to relax his mind completely and think of nothing at all, but that was impossible. His mind was like a sailing ship with no wind at the sails and no helmsman at the rudder. Adrift with the sea, it was free to island-hop randomly from thought to thought.

It started with his being there, the fact that he was in that place at that time, and from there his thoughts drifted to why he was there and how it had come to be. Somehow that question evolved into trying to decipher the immensity and complexity of the universe.

Then, like the captain grasping that the sea's seemingly haphazard currents were taking his ship on a definite, predetermined course, Alex realized he too was heading somewhere. Coming into focus was an uneasy feeling that there was a purpose to his being there, in Los Alamos, at that particular time. What could it be? What could be special about the summer ahead? Alex Feher, analyst by profession but adventurer at heart, was eager to find out.

He opened his eyes. Black Mesa was directly in front of him in the moonlight. It seemed darker than he remembered—probably more vegetation from an unusually wet spring, he thought. He looked to the heavens again. The stars too seemed different, brighter and closer—must be the thinner air.

Back to Black Mesa: why had he never been there? So near and so distinctive, yet he'd never seen it up close. Maybe there was no road. According to stories it was a sacred place for the local Indians. Was it really? Did that mean he couldn't visit?

It was silly, he knew, but the dark, round mesa seemed to be beckoning, calling him there. He would answer it. He promised himself that if he were allowed, he'd spend a weekend there exploring.

Now he noticed his breathing: slow and easy. He could hear it amid the stillness. It was normal, but in thinking about it, he relaxed more completely, and the more he relaxed, the slower his breathing became. At the point of unconsciousness a tingling sensation invaded his body and triggered it into responding. His breathing returned to normal, but for an instant he had had the odd feeling that he was a part of the mesa, and it was a part of him.

Out of his trance and momentarily refreshed, Alex walked back the same way he had come, descending the mesa at the deer trap. The moon, like a half-open eye, stayed with him, peering over his left shoulder. After reaching the house, he peeled down to his underwear, flopped onto the unopened bed, and quickly fell asleep.

He slept fitfully and dreamt furiously, about Indians and bombs and Lisa and a dozen other seemingly unrelated subjects. They were gone and forgotten when he awoke the next morning.

# Prologue, Part 5

## Turning Point

*The flesh healed quickly for Wiloloaneha, but the bones were never quite right, because he rushed his recovery, spurred by thoughts of hatred and retaliation. He never admitted to the pain, but it was always there and Wiloloaneha walked with a noticeable limp for the rest of his life—a constant reminder to him, a visible sign to others, of what the Nopeka had done.*

*Wiloloaneha's hatred of the Nopeka and his desire for vengeance, for the complete and utter destruction of the Nopeka, spread like a virus through the tribe. Some of the elders questioned the wisdom of letting blind hatred guide their actions, but their objections went unheeded, and the fatal disease took hold.*

*So the slaying of Kiakiali Ahona marked a turning point in the war between the two tribes, but it was not the one for which the Nopeka had hoped. The tone and nature of the fighting changed from territorial skirmishes to a drive by the Hachonee to completely obliterate the Nopeka, evidenced by the frequency and ferocity of their attacks.*

# Chapter 5

Dr. Sandy Jeffers wheeled the gurney swiftly and skillfully through the doorway and into Room 594A of Riverside Memorial Medical Center. There was no danger of the patient falling off the small hospital bed; three two-inch cowhide straps held him tight. And there was little danger of being seen, not at 2:20 in the morning. One or two of Santa Fe's rowdies might show up in the emergency room to have their heads patched, but no one would be up on the fifth floor near the back of the hospital where the walls were plain white and without any cheery posters, Ansel Adams photos, or R. C. Gorman prints.

The room was L-shaped, with the door to the hallway at the foot of the L. Inside, another door, halfway up the L, led to an anteroom that also shared a heavy plate glass window with the larger room. Once used for dental X-rays, the rooms were now nearly empty. On the floor at the top of the larger room was an odd assortment of computer-like equipment, something that appeared to be a CPU with several monitors and printing devices attached to it. Otherwise the room contained only a small Formica table that stood empty by the hallway door, and a wooden crucifix that hung on the wall above the table.

Dr. Jeffers—the name was stenciled in maroon on the right side of his lab coat—pushed the gurney around the corner and back to the far wall, next to the bank of equipment. He carried with him, slung over his left arm and head, a kind of duffel bag, which he now slipped out of and placed on the table by the door.

His white lab coat, yellowed from cheap laundering, hung open, and underneath he was dressed casually in a long-sleeved lightweight flannel shirt, black and gray checkerboard, tucked loosely into brown cotton slacks. He wore Timberland boat shoes without socks. On the left breast of his lab coat, no longer hidden by the duffel bag strap, were the letters "W R A M C," above some kind of crest or logo, both also in maroon but faded lighter than the lettering on the right side.

The patient on the gurney lay motionless, his eyes closed. He looked to be at least seventy years old, with thin white hair and an emaciated face. An IV bag, suspended above the left side of the gurney, provided sustenance. His arms rested on top of the sheet covering his torso, free of the straps. Between his arms, rising and falling with his slow and regular breathing, was a mass of loosely coiled cords, connected to more than a dozen electrodes taped at various spots around his body.

Dr. Jeffers separated the cords, and one-by-one, plugged them into the equipment on the floor. He flicked a switch and the monitors and printers came to life. He re-checked the connections, to make sure they were secure, and he checked the printers, already spitting out their products, to make sure there was enough paper and that it would continue to feed without fouling.

He glanced at the patient, known to him only as #243, then to the monitor with vital signs. They were regular but weak. Patient #243 was dying, life draining away like the last grains of sand in an hourglass. Dr. Jeffers gave him maybe four hours to live, eight tops.

The doctor lifted the patient's right arm and, quite unnecessarily, felt for a pulse. There it was, weak and slow, but still proof of life. Dr. Jeffers looked at his watch and timed the beats….eight, nine—the arm so light and withered, there wouldn't be any strength even if he were awake.

He had to start counting again….five, six—in a while it would be gone—the man would be gone. And only a few people even knew that he was alive, and because #243 was like all the other patients, Dr. Jeffers was probably the only person on the face of the earth who cared that he was alive, and the only one who would care when he died—and Jeffers didn't even know his name.

He laid the arm gently back down onto the bed, placing it like the left one, wrist up and alongside the torso. Patient #243 remained impassive. His hands lay open and seemed to be sending a suppliant message for help, but that was nonsense.

Dr. Jeffers turned his attention to the duffel bag and opened it. He removed a gleaming canister, which he set on the table. The canister was about the size of a football with blunted ends. It rested on a flat bottom and on one side had a seam that ran from end to end and looked like meshing teeth, and on the other side had four small dial-like controls. He bent over the canister and, holding it steady with his left hand, he very carefully twisted the dials to the settings he wanted. Then he slid the Formica table across the room, placing it next to the gurney. He turned the seamed side of the canister to face patient #243.

From the duffel bag, Jeffers removed a small black transmitter, like the kind used to open garage doors, but this one was different. Not just stronger, it was specially designed. Its signal would pass through the leaded walls of the X-ray room.

He looked around one more time, reviewing his preparations and checking the visible cord connections. Then before closing and locking the door to the hallway, he checked the corridor, looking and listening to make sure no one was nearby.

Working quickly, Dr. Jeffers went into the anteroom and fastened the heavy door shut. Beads of sweat formed on his brow and rapidly grew larger. He glanced through the window at the patient and at the monitors. Vital signs were still normal for a man slowly but steadily dying.

The transmitter seemed heavy and slippery in Jeffers' hand. He was sweating profusely now; sweat ran down from his temples and dripped onto his lab coat. He tried to swallow, but swallowing was hard and incomplete. His breathing was becoming labored, and he had to steady himself against the wall by the window. Relax, he told himself, relax.

In a moment he felt well enough to continue. Even so, he squeezed his eyes shut and hesitated for several seconds. He opened his eyes, looked into the other room, and pushed the transmitter button.

The canister moved slightly; the seam was opening. The monitors and printers went wild, like seismographs recording an 8.5 earthquake. Then abruptly they stopped. Patient #243, who never moved, was dead. The canister closed automatically and re-sealed itself shut.

Dr. Jeffers waited several minutes, just to be safe, before retrieving the data from the monitoring devices and storing it with the canister in the duffel bag. He slung the bag over his shoulder and returned the body to the room from which it had come. When he finished disconnecting the electrodes, he notified the nursing staff that the patient had died. The nurses prepared the death certificate, citing natural causes per Dr. Jeffers' instructions. He quickly signed it and left without ever having learned the dead man's name.

Well, he thought as he walked in the darkness to his car, now he should have what he needed. But was it worth it? Yes, and it was O.K.—#243 was about to die anyway. Yes, he kept telling himself, it was O.K.

# Prologue, Part 6

---

# Survival on Black Mesa

*The Nopeka survived by moving onto the top of nearby Black Mesa. The mesa was round, nearly a mile across, with vertical walls one hundred feet high. It was easy to defend and large enough to farm: a place where the Nopeka could be almost self-sufficient.*

*The attacks continued for nearly four years, and while the Nopeka survived, they grew steadily weaker. The stranglehold by the Hachonee grew tighter on the isolated tribe of farmers, whose numbers dwindled, until both sides knew that the next full assault by the Hachonee would be the last.*

# Chapter 6

Alex was awake and up well before the sun. The first thing he did was make coffee the way he liked it, strong and hot. Next he fed the cats, a mixed-breed mother and her kitten. Still operating on Eastern time, two hours ahead of the Mountain-zone time of New Mexico, he had a chance to unpack, then he showered and shaved before downing his third cup of coffee and leaving for the Los Alamos National Laboratory.

The city of Los Alamos is for all practical purposes the laboratory. Both, Alex knew, owed their fame—or maybe their infamy—to the World War II Manhattan Project. Before that, Los Alamos was just a small town, unheard of and difficult to find, with Route 4 entering from the east and the Jemez Mountains forming a natural barrier to the west.

Someone—he couldn't remember who, although it was probably Mrs. Andrews—once told him the Indian word Jemez meant "place of the boiling springs." Like the rest of the area, and certainly befitting what was to come, his historian had said that the Jemez Mountains were formed out of fire and violence, by volcanoes erupting time and again, over thousands of years.

The countryside surrounding Los Alamos is a jigsaw puzzle of mesas and canyons. The town and laboratories sit atop the Pajarito Plateau at an elevation of more than seven thousand feet. The original laboratory was located on an eight-mile-long mesa, separated from the rest of the plateau by two deep canyons; a simple guard tower gave ample warning and protection. The natural landscape provided Los Alamos with isolation and security, and this, together with its remoteness, distance from enemy air attack, and proximity to a test site, made it the ideal place to design the world's first atomic bomb.

Los Alamos: where theory became reality and a small amount of mass was converted into a tremendous amount of energy. But Alex had a feeling it was more than that, a place where Past is linked to Future, but not merely by passage of time. The connection seemed more complex, the way Mass is linked to Energy in Einstein's famous equation. Maybe, he thought without knowing why, the Los Alamos connection links man's heritage to his destiny.

The University of California runs the Los Alamos National Laboratory, which employs eight thousand people and is funded mostly by federal contracts with the Departments of Energy and Defense. The lab's main business is atomic energy research, with both peaceful and military applications, and Los Alamos serves as a repository for the materials, devices, and expertise required to conduct that research.

Alex's drive to the lab took him from Barranca Mesa, past the small, one-airline airport (you could see it but had to go well around the canyons to get to it), onto Diamond Drive and past the golf course, then past the business district, across Diamond Drive Bridge, and right onto West Jemez Road where the main entrance is located. He parked in one of the Visitor spots and reported to the Badge Office of the Administration Building.

Dr. John Canaday, his supervisor and old friend, was waiting for him. They said warm hellos, then John vouched for Alex to the security staff. Alex filled out and signed a half-dozen security forms, then had his ID-card picture taken by the same man who'd taken it the other summers. In less than a minute the security badge was ready.

With the badge, Alex could enter the laboratory and most of its facilities. The cryptic markings arrayed vertically next to Alex's picture meant, to those who understood, that Alex had been cleared for Top

Secret material as well as seven different categories of Critical Nuclear Weapons Defense Information, or CNWDI "Sigmas," as they were called. If he wanted to, Alex could access almost all of the lab's data.

John escorted Alex to the security gate, where the guard took Alex's badge in hand and closely scrutinized it, just as he did every badge of every worker and visitor.

"Alex, I've got to get to a meeting," John said as they passed into the secure laboratory complex, "but I'll be free in about an hour. Why don't you stop by my office then, and we can talk specifics about your work this summer."

"Fine, John, I'll see you in an hour." Alex's feet steered him automatically through the corridors to his old office. On the way he nodded, waved, and said brief hellos to several familiar faces, and he stopped to chat for a few minutes with Sarah Hall, the dependable secretary with over forty years of service who would again see to his administrative needs. Alex knew Sarah would be retired already if she lived or worked elsewhere, but New Mexico is revitalizing, and the lab wasn't the suffocating bureaucracy of other government agencies.

Back in the same office he used each summer, Alex still had forty-five minutes before his appointment with John. He picked up the phone and without having to search his memory, pressed the four digits that he'd known so well.

"Library, Research Department. Brenda speaking."

Alex's heart sank just a bit with the unfamiliar voice.

"Is Loyola Sanchez there?"

"Just a moment." There was hope.

"This is Loyola."

So, she was still there. For just a moment he felt oddly, indecisively reluctant, like a little boy about to steal the last cookie from the cookie jar, but the pleasant twinge that her voice inspired helped him overcome it.

"Hi. It's me." She'd know who it was, even though ten months had passed since the last time.

"Hi. I thought I'd be hearing from you. Are you in your office?"

"Yeah, just got in. Everything seems about the same. How are you? Married yet?"

She laughed. "You know the answer to that—never again. Oh, but—"

"Well, in that case I can invite you for coffee. Do you have the time?"

"Sure, Alex, I'd like that. Come up to my office—just give me two minutes. Oh, I'm not up front anymore. Look for me in the back—to the far right."

"Great. Be there in two minutes."

*       *       *

Loyola Sanchez was an American Indian who had become "Americanized." Great-granddaughter of the last great chieftain of her tribe, she was the first in her family to attend college, the first to leave pueblo life. After graduating from New Mexico State University with a degree in library science, looking for an excuse not to return to her village, she married Osbaldo Gonzalez, a local mechanic, and they lived in the nearby town of Jemez Springs.

A year after she was married, Loyola gave birth to a daughter, Sabrina. Soon afterward, ignoring Osbaldo's objections, protestations, and ultimatums, Loyola took a job at the lab.

Osbaldo was furious. Women did not need college educations, and they were not supposed to work. Except at home. His masculinity threatened, he began to see other women. He went so far as to flaunt his affairs, first to his friends, then publicly, finally even to Loyola.

Loyola was no less innocent, though she was certainly more discreet. She had been having an affair of her own, but she never flaunted or even confessed it to Osbaldo; he would have killed her.

On her third wedding anniversary, Loyola filed for divorce. The proceedings dragged on, and reaching a settlement was hard, even the splitting of assets, small as they were. The most bitter issue was custody of Sabrina, but Loyola won using Osbaldo's affairs against him, hoping and praying her own indiscretions would not be discovered.

After the divorce Osbaldo had little time for Sabrina. His real objective had been to defeat Loyola, not to win his daughter.

Loyola could easily have found another husband, if she wanted one. She was attractive, petite, and yet deceptively strong, with long black hair that reached down to small, round and firm buttocks, and big brown eyes that rested above large, strong cheekbones. She was, or at least appeared to be, carefree and happy-go-lucky, with a flirtatious smile and a look that said she knew what you wanted, and you might get it, but if you did, it would be on her terms—she would be in charge. With men, she was the fish playing the fisherman.

Now thirty-two and a resolute if not confirmed bachelorette, Loyola concentrated on her job and on raising Sabrina, with the somewhat ironic desire to bring Sabrina back into the Indian way of life. As for her career, she attended classes part time toward a master's degree, with the goal of moving higher in the lab's administration.

Two summers before, she and Alex had begun dating. At first she thought Alex was out of her league, since her usual dates were local roughnecks too much like Osbaldo. Alex, too, wondered about the attraction; he had fallen in love only once in his life, with Lisa Martin, and Loyola was nothing like Lisa. But what Loyola and Alex lacked in common background was made up for by a commonality of spirit. An excitement had existed between them. They were two adventurers, and for each one, the other was the adventure.

Early on they developed an enjoyable, comfortable relationship, with no commitments, no jealousies, no intrusions into other parts of their private lives. They had plenty of opportunities to be alone, since

Sabrina liked spending time with her grandmother, learning and experiencing Indian lore at the pueblo, which was only a few minutes away.

But this summer Alex had mixed feelings about resuming their relationship. Something just didn't seem right. He'd have to play it by ear. On the one hand it was such a pleasure, especially—but not entirely—sensual, to be with her, but, on the other hand, he had had the feeling when he left last year that she was close to falling in love with him, and he knew he could never respond in kind.

*          *          *

The laboratory's library is open to the general public, though portions of it are off limits to anyone without the proper badge, and guards are stationed at those entrances. The library is also connected via guarded passageways to the building in which Alex worked, so he had only to climb some stairs and walk a few hundred yards of corridor to get to Loyola's office.

Alex found his way back to her new location. When she saw him coming, she rose from her desk and walked around it to greet him. "Hi."

"Hi."

She wore a loose gray sweater, which hid more than highlighted her small firm breasts, and a tight black skirt that didn't quite get to her knees. Alex took it all in. "You're looking great."

"Thanks, you too."

Alex took her hands and looked into her deep brown eyes. "I'd forgotten what heaven was like," he said.

She waited a moment, and then squeezed his hand playfully. "Bullshit, white man. You've probably been getting plenty of *heaven* from those southern belles back in Virginia."

Alex laughed heartily. "I wish," he said. "Come on, let's get some coffee."

They left through the library's front door and walked across the street to the Otowi Building. The cafeteria was nearly empty after the early morning breakfast rush. Alex got their coffees while Loyola retrieved a cheese Danish for herself.

They had barely settled into their chairs, politically correct on opposite sides of the square dining table, when Loyola announced, "Alex, you need to know, I'm kind of dating someone right now."

Alex wasn't sure if he was relieved or disappointed. He put his hand on hers. "Good for you. Is it serious?"

"No, at least I don't think so. But he's a nice guy, and he's fun. Only problem is, he's temporary, like you."

"Anybody I might know?"

"Doubt it. He's military and this is his first time here."

"Does Sabrina like him?"

"Adores him, probably more than I do."

"Well, that's good enough for me. By the way, tell her I have something for her in my suitcase."

They shared general news over two cups of coffee, until Alex said he had to leave for his meeting with John.

"Do you think we might be able to have dinner sometime? As old friends—if your new beau doesn't mind?"

"He wouldn't and I'd love to."

"Great. I heard there's a new French restaurant in Santa Fe—Le Mistral. Do you know anything about it?"

"No, but I'll try anything once," she said with flirty eyes and a mischievous grin.

"I know," laughed Alex, remembering and suppressing a melancholy sadness.

# Prologue, Part 7

## Year of Dry Storms

*Historians are uncertain of the exact year, but the tribes of New Mexico, particularly the Nopeka, knew it as the Year of Dry Storms. Every afternoon, or so it seemed, dark clouds gathered on the horizon, sometimes in the east, sometimes in the west. Forming into billowy mountains, ranging in color from slate blue to gray-black, the clouds journeyed slowly in the direction of Black Mesa until they passed directly overhead. The Indians desperately needed rain for their withered crops and parched animals, but the clouds seldom delivered more than a few drops, hardly enough to settle the dust.*

*With the storm clouds came the wind, blowing in low tones at the base of the mesa, but whistling and howling across the top, driving the few droplets of rain sideways into the dust, forming little craters of oblong O's.*

*Off in the distance with the gathering clouds, warning of the coming wind, were lightning, flickering softly, and thunder, booming gently. Brighter and louder, flashing and crackling, they accompanied the wind as it swept to and over the mesa, like hunting dogs at the heel of their master. Lasting until the storm had moved well past, lightning and thunder were also reminders of the violence that had come and gone.*

# Chapter 7

The day promised to be beautiful. There wasn't a cloud in the new, white-blue sky as Alex and Loyola left the Otowi Building. An early morning crispness held the air, offset by only a hint of warmth as the sun had now climbed twice its diameter above the horizon.

Before descending the steps of the Otowi Building, Loyola at his side, Alex paused. He closed his eyes and took a deep breath. In a fraction of a second his mind raced with thoughts about her, his day to come, and the rising sun. Nothing specific, just passing reflections, lightning quick. While Loyola, although now more past than future, was pretty much a known quantity, the day ahead was an unknown quantity. And the rising sun, well, that was just an illusion, a trick caused by the earth's turning and his limited perspective, a stationary figure glued to earth by gravity. But that triggered another thought from somewhere within the depths of his subconscious. "Remember," it said, "all is not what it seems."

A few minutes later he was in John Canaday's office, waiting for John to bring him up-to-date on ballistic missile defense. John's office was small, cramped with a desk and matching chair, several bookcases, a round conference table with four chairs, and a well-used, overstuffed recliner that did not fit in with the rest of the standard issue, modular furniture. The recliner, great for an occasional nap, was where John did most of his hard thinking. He insisted, as always, that Alex sit there while they talked.

John was a big man, slightly overweight, but more big than fat. He had been at the lab nearly twenty years, after receiving his Ph.D. in nuclear physics from Stanford. Now forty-five, he was balding, with a mass of thick, curly black hair on the sides of his head, and a patch of black on the top, leaving a horseshoe of pink crown. His white shirt-sleeves were rolled up to the elbow, and the tie he'd worn to work that morning had already been removed. He looked as if he'd been in some kind of tussle, and figuratively he may have been, at least a bureaucratic one, since now he was more administrator than physicist.

But even with the burdens of administration, John was usually in a good mood, and today was no exception.

"It's really a pleasure to have you here again, Alex. You know, I get more out of you in two or three months than some of my full-time workers in a year. Sure you don't want to come here permanently? I could arrange it—at a lot more than your university salary."

"Thanks, John, but no. I enjoy teaching too much, being around college-aged kids. I only wish it paid more."

"If you ever change your mind, let me know."

"Will do. Now tell me, what's new in the missile defense business?"

John spent about twenty minutes reviewing recent technology advancements and followed that with the latest theories about deployment and counter-deployment of defense systems. Much of what he said was classified, ranging from Secret to Top Secret. John handed Alex several binders of information to read when he had the chance. Secret binders had red covers, and binders with Top Secret information had yellow covers.

Finished with the preliminary, background information, John asked if Alex had any questions.

"No, but I might after I sort through the papers. Just tell me what you want me to do this year."

"About the same as last year, Alex. I'd like you to continue looking at satellite configurations—for both sides—until you're comfortable with their potential capabilities and limitations."

This meant, as in prior years, Alex would be analyzing various configurations of satellite weapons—weapons designed to orbit the earth as a defense against missile attack. How well a configuration could defend depended upon many variables, including the number of missiles, their initial locations, the number of warheads each missile carried—dummy and real—and the hardness of the missile body. He also had to consider assumptions about the weapons in orbit, such as how powerful they were, the source of their power, the time required to retarget following a kill or a miss, and the orbits themselves.

"Then after we've discussed what you've found," John continued, "I'll want you to get into the question of offensive capability." John paused briefly to peer over his reading glasses at Alex. "At least for the other side."

John had hit upon the one sensitive area between them, a source of numerous debates, albeit friendly, but where their points of view differed sharply. Alex thought it amusing, studying how well a configuration of satellite weapons, ostensibly designed for defensive purposes, could perform in an offensive capacity. He and John had discussed the irony many times, but the sore spot was John's position that the United States was not interested in an SDI offensive capability. Alex was always assigned to look at "the other side," but he knew someone was working the U.S. side, probably under a security classification higher than his own, and most certainly under John's direction.

But on this, his first day back to Los Alamos, it was too soon for Alex to give John a hard time. "Great," was all he said.

John rose and Alex followed suit, having to extricate himself from the recliner.

"Would you like to join us for lunch?" John asked.

Alex wasn't sure who the "us" was, but it didn't matter. "Yes, thanks. Do you still eat lunch at the Otowi Building?"

"Most of the time. Can't seem to get away from the lab without somebody looking for me about some puny budget matter. Today I have to be back for a one-thirty meeting with Al Chen—next year's budget— so it'll have to be Otowi. We'll leave from here about noon. Do you have dinner plans? Amanda said to invite you as soon as possible."

"Thank Amanda for me, but I think I'll rest tonight. Maybe later in the week. In fact, Wednesday or Thursday would be fine. And I'd love to play bridge if you can find someone."

Amanda, John's wife, was not only an excellent cook, but an avid and very fine bridge player as well. They usually played a few rubbers of bridge after dinner, provided they could round up a fourth. Alex looked forward to bridge with the Canadays as much as the meal.

"I'll check with Amanda and we'll firm up Wednesday or Thursday. And don't worry, she'll find a fourth. Probably have the two of you married before you go back to Virginia," he muttered.

As they walked out of John's office, John suddenly said, as though it had almost slipped his mind, "Hey, there's someone I want you to meet. I think the two of you might have a lot in common—oh, and he's a doctor."

# Prologue, Part 8

## Amitolanne and Tepi

*The night before the last battle, a small but erect figure could be seen on top of Black Mesa, near the edge, facing west, watching the last flickers of lightning from that afternoon's storm. Amitolanne, Bright Rainbow, held her three-year-old son cradled in her arms. Tepi was named after the wildcat.*

*Amitolanne looked into Tepi's face. Even with his eyes half shut after a youngster's full day of play, she could see Atopu, the boy's father. Atopu had been dead now for nearly a year, killed in a Hachonee ambush while hunting for deer in the valley below the mesa. Amitolanne wondered how long the rest of their tribe could hold out.*

*"What will tomorrow bring, my son?" she asked softly.*

*Tepi murmured something in response, then closed his eyes.*

*Would they attack? It had been more than two weeks since the last time. Maybe they, too, were sick of warring. Maybe they would offer a truce. Not likely, she knew.*

*The storm's thunder no longer reached the mesa, and flashes of quiet lightning illuminated only the distant night sky. Amitolanne lost herself momentarily in nature's beauty, forgetting the war. As the fading, flickering lightning passed over the horizon and out of sight, she cautiously shifted Tepi in her arms, then carried him back to their bed. Whatever might happen tomorrow, a young brave needed his sleep.*

*Curled up next to Tepi under a heavy buffalo hide, she thought about the storm, which once again had passed without providing rain. What good was a storm without rain? She drifted toward sleep with her mind empty but for that question. An answer came to her: like everything else in nature, the storm was a gift from the gods, in this case a gift of beauty. She fell asleep with a prayer of thanksgiving.*

# Chapter 8

John led Alex through a maze of basement-level corridors painted light blue and filled with overhanging, color-coded pipes until the two men finally reached their destination, a sparsely furnished office that had *temporary* written all over it. A tall, lanky man in an Army uniform sat with his back to the door, pecking away on a computer keyboard, one hand at a time, left, right, left, right. The officer turned and stood when he heard them enter.

He was well tanned, with disheveled hair the color of Coors Light. A wide grin split his narrow face at the sight of John. "Howdy, partner," he said.

"Good morning, Sandy. I'd like you to meet Alex Feher. Alex is from the math department of Virginia Tech, a summer regular here." Turning to Alex, John continued, "Alex, meet Dr. Sandy Jeffers. Sandy is an Army physician. He comes to us from Walter Reed."

"Well, the name of the place is Forest Glen," Sandy drawled in what had to be Texan, "but it's part of the Walter Reed spread."

"Sandy's a neighbor of yours, Alex. He's renting a house just down the street from you. I thought you might be able to ride in together. Sandy's also a mighty fine tennis player."

John shifted his glance to Sandy. "Alex likes to play tennis, and if he's kept up his game, he should give you a pretty good match."

Alex stepped around John to shake Sandy's hand. "Good to meet you, Sandy."

"Likewise, partner."

"Been able to play much tennis here?"

"A mite, mostly with John, but I need to get out some more. Got to keep in shape for when I get back to the Army."

"How's John's game? Does he still have that wicked first serve and notoriously bad second?"

"Yup, that about describes it. I keep telling him he ought to lose a few pounds. He's like a lumbering bear out there. But I think it's a lost cause," Sandy said with a wide grin.

"It's all those damned meetings I have to go to. I just can't get any exercise."

"And I know Amanda's great cooking doesn't help," Alex said.

"Look," John said, "I'll leave so you can make fun of me behind my back. I'm already late for another of those damned meetings. I'll see you guys later."

John left and Sandy grabbed the chair located at the computer terminal and slid it in front of Alex. "Please, Alex, sit a spell."

Alex sat down, and Sandy pushed a pile of papers on his desk out of the way and sat down where the papers had been.

"I know about Walter Reed, but I've never heard of Forest—what was the name? Forest Cove?"

"Forest Glen. No, it's pretty much unknown, and the Army would like to keep it that way."

"Oh?"

"Well, that's because of the medical research, but it's all got to be done, I mean if you want to be ready for whatever the next war might bring.

"Most people know about Walter Reed Army Medical Center. It's hosted presidents, foreign heads of state, and other dignitaries, but Forest Glen is a mite more interesting to look at."

"Where is it, in D. C.?"

"No, in Maryland, between Kensington and Silver Spring, just a couple of miles from Walter Reed proper."

"I know about where that is."

"People walk by it every day without knowing it's there, but if you ever do get that way, you ought to look it up. The Forest Glen Annex to Walter Reed. It's really something to see—a grotesque combination of old, decaying structures and a bunch of newer government buildings, and they're not in great shape either. Forest Glen is out of place and out of time, like something from the Twilight Zone."

"Sounds weird. How'd the Army get involved with a place like that?"

"Interesting story. Over a hundred years ago the B & O Railroad and a local trolley company laid down track there, then real estate speculators built a hotel to make sales pitches. They called it 'Ye Forest Inne.' It was a fancy place, with flagpole-topped Queen Anne turrets and a Texas-sized ballroom with beam-buttressed dormers more than sixty feet high.

"The sales scheme didn't work, so they converted the hotel into a casino. That didn't pan out either, so the property was sold. The buyers turned the hotel into a girls' school called the National Park Seminary, but it wasn't really a seminary. To match the grandeur of the hotel and give the seminary an international air, they converted the grounds into a statuary and added buildings like a Greek temple, a pagoda, a Swiss chalet, a Dutch windmill, an English castle, and a Tuscan villa. This was around 1908. The property changed hands a few more times after that, and the Army bought it in 1942."

"That's a coincidence," Alex said. "Los Alamos was bought by the Army about the same time, and it used to be a boys school."

"Didn't know that. The Army bought Forest Glen to use as a rehabilitation center. The government turned the old girls school into a mental hospital for soldiers returning from World War II.

"According to old-timers still working there, the patients were a sight—had to wear bright red pajamas so they could be spotted easily. I've heard they'd roam the grounds like machines. Some were lethargically slow, others agitatedly fast. Some had to be escorted, and some never moved at all, just stood or sat like the marble-white statues. Some thought the statues were ghosts—ghosts of their buddies who didn't make it back from the war. They say those patients used to sit and chew the fat with their ghostly friends—mostly when the moon was full." Sandy laughed and tried to make an eerie-sounding "WooOOooOOooOO."

Alex laughed, too, though he felt a little sad for the patients. And maybe they really were conversing with something. Alex was reminded of the ghosts he thought he saw on Deer Trap Mesa.

"Most of the original seminary buildings are still there," Sandy continued. "But they're rotting and decaying. It's a darn shame. The Army maintains them to a degree, but it gives priority to the newer, bland buildings, like the one where I work. Or usually work, when I'm not hogtied here."

"So what are you doing here at the lab?" Alex asked.

Sandy seemed to be contemplating his reply. His eyes avoided Alex's gaze. "Well, it involves radiation. It's not very interesting, not really. What about you?"

Alex explained briefly that he worked on strategic missile defense systems, "and I also look at *offensive* capabilities," he said, underscoring the word with cynicism, "at least for anything the Russians might put up."

At that Sandy raised his eyebrows and tilted his head, a clear invitation for Alex to let loose whatever he was holding back.

"O.K., but first some background. The United States envisions its defensive satellite system like an umbrella, with satellite weapons continually in position to defend against attack. In the ideal situation, each satellite would stay in position above a particular point on the earth.

But that can happen only with geosynchronous orbits directly above the earth's equator.

"For missile locations not on the equator, satellite coverage becomes complicated. Satellites orbit the earth while the earth rotates. It turns out that for adequate defensive coverage, say against the known or suspected missile locations in what used to be the Soviet Union, a large number of satellite weapons is necessary. By the way, the USSR would have required twice as many satellites for its own SDI. That's because U.S. missiles were more densely situated, requiring more satellite weapons overhead at any one time. So in 1985, when Gorbachev told Reagan the USSR would match any U.S. SDI system, Reagan said 'Go ahead.'

"But the main concern of the USSR wasn't the prohibitive cost of building a defensive satellite system. It was a fear of the offensive capability that SDI would give the United States.

"While a defensive system has to provide continual coverage, an offensive system does not. It only has to suppress enemy missiles for some twenty-or-so minutes while its country's own missiles are on the way to their targets. These satellites would circle the earth in seemingly random and unrelated orbits, but every so often they would be in position to offer total or nearly total missile suppression."

"So if I understand this right, it might take, say, five hundred satellite weapons to provide defensive protection, but maybe only fifty to support the kind of preemptive strike you described."

"Right, and your numbers aren't too far off, by the way. So after all the ballyhoo about a Strategic *Defense* Initiative, I think it's ironic that any defensive satellite system would provide an even greater offensive capability—and very early in the deployment schedule. No wonder the Soviet Union was so concerned about SDI! They couldn't afford to deploy their own, yet they couldn't allow the United States to have such a strategic advantage."

"So what's your beef with that?"

"Nothing, except John confines me to looking at offense by the Russians, and he pretends we—the United States—don't do offensive planning. But I know better, and when I want to get his goat, all I have to do is refer to our work as 'SOI'—Strategic *Offensive* Initiative."

Alex and Sandy talked for another hour, mostly about tennis and their neighboring homes. In that brief time they had become friends. Yet when Alex asked Sandy again about his work, he answered in vague terms and steered the conversation back to another topic. He seemed tentative, guarded, as if he were letting Alex meet only three-fourths of him, and Alex was curious about the missing fourth.

The telephone rang, but Sandy ignored it.

Alex waved toward the phone. "Go ahead," he said.

"Dr. Jeffers here. Oh, hi sweet thing. Can I call you back? I've got someone here—Alex, uh, Alex…?"

"Feher."

"Feher. You're kidding. Well I'll be darned if that don't beat all. Listen, honey, I'll call you back in a little while. We're still on for tonight, right? Great."

Alex heard the click on the other end. "What was that all about?"

"You. You're the one. She told me an old friend would be coming soon."

Alex still didn't understand.

"I think you know the lady. We've been going out. Loyola Sanchez."

"I'll be damned. And she told me about you. I hope there's no problem."

"Shoot, no. It's not really serious anyway. There's a young lady back in Washington I'm fixin' to go after when I get back. You know, Alex, maybe the three of us ought to get together for drinks or dinner. What do you think?"

"Fine by me, but right now I'd better get back to my office. Would you like a ride tomorrow morning?"

"I'm going to need my car, but if you'll mosey over to my house in the morning," Sandy said, "you can ride with me. Bring your tennis gear, and we can play after work."

"Great. I'll get a reservation on one of the lab courts."

Talking about Loyola and tennis seemed to have relaxed Sandy again. As Alex was leaving, Sandy clapped him on the back. "Better rest up tonight, partner, so you won't have any excuses if you lose."

"You too, partner," Alex said, smiling knowingly.

*　　　　　*　　　　　*

Alex thought back to the first time he and Loyola had been together. She came to his house for dinner, bringing a tossed salad of garden vegetables topped by her homemade ranch dressing. He contributed two thick pieces of tenderloin, which they cooked to a bloody rare and devoured quickly. The bout of lovemaking that followed was much the same.

They talked, then began to make love again, more slowly and leisurely. Alex watched her move, admiring her body. Though feminine in every way, it reminded him of a flyweight boxer's. She had small, firm breasts, and strong, wiry arms and legs. After a few minutes she climbed on top of him. "Now I'm going to show you what it's like on the bottom," she said, and she drove hard and powerfully to completion, seemingly ignoring him. It was an equalizing moment for them, something she needed to have, and something he had never forgotten. After that the lovemaking was mostly giving for each of them, which was as good as the taking in the end. Now Alex could only envy Sandy.

# Prologue, Part 9

## Attack!

*A few hours later Amitolanne was awakened by shouts from a lookout at the edge of the mesa; the Hachonee were attacking. Instinctively she reached for Tepi, resting against her body. There were more shouts, closer, and the muffled patter of moccasined feet running close by. It was still dark, and although the Nopeka had been caught by surprise, they were not unprepared, as each able brave scrambled quickly to his station.*

*Several foot trails ascended Black Mesa, but they were difficult to climb and one man at the top of each path could easily defend against warriors scaling the cliffs one at a time.*

*Getting to the top of the mesa by horseback was even more difficult, though not impossible. Only one of the footpaths was traversable by horses, and its winding route around and up the mesa made easy targets of the attackers. As the path approached the mesa top, it became narrow and steep, until the finish was nearly vertical, and not every horse or rider was equal to the final task. But it was the only practical point of assault for the Hachonee, and so it was here they came, here where the Nopeka concentrated what was left of their defensive forces.*

# Chapter 9

---

Army officers are strange people. That was Alex's assessment. He'd met officers before, he'd even worked and socialized with them, but that was on his turf, at the lab or back at the university in Blacksburg. When they were out of their element, Alex had concluded, away from the military establishment with its rules and order, Army officers were ill at ease and just plain uncomfortable mixing with civilian society.

Professional officers weren't just reticent; they selected their words carefully, guarded them closely, not revealing anything too personal, as if personal disclosures would come back to hurt them. Name, rank, and serial number. That was all. Anything more could be destructive, or so they were taught. Don't volunteer any information to the enemy, not even wrong information, because a smart enemy can discern truths out of falsehoods. And who was the enemy? If you were paranoid enough, and some individuals and even some institutions within the military were, then anyone outside of the military establishment would be the enemy.

Sandy Jeffers wasn't like that, at least not with Alex. He willingly discussed his personal life, including his fears and his shortcomings. But talking about work seemed to make him uncomfortable, and Alex sensed he was holding something back. Alex chalked it up to lab security.

They played tennis as planned on Alex's third day in Los Alamos. Throughout play the now good friends carried on a lively conversation.

Sandy won seven games to five, although Alex thought Sandy had eased up to keep the set close. After match point they moved to towel off on one of the benches just beyond the chain link fence enclosing the lab courts. The talk turned to marriage.

"Shoot, Alex, I'm thirty-four years old, been divorced more than ten years, and I'm still kicking myself for not being able to make a go of it with my wife. The whole thing, the breakup and divorce, was my fault. Maybe the biggest mistake was getting married in the first place."

"That's hard to say. I'm sure your wife shared some responsibility for the divorce."

"Well, maybe, but there's more to it than she ever realized, and it all comes down to me being responsible. What about you, Alex? You ever been hitched?"

"No, I screwed up with the only person I could have married. But maybe someday."

"Were you ever interested in Loyola—I mean as someone you could marry?"

"No, it couldn't have worked. Too many differences, and in the long run they'd clash. Besides, the deep feeling just wasn't there for me.

"I did have that feeling once. When I was in high school I fell in love with a girl, head over heels—the perfect girl—named Lisa. It was love at first sight, but I was too shy, too insecure, and I never did anything about it. Now she's married and I've missed my chance. Oh well, that's life I guess."

The sun was down and Alex draped the towel over his shoulders, protection from the evening chill. "It sounds like maybe you're not completely over your ex-wife. Ever talk to her?"

"Yeah, from time to time, but she's remarried now, and besides, I've been getting interested in someone—Christine—back in Washington. But it did take me a long time to get over the divorce.

"Heck, at first it was total system shock, and I guess that's to be expected. But later, after I matured a bit and could look more objectively at the mistakes I made—mistakes my big ego and the pain of the breakup wouldn't let me see—I think the divorce hit me even harder. But I've learned from my mistakes, and now I think I could get married again. In fact, when I get done with this stint in Los Alamos and get back to D. C., I may talk to Christine about it."

"Well, great. I wish you luck. How soon will you go back home?"

"That's hard to say, but it can't be soon enough. I don't much care for the work I'm involved in."

"Can you tell me about it, or is it too hush-hush?"

"It's hush-hush, probably the most secret stuff around here, but that's not the issue. Can we change the subject?"

"No problem. Tell me about your work at 'Doe-dimmer.'"

Sandy was on loan to Los Alamos from the Department of Defense Institute of Medical Research, or "Doe-dimmer," as he pronounced its acronym.

"Be glad to. Our research includes the prevention and treatment of tropical diseases, the effects of nuclear, chemical, and biological weapons, and how to protect against those weapons. We also look at the physiological effects of bullets, bombs, and shrapnel."

"I take it you work with radiation."

Sandy nodded.

"Been there long?"

"Four years, but my first assignment was different—studying the medical effects of blast overpressure on soldiers."

Alex raised his eyebrows, picturing soldiers forced to volunteer for "bomb blast" duty.

Sandy seemed to read Alex's mind. "Well, shoot, you can't experiment on real soldiers. We used goats. Their torsos are similar."

"Ah."

"All you have to do is tie up a goat near an explosive device, set it off, then examine the carcass. I've written a bunch of monographs on the subject, but you won't find them in your public library. This kind of research—using animals—is sensitive, and that keeps the papers confined to military channels.

"After two years I reckoned it was time to move on to something else, so I asked for a transfer. I guess I was pretty well thought of at Doe-dimmer, so the director asked me to stay, but he wanted me to take on a new assignment, less grisly and more theoretical—the effects of nuclear weapons."

"You mean how radiation kills?"

"Yup, but it's more than just radiation. Nuclear weapons can kill in three ways. The blast, of course, and the release of thermal radiation, or heat, will kill in the vicinity of detonation—'ground zero.' The third killer is nuclear radiation, from the blast in the form of gamma rays and neutrons, or from radioactive fallout of gamma rays and electrons.

"Gamma rays and neutrons are the most dangerous forms of radiation to humans, but neutrons don't occur in fallout. That's what led military scientists to design the neutron bomb. What they ended up with was a tactical weapon that could kill hundreds of soldiers by releasing neutron radiation, but without much blast damage or fallout. This was perfect for the European theater, where NATO forces would have been defending within their own borders. Enemy tank crews could be killed easily without much collateral damage to the cities or countryside.

"When I saw that nuclear radiation and its tactical uses were becoming important to the Army, I took at interest in the subject. I read papers, consulted textbooks, attended professional meetings, and even made a point of seeing patients suffering from radiation poisoning. I guess I'm not being very modest, but pretty soon I became something of an authority on radiation and on all of its forms.

"My basic research dealt with soldiers exposed to radiation from enemy nuclear weapons. The main question is how much radiation can be absorbed safely, and how much will incapacitate or kill a soldier. From the pure tactician's point of view, my most important research was on how long a soldier might function with a lethal—but not incapacitating—dose of radiation.

"You can evacuate soldiers exposed to nonlethal doses, and they'll recover. But soldiers who are going to die from it in a day or two, usually they can function normally for several hours. Well, they can be very effective, like the Japanese kamikaze. They're already on the battlefield, and they have nothing to lose. Shoot, all you have to do is motivate them to keep fighting, to do what they can while they're still able.

"As grotesque as it may sound to make canon fodder of dying soldiers, in the real world of war it might mean the difference between defeat and victory. 'For want of a nail…,' I tell myself, and I always look at my work in a positive light. If my research can prevent our soldiers from being killed or injured, or can extend their capabilities, then it could be a contribution to keeping the other side from starting a war."

"I take it that's what brought you to Los Alamos—your expertise in the area of radiation."

Sandy stood up, stuffed his towel with the other tennis gear in his large red and blue gym bag and threw it over his shoulder. "That's about right. Ready to go?"

*      *      *

On Alex's fifth day at the lab, Friday, he met Sandy in the parking lot for the ride home.

Sandy was leaning against his car, arms folded and head bowed. Alex approached but Sandy did not look up. "T G I F, Sandy. Ready to head home?"

Sandy said nothing until he had unlocked the passenger car door for Alex. "Want to stop for a tall, cold one on the way? I could use it."

"Sure. I owe you one, anyway."

Sandy looked at Alex, confused.

"From the other day—tennis."

"Oh, yeah."

Not until they reached the parking lot of the Ramada Inn, where Happy Hour was just beginning, did Sandy say anything else. "One of these days I'm going to belt that man, colonel or not."

"Who?"

"Colonel Billy—not William or Bill—but Billy Hollis the Third, that's who. My boss and the biggest asshole in the Army."

# Prologue, Part 10

## Success

*On this day, fed by a sense that the war's end was at hand, fierce determination colored the faces of the Hachonee like war paint, and brave after steeded brave attempted to breach the top. Most of the early attackers died trying, ending up sprawled heaps, often next to or under their horses. Those not killed were forced to turn back, forced to queue up with fresh volunteers to try again. Wiloloaneha was there to urge them on, though no urging was necessary.*

*One at a time the riders came, seemingly from an endless line. And as the suicidal charge continued, so did the accumulation of bodies on the side of the mesa.*

*At the base of the mesa and well out of range of Nopeka arrows, Hachonee foot soldiers waited for the order to move out. When it came, they rushed the trail, taking up positions alongside fallen bodies.*

*The inevitable toll of attrition finally weakened the Nopeka defense, and the Hachonee gradually moved their positions forward—by inches, then feet, then yards. By mid-morning they were at the edge of their objective, the mesa top, and only a few defenders remained. When the last one fell a short time later, the Hachonee swarmed the mesa with speed and superiority in numbers.*

*The killing would be easy, as resistance on top of Black Mesa was spotty and loosely organized at best. Wiloloaneha gave the signal for the slaughter to begin, then he rode around the mesa, surveying the carnage.*

# Chapter 10

Sandy continued his tirade. "Hollis thinks he owns this place and everyone in it. He orders people around like they're all recruits and working for him. You know he makes me call him 'sir' whenever we talk, even if it's just shooting the bull. And he thinks because I'm a doctor, I'm not really an Army officer. He looks at me like an outsider, someone not to be trusted. Shoot, he's the one not to be trusted!"

He paused for a moment, pain evident on his face. "It's bad enough that he treats me like dirt, but today he had a secretary in tears. First he blames her because the computer goes down and she can't type his report, then he accuses her of holding onto his papers to learn about the project, like she's a spy or something. I think the guy's severely paranoid."

*        *        *

On Monday, after work, Sandy and Alex changed clothes at the lab and left from there to play tennis. The courts were within walking distance, but Sandy drove anyway. Sandy seemed nervous and preoccupied, and without saying why, he told Alex there was a chance he might be called away.

They were just into their third game when Sandy's cell phone sounded. "Sorry, partner," he yelled as he ran to his equipment bag. He huddled over the bag for about ten seconds, listening into the phone then speaking a few muffled words. In less than a minute he was back.

"Sorry, but I've got to drive into Santa Fe. I'm really in a hurry. Can you hitch a ride home?"

"Sure, Sandy, but what gives? What's in Santa Fe that's so important?"

As he got into his car, Sandy said, "No big deal. I've just got to be there. I'll tell you about it some other time."

Sandy threw his car into first gear, popped the clutch and hit the accelerator. The car hesitated, tires spinning, gravel spitting, then he sped away as if the devil were after him.

Alex just stood there puzzled.

The next day Alex had to drive alone. Sandy had left a message on Alex's answering machine saying he would be late to work and for Alex not to wait for him. Sandy did stop at the lab briefly, said hello to Alex and made arrangements for tennis the next day, but he didn't say anything about Santa Fe, and Alex didn't want to press him.

*        *        *

A week later Alex finally beat Sandy at tennis. Tennis and the single beer after it paid for by the loser had become an almost daily habit. The waitress, who by now knew the terms, placed the two drafts in front of them and looked to Alex.

He grinned. "Not today," and he jerked his thumb in Sandy's direction.

"Well, congratulations," she said to Alex as Sandy tossed a five-dollar bill onto her tray.

"Don't look so glum, buddy. You'll probably beat my socks off next time."

Sandy shrugged and took a sip of beer.

"Besides, losing once in a while is good for your soul."

"Oh, it is, is it? If you only knew…," and Sandy laughed a dry, hollow laugh.

"Knew what? Come on, Sandy, tell me what's going on."

"Well, maybe I can tell you something, but it's a two-beer story."

"Got nothing better to do. Fire away."

"To start, the day I was born was the day my mother died."

"Sorry, I had no idea."

"It's O.K. Her name was Annie. She was forty-four, a little overweight and a heavy smoker, and her heart gave out after the delivery. My daddy and my brothers and sisters—the youngest was twelve—they kept her memory alive for me. From my earliest recollection, I felt I knew her, what she was like, and what she would have wanted for me.

"I know she was with me in spirit my first day in school. When I was scared or lonely, I pretended she was there. She became my companion and confidante. I talked to her, silently, and had this sense of having been heard and understood. My mother was gone, but she was also a part of me, somewhere inside my being.

"As I grew older, I became curious about how the mother I'd never seen could be so close to me."

Sandy's eyes focused on his half-filled glass of beer. "Well, the curiosity I had about my mother evolved into something deeper, a kind of fascination with the difference between life and death. That's why I became a physician.

"Like I said, this is a long story, so let me see if I can move it along. I got married in college. I didn't know it, but what attracted me to Anita was how much she looked like my mother. Even the names were similar. Annie and Anita. Anita was the mother I'd been deprived of.

"The mother-son conflict didn't come into play until I accepted Army funding for medical school and with it a long-term obligation for Army service. Anita was dead set against a military career, but I desperately wanted to be a doctor and it was the only way I could get to medical school. When the bickering started, it was like my mother scolding me, and I withdrew from her as a husband. Sex became revulsive. I couldn't even touch Anita, and I didn't understand any of it.

"Anita couldn't figure it out either. She tried to accept my decision about the Army, but we just grew farther apart. We separated, then each of us found a new partner for support, and we were divorced before I finished medical school.

"I didn't understand what happened until a few years later, and then there was nothing to do except learn from the experience and put it behind me. I could have tried explaining to Anita, but she'd already remarried, so what was the point?

"But I did take stock of where I was in my life, how I got there, and the role my mother had played. And I was surprised to discover that my life seemed to have a purpose to it. A single, pointed purpose. Since then I've spent my leisure time, except for tennis, chasing a dream. I reckon the dream was born when I was born, then nurtured by a mother who wasn't there."

"O.K., so what's the—"

"I've been searching for the secret of eternal life—life after death."

# Prologue, Part 11

# Atrocities

*Amitolanne was one of the last Nopeka alive. Tepi had remained close to his mother throughout the battle, and despite the terror and pandemonium, she had kept a careful watch on her son. The position she was helping to defend had just been overrun, and death was all around her now.*

*Amitolanne was not afraid to die, but she was afraid for her son. Should she fight to the death, or should she run, not like a coward, but to try and save Tepi?*

*To her left and in a cloud of dust, three Hachonee brought down a Nopeka warrior. They beat him until he was unconscious. Amitolanne watched in horror, lying behind a long-ago fallen piñon tree, shielding Tepi from the sight.*

*Working quickly and with a precision that comes only with practice, one of the Hachonee scalped the Nopeka brave, and the other two castrated him, all while he was still alive. Then they left him to die in dust fast becoming red mud.*

*Just a few feet away and directly to Amitolanne's right, a seven-year-old boy sat crying. A Hachonee on horseback galloped to a stop near the body of the boy's mother. Using a lance, the horseman worked the woman's clothing open, intent on some obscene mutilation. The boy leaped to defend the body and succeeded in pulling the lance away from the man. But the Hachonee also had a tomahawk, and he beat the boy down. Then without dismounting, leaning low from his horse, he finished his task with one violent blow, splitting the boy's head open.*

*Sickened, Amitolanne pulled Tepi to her, and they hid behind a large juniper bush between them and the boy's killer. When the warrior rode away in search of another victim, she gathered Tepi into her arms and made a break for the mesa edge, hoping, praying, to reach it and scale down to some hiding place before the Hachonee could take her. She was still more than fifty yards from safety when one of Wiloloaneha's lieutenants spotted her.*

# Chapter 11

"Say that again? You want to live forever?"

"No," and Sandy looked directly at Alex, "I've been searching for the human soul and I think I…, we're onto it."

Alex had been gazing in Sandy's direction, not looking at anything in particular, but now he lifted his head. He fixed his eyes on Sandy's, then screwed his face into a look of shocked disbelief.

"What?"

"Let me back up."

"Please do, and hang on—want another beer?"

"Why not?"

Alex signaled to the waitress. "O.K., shoot."

"For years I've been interested in the question of immortality. I don't mean prolonging human life, but does something, some part of us, survive when our bodies die? A soul, if you will. We're obviously different from other animals because we can think, reason, and emote. But is that unique part of us also immortal? Most of the world's religions teach us it is. But where is the scientific evidence?"

Alex shifted in his chair, aware Sandy was about to answer his own question, even though he'd paused to let what he was saying sink in. In that brief span Alex recalled his mother and sister and all the philosophizing he'd done after their deaths.

Sandy continued. "A couple of years ago I learned about a small group of scientists, real scientists, not pseudo-intellectual crackpots or religious zealots, who were looking for evidence of a soul. They referred to their project as 'S-cubed'—three S's. It stands for Scientific Search for a Soul. I was interested in what they were doing, so I started corresponding with them.

"Most of their work, which is very low-profile by the way, was being done either in Switzerland or here in the United States, on the West Coast. Well, a few years ago, when the federal government started to emphasize partnerships between the public and private sectors, facilities like the Los Alamos lab began to look for suitable commercial ventures to support, and elements of the private sector likewise looked for federal agencies that might assist them.

"At that time there were people at the lab who supported the S-cubed research. The lab itself couldn't sanction the work, so it declined to become a partner. But the lab did allow the S-cubed group to use some of its equipment. The only limitations were that the work not be done on lab property—yet it had to be close enough so the equipment could be returned on short notice—and it couldn't appear that the lab was a participant.

"S-cubed then found a medical center in Santa Fe, Riverside Memorial, willing to give them space to conduct their research. More important than space, though, was the chance to study patients who were at or near the point of death. When I knew I was coming here, I let the S-cubed group know, and they invited me to participate."

The waitress arrived with their beers and Alex paid the tab.

Sandy took a fresh sip before continuing. "Riverside Memorial is ideal for this kind of work because it has a large geriatric patient load. Many of the patients come from institutions—nursing homes—and they have no close next-of-kin. For some of them, we provide the only companionship they have during their last hours."

Alex felt he had to say something. "You experiment on these people?"

"No, it's not experimenting, or at least it's not supposed to be." Sandy tightly shut his eyes for a moment, as if fighting off a wave of pain, then he swallowed and continued. "The testing we do uses state-of-the-art equipment to detect energies of various kinds and in various states. It doesn't harm the patients in any way; it only monitors them. Each patient, or his legal guardian, has to approve the monitoring. But I have to fess up we don't tell the whole truth. While they know we're interested in changes in energy levels, what they don't know is that we're searching for the soul.

"When a patient who's agreed to be monitored slips toward death, one of us is notified, and we set up the equipment. Last week I was on call, and there was no one closer to the hospital. That's why I had to leave in the middle of our tennis match."

Alex, at a loss for words, sat silently for a moment. Then he said, "And you say you're 'onto it?' What's that mean? You've found the soul?"

"Maybe. But I'd rather not say any more now."

"Sandy, this is important to me. I want to learn a lot more about S-cubed, maybe even participate. You see, my mother and my sister died recently—"

"I'm sorry, Alex."

"Thanks. It's just that this is exactly the kind of question I've been hammering at ever since they died. Is there a God, an afterlife? Can we ever be reunited?"

"Look Alex, I'll introduce you to Doctor 'B.' He can tell you more and explain things better than I can. Excuse me, that's Stanley Bershinski. We call him Doctor B. Stan's in charge of S-cubed, and he's also our best researcher. He has Ph.D.'s in both physics and philosophy. You two probably have a lot in common. His philosophy degree is really in logic, and Stan says that's the most abstract form of mathematics."

"That's true. Your Doctor B probably understands more of the *essence* of mathematics than I do. When can I meet him?"

"As a matter of fact, I've invited Stan for dinner this Thursday. You can meet him then. And if you don't mind, I'll invite Loyola. She doesn't know anything about this, and it's time I told her what's been keeping me so busy. But I need to ask you to keep this a secret, the soul work I mean."

"I understand. I won't say a word to anyone."

Alex drained his beer as he thought about the S-cubed work and its potential ramifications. He shook his head and mumbled something indecipherable.

"What'd you say, partner?"

"Oh, I just said 'goddammed.' It's not going to be easy to comprehend what you've just told me. You haven't got any other monumental secrets, have you?"

# Prologue, Part 12

## Oholi

*The man, on horseback, was thin but powerfully built—Oholi, named for an albino antelope because he had the fairest skin and lightest hair of all the Hachonee. Oholi was on top of Amitolanne and Tepi before they had gone twenty yards. Three of his tribesmen joined him as he dismounted and struggled to hold the woman.*

*Amitolanne was small, but she was wiry and strong, and she fought like a mountain lion. Wiloloaneha rode over to see what the commotion was. By then, with the help of the others, one fully occupied with Tepi, Oholi had a tight hold on Amitolanne.*

*"What do I do with her, Wiloloaneha?"*

*With a sneer he answered, "What is it a woman is good for, Oholi?" Then Wiloloaneha kicked his horse and rode away.*

*The man holding Tepi knew what would happen to the woman and he did not like it. He headed back with the boy to where others were already regrouping.*

# Chapter 12

The next day, after work, another secret from Sandy. But not the secret itself, only about the secret.

*　　　　　*　　　　　*

Sandy met Alex at the Mercedes. Alex unlocked the doors. He settled into the bucket seat, then started the engine. Sandy remained outside the car. Alex had to reach over and rap on the window to get his attention. Sandy absentmindedly climbed in.

"Mind on your work?"

"What's that? Oh, guess so, Alex." Pause. "It's a weapon," was the announcement. "I'm workin' on a friggin' weapon."

"Weapon? I didn't think physicians worked on weapons."

"I'm not building the damned thing, just trying to figure out what makes it tick."

"Does that mean the weapon has something to do with radiation?"

"Yup, and it's what brought me here. The Pentagon handpicked me because of what I know about radiation—to work for Hollis, just to study a new radioactive material. And I'm telling you a tall bit more than I should."

"You don't have to. It's none of my business. I don't have any 'need to know,' as they say."

"I know that, and I'm plumb being torn in two. I wish I could tell you the rest—but it wouldn't be right."

"How hot is this stuff?"

"Hot. The hottest stuff around. Only a handful of people know anything at all about it. Hollis and I are the only ones with full knowledge of the project. It's got the highest security classification in the lab."

"Am I supposed to guess? Is it something that makes a more powerful atomic bomb?"

"No, it's the radiation itself. Different. Lethal. More lethal than it should be."

"So what's the problem?"

"The problem is ethics, morality, maybe something higher. For Hollis there is no problem. But I'm not Hollis. Maybe you were right. Maybe physicians shouldn't be working on weapons."

*　　　　　*　　　　　*

After hearing Sandy talk about Colonel Billy Hollis for two weeks, Alex finally got to judge for himself when he went to Sandy's office to meet Sandy for lunch. Hollis was there, lecturing Sandy in an angry tone of voice, when Alex knocked to let them know he was within earshot. Hollis snapped his mouth shut in mid-sentence, and Sandy introduced him to Alex.

"Sir, I'd like you to meet a friend of mine, Alex Feher. Alex is a mathematician from Virginia Tech, working on ballistic missile defenses here. Alex, this is Colonel Hollis, my boss."

"Pleased to meet you, Colonel. Hope I didn't interrupt anything important."

"No, we were just discussing my philosophy on military appearance."

Alex noticed then how Sandy's hair had begun to creep over his ears, obviously not the military standard. Hollis, who was a short man, at most about five feet seven, had a crew cut and what is known in military circles as "white sidewalls," meaning the hair on the sides of his head had been cut down to skin. Although he was clean-shaven, it was obvious he had a heavy, dark beard, making Alex wonder if Hollis's five o'clock shadow wouldn't be longer than some of the hair on the top of his head.

Colonel Hollis was wearing the complete Army green, or "Class A," uniform, as Sandy later identified it for Alex, meaning an olive jacket and slacks and black necktie. His heavily starched shirt was a lighter shade of green.

With all of his decorations and ornaments, Hollis could have been a Christmas tree in an abstract painting. He wore silver colonel's eagles, bronze unit crests on his epaulettes, the "Big Red One" patch of the First Infantry Division on his right shoulder, a Ranger Tab and another patch on his left shoulder, and gold "U. S." symbols on his lapels, each one above the "shell and flame" insignia of the Ordnance Corps.

His right breast pocket had a black plastic name plate, and above it were two ribbons, one blue and one red, and above them the Ordnance Regimental Crest. Above his left breast pocket were four colorful rows of three ribbons each. Hollis's highest ribbon was the Silver Star with a bronze oak leaf cluster in the center indicating it had been awarded twice. The only other ribbon Alex recognized was the Purple Heart, also adorned with a bronze oak leaf cluster, meaning Hollis had been wounded twice in wartime.

Above the ribbons, nearly reaching the epaulette, was the light blue Combat Infantryman Badge. Below the ribbons, on the pocket were Master Parachutist and Explosive Ordnance Disposal Badges. The blouse was fastened with a row of gleaming gold buttons and covered a brass belt buckle polished to a reverent shine. Black officer stripes ran down the outside of his trousers, and razor-sharp creases in the front met spit-polished black shoes. Hollis had to be one of the few officers who still spit-shined his shoes.

Lieutenant Colonel Sandy Jeffers, on the other hand, wore a more casual form of the Army uniform. His light green shirt was short-sleeved and open at the collar, exposing a wad of chest hair. His pants were bound with a belt not cut to size, leaving about two inches of fabric and a tarnished tab dangling beyond the buckle. The buckle itself looked as if it had never been polished and was adorned with scratches and a good layer of tarnish. He wore Rockport shoes with thick, spongy soles, and made of a wrinkled leather that could never maintain more than a dull gloss, let alone a shine—not at all traditional military.

Hollis squinted at Alex. "So you work on Star Wars, eh? You're wasting your time. Next one'll be a conventional war," he said with conviction, "and we're going to win it. Then there won't be a Russia or Iraq or North Korea to worry about."

What Hollis had said was not completely logical, since the existence of strategic defenses, assuming both sides had them, would *force* the next confrontation to be conventional. Unless, and this thought bothered Alex, one side thought it could easily win a conventional war now and prompted the issue. "You wouldn't have any special way of winning that war, would you, Hollis? Like a secret weapon?"

Hollis moved between Alex and Sandy, next to the standard, government issue gray filing cabinet. He looked suspiciously at Alex, then at Sandy. "You didn't—"

"Course not, sir."

"I hope not, because if curiosity killed the cat, then knowing and telling too many secrets will certainly kill the rat." Wham! Hollis's fist exploded into the side of the filing cabinet. An imprint of his knuckles remained in the metal a half-inch deep.

Someone rapped sharply on the doorjamb. A taller, younger version of Hollis entered the room. His face had a mean look to it, and he didn't acknowledge Alex or Sandy, despite the fact that he was in Sandy's office.

"Colonel, the Pentagon is calling, sir. I put them on hold. You'll have to take it in your office."

"O.K., Major. Tell them I'm coming."

"Colonel," Sandy said, "would you like to join us for chow after your phone call?"

"No. And I expect you to be back in forty-five minutes—standard lunch break. I may need you for something, depending on this call. Understood?"

"Yes sir," Sandy answered, clearly biting back what he really wanted to tell Hollis.

What a pompous jerk. Alex was thankful he didn't have to work with Hollis. He repeated his thought out loud to Sandy. "And who was the other tightass?"

"That was Major Joe Shields. He's just a flunky for Hollis, sort of a military aide. We hardly ever see him, and nobody really knows him personally or knows anything about him. We call him 'the Major' because that's all we do know."

# Prologue, Part 13

# Rape

*Watching Tepi taken from her renewed Amitolanne's fight. She swung out at Oholi, raking at his face, trying to claw out his eyes. Angered by the pain, he released her, but only to get some distance as he swung hard with his fisted right hand, hitting her just behind her left eye. The blow stunned her, and she fell onto the hard mesa ground.*

*Oholi pulled out his knife, leaned over, and began to cut open her clothing. The other two men stood frozen, leering down at Amitolanne until Oholi ordered them to hold her arms and feet.*

*Dazed, Amitolanne felt the mesa rocks at her back, saw the men grouped around her, recognized their intent.*

*Using his fingers to open the way, Oholi forced himself inside her.*

*Now she was fully conscious, aware of what was happening. Sensing this, the two men held her tighter. With the weight of Oholi on top of her, she could do nothing.*

*There was no pain or fear for Amitolanne, only anger. Her arms were pinned to the ground above her head and she struggled to free them, but she could not. She dug her fingernails into the dry mesa soil and arched her body in an attempt to dislodge Oholi. The effort was futile. Snarling like a*

*mad dog, spittle flying, she threw her head and teeth at his neck, but wise-
ly he kept out of reach. Exhausted momentarily, she let her head fall back,
then she tossed it forward again, this time spitting into his face.*

*He ignored the empty insult, concentrating instead on his rising pleas-
ure. Oholi finished with a warlike scream, and the other two men joined
in with their own whooping. As Oholi and the man holding her arms
exchanged places, Amitolanne tried to escape, but Oholi once again hit her
into submission with a single, smashing blow to the side of her head.*

# Chapter 13

Alex had dismissed Hollis and was thinking about Sandy's S-cubed revelations as he fumbled with the key to his front door. He heard the telephone ring, and in his hurry he dropped the key. Easier if you don't rush, Alex reminded himself. Then he calmly picked up the key, opened the door, and grabbed the phone on the fourth ring.

"Hey, Alex. It's me."

"Loyola, this is a pleasant surprise." And it was.

"Sandy had to cancel out on our date tonight, and he suggested you might like some company. Got any dinner plans?"

"No, if you don't count doing a load of wash."

"Sabrina will be with her grandmother all evening. Feel like going to that new French restaurant in Santa Fe you told me about? What was it called?"

"Dinner sounds great, and the restaurant is Le Mistral. Their full-page ad in the Yellow Pages says it's the best restaurant in the state and the only Five-Star restaurant. We can decide for ourselves. I'll call for reservations, and I can pick you up in half an hour."

Alex loved dining in Santa Fe. It had become one of his favorite cities, behind only San Francisco and New Orleans. San Francisco he loved best—its colors, sounds, even its smells, maybe especially its smells. The sea and sourdough fragrance of Fisherman's Wharf and the metal-on-metal, cordite smell of a cable car braking were as heavenly to him as once was the sweet, musky scent of Loyola's perfumed body. But like Loyola, San Francisco had no permanence for Alex. It was too exciting and seductive, a place of magic, but only if you didn't get too close or stay too long. Because if you did, the magic would become commonplace, and what's commonplace isn't magic. And once spoiled, the magic would never return, and even the memory of it would be sour. That's why Alex could never marry Loyola, why he could never live in San Francisco. But he could cherish the visits.

Santa Fe was not San Francisco, but it didn't have to be. It had its own place in American history and its own charms, a city teeming with life amid a sea of tranquillity, a hot campfire on a cold night in the wilderness. A person could have as much—or as little—heat as he could handle. It was someplace, Alex was thinking, that a body could retire to.

The heart and soul of Santa Fe is its Plaza, a one-square-block area smack in the center of downtown and once the end of the notorious Santa Fe Trail. The Plaza is a place for festivals. On its streets are cafes, shops, and historic buildings, including the Palace of the Governors. Built around 1610, the Palace of the Governors is the oldest public building in the country and has served as the seat of government for Spanish, Mexican, and U. S. Territorial rule. Shops and restaurants spill over into the narrow side streets surrounding the Plaza, and just a few blocks away is the Mission of San Miguel of Santa Fe, one of the oldest churches in the country.

Alex found a parking place between the Plaza and the Mission of San Miguel. He locked his car, then he and Loyola walked arm-in-arm to Le Mistral, only two blocks away, one block east of the mission.

It was on their way to the restaurant, as they strolled through the cold evening shadow of the Mission of San Miguel, that Alex told her about meeting Hollis. She stopped walking, and Alex had to tug on her arm to get her moving again.

"Yes, I know who Hollis is. I think most everyone in the lab knows about Hollis. I was even introduced to him once, when the director was giving him a tour of the facilities. He had this major with him, tagging along like some kind of flunky."

Interesting, Alex thought. It was the same word Sandy had used to describe the Major.

"I didn't like Hollis when I met him, and I don't like him now. He looks at you like you're meat. And he has these friends, they're not military—I've heard they're CIA or some other kind of spooks, but they look like thugs. I don't trust Hollis. I think he's dangerous."

"Well let's forget about Hollis. There's Le Mistral up ahead—not exactly what I'd pictured." Alex purposely changed the subject as they came within sight of the restaurant. And Le Mistral did not look like a restaurant, at least not the fine one it was touted to be. Constructed of white adobe, its simple style matched its surroundings perfectly.

The maitre d' seated them in a bright open-air room and presented them with menus as simple as the decor. The menu listed only eight entrees, standard supper fare, but after the last entree there were "additional, daily specials." After taking their drink orders, the waiter recited the specials of the day, and his list outnumbered the items on the menu.

Alex and Loyola each selected from the list of specials. For their appetizers, Alex ordered a plate of crisp, light, fried yucca topped with chunks of pork.

For her entree, Loyola ordered fettuccine with salmon. The fettuccine was prepared al dente, with chunks of salmon, grill-striped and crusty but lusciously moist, flavored with shreds of basil, double-blanched garlic, and a drizzle of olive oil, all topped with diced, garden-fresh tomatoes and deliciously tangy Parmesan cheese.

Alex's choice, after asking the waiter for his recommendation, was more basic: venison prepared with mushrooms and red wine. The full-bodied, gamy venison flavor was tempered perfectly by the tasty wine sauce, and the result was the tenderest, tastiest meat he had ever eaten.

But what impressed Alex most at Le Mistral was the dessert menu, also recited by the waiter. Once again he rattled off about a dozen items, all sounding elegant and scrumptious, with one exception: red raspberries. Alex loved red raspberries, but the waiter did not say how they would be prepared.

"Raspberries? How do you serve them? With cream? Or with a liqueur?"

The waiter seemed to be waiting for this moment. Like a haughty English butler, he responded matter-of-factly, "How would you like them served, sir?"

When Alex didn't immediately respond, having been taken aback somewhat, the waiter offered several innovative suggestions. Alex's choice was to have them over peach shortcake, then topped with freshly whipped cream.

Alex and Loyola didn't discuss or even mention Hollis during their dinner—yet his specter was present, like the lingering smell of a bad cigar. Afterward, Alex took her back to her house.

"Wouldn't you like to come in for a while?" she said seductively. "Sabrina can spend the night at the pueblo."

"I don't think I should," he answered, though not very convincingly, he thought.

"Actually, Alex, I'm feeling kind of upset. Could you just stay with me for a while?"

"Sure."

Loyola was inexplicably nervous, and Hollis seemed to be the only explanation. "No, it wasn't talking about him," she said. "I don't know what it is, exactly. It's more like a premonition."

Alex wanted to ask what, if anything, she knew about S-cubed but decided to stay on safer subjects. An hour later, he offered to get Sabrina and bring her back home, but Loyola didn't want to stay by herself, so she rode with Alex to the pueblo.

Alex helped tuck Sabrina into her bed. As he was leaving, Loyola suddenly pulled him to her and kissed him goodnight. "Thanks, Alex, for everything," she said.

*     *     *

The next day at his mid-morning break, Alex saw Loyola seated at one of the outdoor tables behind the Otowi Building. He brought two Danish and two coffees, and asked if he could join her.

"Sure, Alex, and thanks again for last night. I don't know what got into me."

"No problem. Hope it wasn't the food."

"No," she laughed, "it better not be. Not at those prices. By the way, Sandy thanks you too. And he says we're both invited tonight to meet some professor he works with. Do you know what that's all about?"

Alex briefly summed up what he knew about the S-cubed project. She didn't seem as impressed with the news as he'd been, but then again, she was getting it secondhand. Besides, he hadn't allowed it to sink in fully yet, postponing that until he could meet and hear from Doctor B, so he wasn't even sure what he thought about it.

"And Sandy asked if you would you mind picking me up. He'll be busy, and my car is in the shop." They made their arrangements, and the rest of the workday sped by.

The evening was cool. Alex drove to Jemez Springs, where Loyola lived, with his windows firmly up and the climate control system set to HEAT but without the fan.

She was out in front of her small, two-bedroom frame house, waiting for him. She had been using her fingers to pinch dead blooms from the rose bushes growing along both sides of the gravel driveway. Rose petals the color of dried blood lay around her feet. She clapped her hands together, scissors fashion, to dust them off, then she headed toward Alex, who had come around the car to meet her and open the car door for her.

"Hi, lover," she said seductively.

"You're oversexed, I swear."

Loyola laughed. "Actually, I'm tired." She was also much more relaxed than the last two times Alex had seen her.

For most of the drive back to Los Alamos they said nothing. Loyola broke the silence. "I love Sandy's house. The owners are supposed to be filthy rich."

"I've only been inside the front door, but from the outside, it looks like it would sell for twice what the Andrews' would bring."

"And I'm glad he invited both of us. Me because this is important to him and it makes me feel like I'm important to him, and you—well, I know how close you two have become."

Alex answered, his eyes on the highway ahead, "Yeah, but I think there's more he isn't telling about his work and about those spur-of-the-moment trips to Santa Fe."

"Maybe he's got another girlfriend there, somebody hotter than me."

"No way," Alex laughed.

Sandy had told them seven o'clock and they arrived on time. He seemed unusually formal as he met them at the front door, kissing Loyola on the cheek and shaking Alex's hand. He guided them to the living room, a huge room decorated in gold and green and obviously furnished by someone with expensive tastes. Sandy poured three glasses of a dry white wine. Alex and Loyola settled into large wingback chairs the color of old haystacks, and Sandy seated himself on the matching couch. Alex, even Loyola, looked at Sandy with anticipation.

"Loyola, did Alex tell you about the S-cubed project?" She nodded. "I'm sorry I've kept it from you, but the whole thing is very secretive."

"That's O.K., I understand. Are you going to tell us more?"

"I guess it's time I did."

The two listeners sat back and waited.

"We think we've found it."

Alex responded first. "Say that again?"

"The soul. We've found it. Doctor B will be here shortly and I'll let him tell you more about it."

"I can't wait that long," Alex said. "You've got to tell us something now. Like what is it, and where is it, and where does it go when we die?"

"Well," Sandy began slowly, "it's an energy form, and it's nowhere specific, at least not that we can pinpoint. We do have definite evidence of it leaving, or changing, at the moment of death, which, by the way, S-cubed defines as the moment when the soul leaves. It gets us into all sorts of difficulty with brain-dead comparisons. And I'll have to defer to Doctor B on the 'where it goes' question.

"To be honest with you, I was aiming to talk about something more serious, if you can believe that. But I don't know—"

# Prologue, Part 14

## Too Much to Carry

*As Amitolanne came to, the second man whooped out his completion, and the third prepared to take his place. Amitolanne began to make peace with her gods. She did not look at the man who was mounting her; she looked through him. Her whole being was based, no absorbed, in her gods, yet focused on these men.*

*She stopped struggling, and the look on her face, at first peaceful, became intent, ominous. As her face changed, the last Hachonee man over her reacted, first with puzzlement, then fear. He forced himself to a climax, but with no war cries or whoops, with only a grimace straining his face, his eyes tightly shut.*

*He stole a glance at Amitolanne's face, to see if that look was still with her. It was, and his shame and fear were so great he felt as though his soul, not his semen, had spurted from his body—as if his soul were no longer his to own.*

*After he righted himself and stood over Amitolanne, he said to Oholi, "Let's take her back. She will make a good mistress."*

*"We already have too much to carry. She has done all she can for us."*

*"Then give her a horse, so she can find her way to another tribe."*

*"I will take care of her. You two go see if Wiloloaneha needs any help."*
*The two men quickly mounted their horses, and without looking back*
*to see what was going to happen, rode off in search of Wiloloaneha.*

# Chapter 14

---

Sandy was cut off and mildly startled by the harsh buzz of the old-fashioned front doorbell. "I reckon that's Doctor B. Excuse me while I get the door."

After Sandy had left the room, Alex and Loyola looked at each other with a thousand questions.

In a moment Sandy returned, ushering into the room a short man, barely five feet tall, about fifty years old and dressed almost entirely in black.

"Loyola, Alex, I'd like you to meet Stanley Bershinski. Stanley is currently on sabbatical from the Technische Hochschule in Zurich and lives in Santa Fe. Stan, this is Loyola Sanchez and Alex Feher."

As he rose to shake hands, Alex had to smother his amusement at Doctor B's garb. He wore a black suit, very old-fashioned and much too heavy for the summertime, with a narrow black tie over a white shirt aged yellow. Draped on his shoulders was a long black cape, and in his left hand he held what looked like a stovepipe hat. In addition, he had a bushy black beard streaked with gray, and the entire apparition reminded Alex of one of the Smith Brothers from the cough drop box.

Professor Stanley Bershinski's voice was deep, too deep for such a small man, and accented, probably Central European. The voice reminded Alex of someone else, but he couldn't place it.

"You are Hungarian, no, Mr. Feher?" Doctor B asked.

Alex replied, as he always did when someone recognized the Hungarian last name, "Yes and no. My grandparents came from Hungary, but I've never been there and I can't speak a word of Hungarian"—a statement not true, since many of the words, expressions, and numbers his grandparents had taught him were ingrained in his memory.

"Alex is a mathematician at the lab, on loan from Virginia Polytechnic Institute in Blacksburg," Sandy added, as he handed Doctor B a glass of wine. Dr. B took a seat in the middle of the couch, and Sandy sat on the floor facing the three others.

"Thank you, Sandy. Ach, yes, it is so, Mr. Feher, many mathematicians are Hungarian. Then it is a pity you do not know the language—a beautiful, mathematical language."

Henry Kissinger. That's whose voice it was. Dr. B's first language must have been German or something close to it. "The" was "dee," "so" was "zo," and "what" was "vhat." Alex smiled to himself at his discovery.

"And you, Miss Sanchez, you do not look entirely Spanish. What, if I may pry, is your background?"

"I'm American. Native American. My ancestors were part of a tribe known as the Tamoneehas. The Spanish name comes from the mixing of the cultures over the last few hundred years."

"Ach, yes, I see now. Thank you."

Alex was set to ask Doctor B about his research when, much to his surprise, Loyola got right to the heart of the matter.

"Dr. Bershinski, Sandy has told us something of your research project, 'S-cubed.' Could you explain it to us? Is there really evidence of an immortal soul?"

Doctor B looked sternly at Sandy, putting him on the defensive. "I was with Alex last week when I got called to the hospital. Alex is a good friend of mine, and Loyola is, well, also a good friend of mine, and I know they'll be discreet about this."

Sandy's remarks seemed to satisfy Doctor B, as his eyes softened a bit and he nodded slightly. "It is a very interesting subject, yes, but also very new and very, how do you say, tentative. It is too early to publicize the results of our testing. We must do much more testing first. Perhaps you would prefer to wait for more firm conclusions. You know, this is a subject that causes many people fear—not just fear of the unknown—that is easy to overcome. But for many people, their lives, their religions are based on theories that they regard as truths, which our work may disprove. However, the answers we find could also give many people hope and a new outlook on life—or death."

"I understand your concern, Dr. Bershinski," Alex said, "and I assure you we'll keep whatever we learn to ourselves. But having heard about some of what you've found, you must understand we're curious and we would like to learn more. You can put us in the category of those who would find hope from any evidence of the soul that you discover."

Sandy pushed himself up from the floor. "I'm sorry to interrupt," he said, "but I have a roast that's been in the oven much too long. Could we chow down now and hold the serious discussion until after dinner?"

They moved to the dining room, where Sandy served an overdone but nonetheless adequate rump roast, over yellow rice his maid had prepared earlier in the day. They made only polite conversation at the dinner table, saving the soul discussion for dessert and brandy. During dinner, Doctor B seemed to loosen up, helped by the wine, a strong and fruity sangria. He downed his fourth glass faster than he had the third. Sandy, however, was still on edge, and appeared anxious to get on with the evening, and to whatever it was he had to tell Alex.

After dinner they adjourned to the living room, brandy glasses in hand. Alex sat in one of the wingbacks, and Loyola took the couch where Sandy could join her. He had gone to the back yard to retrieve four hardwood logs for the fireplace, and now he was looking for a box of matches.

Doctor B had barely seated himself when Alex said, "Please, Dr. Bershinski, tell us what you can about your research and what you've found."

"All right, but only if Miss Sanchez will tell me something about Indian beliefs in this regard, the soul I mean. Although I have done much research, I must confess I have never looked into American Indian lore. Will you do that Miss Sanchez?"

"Yes, certainly, but I need to warn you that Indian beliefs vary widely, almost from tribe to tribe. I will tell you about my tribe, but only after you've finished."

Doctor B chuckled. "Fair enough. Yes, I shall begin." And, after a moment to gather his thoughts and swig some brandy, he did.

# Prologue, Part 15

## Death and Celebration

*Oholi stared down at Amitolanne, who lay on the ground alert but motionless. White semen, man's life seed, dripped slowly from between her dark legs onto the back of her tan leather skirt.*

*Oholi again took out his knife. He placed his right foot on her chest, just below her naked breasts, and grabbed her long black hair firmly with his left hand. She did not resist, but as he forced her head back, their gazes met, hatred in his, something more terrible and frightening in hers.*

*He said nothing and she did not make a sound, although she closed her eyes and once again embraced her gods, as he slit her throat. Amitolanne's lifeblood flowed freely, joining that of so many others, finding its way easily into the thirsty Black Mesa soil and spreading wide and deep, like the roots of some ancient tree.*

*Oholi's knife hand was covered with Amitolanne's blood. He stared at it for a moment, then he wiped it off, rubbing his hand across her naked breasts. Oholi stood, and in a final gesture of contempt, he washed the blood into the ground by urinating on her body.*

*He mounted his horse, then rode to the edge of the mesa, near the trail they had used to climb to the top. The rest of his tribe, gathered there around Wiloloaneha, were already celebrating their victory, trading stories of heroic deeds.*

# Chapter 15

---

Doctor B leaned forward in his chair, stared at Alex and Loyola for a moment, then looked down at his lap in thought. His hands came up, open and slightly apart, shaped as if they were holding a beach ball or cradling a small basket. He looked back up, clasped his hands together, and began.

"I will do my best to put this in layman terms. To talk about searching for an immortal soul, we must consider two things. One is evidence of the existence or the presence of the soul within the body. The other is the question of its immortality. Of course we don't know—can't prove—that the soul is immortal, because we do not know what 'forever' means. But what we can look for, after we have identified what we think is the soul, is proof of it continuing to exist after the death of the body.

"What we have found is evidence for both. Because of the generosity of some of your associates at the laboratory, we have discovered within each human a form of energy unlike anything known before. Even if we had known of such an energy, we would not have been able to detect it or measure it, because it is of such small magnitude. The laboratory's equipment has made that possible.

"We have monitored this energy—call it the soul if you'd like—in a number of subjects. So far as we can tell, it has no specific location. It seems to be spread throughout the body, although a better description might be that it 'belongs to' the body.

"The energy is always the same, regardless of the age or race or sex of the subject. We have not attempted to alter it in any way, nor would we want to try, but from what we can tell, that is not possible anyway—nor should it be. That is God's business."

Sandy dropped his gaze, averting it from Doctor B's darting glances. He shifted uneasily in his chair, then looked back to Doctor B, who had paused as if waiting for Sandy to get comfortable.

"We have spent most of our effort examining the energy in dying patients. By that I mean we have tracked the energy form at the moment of death.

"To explain what happens, I must first give some simple mathematical background. I know that's not necessary for you, Alex, but please bear with me." Alex nodded for Doctor B to continue. "Then I will use an analogy to describe the soul and its transitions.

"We live in a three-dimensional world, yes? But using mathematics, we can describe any number of dimensions. For example, take a piece of paper with x- and y-coordinate axes drawn on it, along with the graph of some curve. A point on the graph is described by two coordinates, or numbers in a specified order. 'One, two' is not the same point as 'two, one.' A point in three dimensions is described by three coordinates, and a point in, say, seventeen dimensions—abstract to us—is described by seventeen coordinates. Now, how do we everyday humans relate to the abstract? Can seventeen-dimensional space be relevant to our three-dimensional world?

"The answer is yes, and I will illustrate this. Information about a curve in two dimensions can often be discerned from knowledge of straight lines tangent to the curve at certain points. Let me give you an example that every student of elementary calculus knows. A two-dimensional curve is known to have a local maximum at some point if tangent lines to the left of that point have positive slope, tangent lines to the right have negative slope, and at the point itself, the tangent line is horizontal, or has zero slope. So tangent lines—one-dimensional spaces—can impart knowledge about two-dimensional curves.

"In a similar way, the idea of slopes imparting knowledge can be extended to three dimensions by examining the orientation of planes tangent to a given surface at certain points. So, three-dimensional surfaces can be described by looking—mathematically—at tangent planes which are two-dimensional. Likewise, we can extend this notion to three-dimensional surfaces, things we can see and touch, imparting knowledge about four-dimensional surfaces, things purely abstract.

"And so spaces and dimensions real for us can be related to the abstract by a ladder-like process from one dimension to the next."

Doctor B paused for breath and to allow for questions but no one spoke.

"In a completely different vein, it is possible to connect higher dimensional spaces with numerically related lower dimensional spaces. For example, we might gain knowledge about an object in six dimensions by examining certain surfaces in two and/or three dimensions, six being three times two. Or, dimensions that are powers of two, like thirty-two and sixteen, can often be related to lower dimensional spaces, and so can those that are one more or less than a power of two, like fifteen or seventeen. My point is that mathematically there is a firm basis for understanding higher, abstract spaces, often in such a way as to be able to relate them to our three-dimensional world.

"Now, what does this have to do with the soul, that part of us that survives our bodily death? We have found, and we have a firm theoretical model based on physical evidence to support this, that the soul is not confined to three dimensions as we—our bodies—are. By monitoring the soul energy we've discovered, and by using sophisticated modeling techniques, we find that the energy detected is only a part of the total. The total soul is an entity in seventeen dimensions. Maybe instead of saying a body possesses a soul, we should be saying that each of our bodies is a part of its soul."

Doctor B paused briefly, as if anticipating a question from either Alex or Loyola, but their minds were playing leapfrog, trying to stay with their lecturer.

"How can this be, you ask? Let me illustrate." Doctor B had been gesturing, looking mostly at his hands, or the ceiling, or at a point on the wall above Alex and Loyola. Now he looked Alex squarely in the eyes, as if to make sure Alex understood this was not all folly and conjecture. "Our findings support this analogy, by the way."

Doctor B's glare softened and he continued. "For simplicity, imagine the seventeen-dimensional soul as a hollow three-dimensional sphere—three will play the part of seventeen. Now our three-dimensional universe of existence will be played by a piece of paper—a two-dimensional plane. Picture the sphere, your soul, passing through space over time. It exists prior to your conception, and it will continue to exist after your death. Picture it approaching the plane of paper. When it first makes contact with the paper, it touches at only one point, or you could say that the paper is tangent to the sphere."

Doctor B had begun to gesture again, his eyes roaming from his hands to the wall, to the ceiling, and back again as he spoke.

"This first contact between the soul and our three-dimensional existence happens at the moment of conception. Now picture the sphere passing through the plane of paper. Again, the paper represents our three-dimensional world. The intersection of the sphere and the plane is an individual's worldly existence, which happens to be a circle in our analogy. Notice that the circle is always part of the sphere, but within the plane it seems to be an entity unto itself, constantly changing throughout its 'existence.' That existence ends at the moment of death, when the sphere is again tangent to the paper, but on the other side—a curious expression, no, Miss Sanchez?"

Doctor B was looking at Loyola, who had not yet caught the pun, but he was obviously amused with whatever he'd said, so she smiled and nodded.

"Then the sphere, or soul, continues its journey through space and time, but without our bodily knowledge.

"Our findings show that at the moment of death, the soul, the energy form, disappears from our world. You have heard of the Law of Conservation of Energy—energy cannot be created or destroyed but only changed from one form to another. This is the first example of the law not holding—at least not holding within our three dimensions. The law is probably still valid in the greater universe. But for us the soul simply disappears. Poof. And in our world, the energy loss is so small it seems to make no difference. It is like a grain of sand disappearing from the ocean. Who would notice?"

With that question Doctor B raised his eyebrows, shoulders, and hands, palm up, all at once. They all came down together, and so did his head as he paused for a second. Then his head lifted and he began again.

"We have likewise initiated studies of conception, and we find that the soul energy mysteriously appears at a certain point very shortly after fertilization. For us, that is the real moment of conception, even though in contemporary science, conception is regarded as a several-day process, no longer the moment when sperm first meets egg."

Doctor B looked from Alex to Loyola and back again. He squinted with his right eye and raised the eyebrow over his left eye as if to underline what he was about to say. "I do not attempt to explain any of the 'why' questions, nor to answer all of the 'how' questions. I just presume there is a higher presence, God, in charge of all of this."

Alex and Loyola both nodded in agreement. Sandy sat passively, staring down, his chin resting on fingertips pressed together as if in prayer.

"By the way, this theory offers an explanation for many of the unexplainable phenomena in our lives. Extrasensory perception, for instance, and out-of-body experiences. Even reincarnation. Using the analogy, our existence is the circle within the plane, but the soul extends beyond the plane. It provides a continuous surface, a medium if you like, for the transfer of information, if only we knew how to make it happen. The things I have mentioned, like ESP, happen without understanding. They are accidents. Perhaps one day we will be able to control the passage of information beyond our plane." He paused. "Then again, maybe that would not be such a good idea."

"You mean," Alex said, "the reason I might know what's happening right now fifty miles from here is that some higher dimensional path exists connecting me to that spot?"

"Precisely," Doctor B said. "And an out-of-body experience could just be an extension of awareness into the other dimensions of your existence—not really a departure from the three dimensions of your body."

Loyola also thought of metaphysical possibilities. "And reincarnation could be a second passing of the sphere through the plane—the same soul energy in a new body."

Alex had another observation. "And soul mates—" Lisa Martin suddenly came to mind, but he ignored the intrusion into his thought process and continued. "People destined to be together—could be a literal reality. There might be some overlap in higher dimensions."

"Yes, certainly."

"Now," Doctor B asked like a good professor, "what other questions do you have?"

Alex and Loyola alternated asking a few more questions, Alex's generally more technical, Loyola's more philosophical. Doctor B fielded most of them comfortably. Sandy occasionally contributed, usually restating what Doctor B had said, but in simpler, more understandable terms. It was obvious to Alex that Sandy understood a good bit more of the technical theory, the mathematics and the physics, than he had professed earlier. Alex also had the impression that Doctor B had given much thought to the implications of his research, the only source of discomfort Alex could detect.

# Prologue, Part 16

## Rain and Remnants

*The Hachonee withdrew from Black Mesa the same day, leaving the Nopeka bodies for scavengers. In a few days nothing would be left but bones and the clothing that had not been stolen from the dead.*

*That evening, wind, lightning, and thunder came to Black Mesa. This time they brought rain. The constant, pelting rain cleared the air and washed the footprints and bloodstains from the mesa top, but the rain was not strong enough to wash away the deeds of the Hachonee, who left not as victors but as butchers, their deeds now as much a part of the mesa as any rock or cactus.*

*Amitolanne's son, Tepi, was taken back to the Hachonee village, where he was brought up as one of their tribe. He was a good hunter and lived for many years, though he never forgot what had happened to his own people. He knew in his heart that the gods were just. They would somehow punish those responsible for the cowardly acts on Black Mesa. A few years after Tepi's death, the Hachonee themselves were defeated in war, the remnants of their tribe scattered across New Mexico and Arizona like so much wind-blown chaff.*

# Chapter 16

Loyola and Alex finally ran out of questions for Doctor B some two hours later. They stood and stretched, and Sandy refilled their wine glasses before putting two more logs on the fire. Doctor B waited patiently until the others had resettled into their chairs, and then he reminded Loyola of her promise to tell them about the Indian version of the soul.

"O.K., but as I said, beliefs vary widely, and I can only speak to what was handed down within my own tribe."

Loyola moved to the fireplace and leaned close to the warmth of the fire for a moment before turning back to her audience. She arranged herself comfortably on the floor and slipped her shoes off.

"My ancestors believed that when someone was born he possessed an immortal soul given to him by God, the supreme deity. He was also 'loaned' a secondary soul, from a lesser god, to be carried with him throughout his life on earth. Upon his death, the secondary soul was 'weighed' to determine the fate of the immortal soul. That soul could either move on to what you would call 'heaven,' or remain somewhere in between life and death, sentenced forever to a state of limbo.

"Indians—supposedly—didn't lie or steal, so the lesser soul wasn't weighed according to an accumulation of good or evil as we might think of it today. Instead it was weighed according to the courage of its bearer. By the way," she added, "many of the qualities you and I ascribe to good, such as kindness, compassion, and justice, were also regarded as qualities associated with courage.

"Let me tell you a story you may find interesting. You know the mesa called Black Mesa, the round one that sits by itself between here and Santa Fe?"

Alex nodded with the others, picturing the mesa in his mind. From the distance it did appear black, darkened by the scrub vegetation around the sides and the thick shrubs and short trees on the top.

For Alex the memory was fresh and still unsettling. Black Mesa had been gnawing at him since his arrival that summer. He could see it—couldn't help but stare at it—during his nightly walks on Deer Trap Mesa. He recalled having been told it was the scene of a great Indian battle, and also that he'd made a promise to himself to explore it some-time. Funny he'd never asked Loyola about Black Mesa, he thought.

Loyola continued. "There are many stories about Black Mesa. During the late 1600's, pueblo Indians revolted against Spanish control. By tak-ing refuge on Black Mesa, the San Ildefonsan Indians held out against the Spanish two years longer than most other pueblos.

"But the oldest story is about a series of great battles between two tribes, the Nopeka and Hachonee, well before the Spanish arrived. The Nopeka were farmers, living peaceably in the Jemez valley. Then the Hachonee invaded, looking to expand their hunting grounds. The Nopeka defended well, but they were outnumbered. Slowly their forces dwindled. As a last resort, they moved onto Black Mesa where it was easier to defend themselves. Even so, they had no hope of winning. They could only postpone defeat. The Nopeka fought in an inspired way and held out for years."

Loyola's tone changed; she became more somber. "I live within sight of Black Mesa. I see it every day, and I grew up with it peering over my shoulder. Yet I still have an uneasy feeling when I look at it. They say the Hachonee should have stopped their attack. Annihilation of the Nopeka may have been inevitable, but it wasn't necessary, especially with the courage shown by the defenders. But to stop the onslaught required more courage from the Hachonee leaders than it took to lead the attack, so they kept killing until every defender was dead.

"Each woman was a defender, as was every child old enough to carry a weapon. Most died in the fighting, but many were wounded and some were captured. Those still alive were tortured before being killed. The women were raped and the men mutilated. Only the smallest children survived, babies really, who were taken back and brought up within the Hachonee tribe.

"The Hachonee withdrew from the mesa after the battle. Black Mesa itself wasn't important, only annihilation of the Nopeka. The ground there is now sacred, to commemorate the bravery of the Nopeka. But we do not go there, not because the mesa is sacred—but because we're afraid of the mesa.

"Shortly after the battle was won, the Hachonee moved elsewhere. Many lived long lives. But it's said that as they died, those who fought the Nopeka, one by one their souls were found deficient—and condemned to remain at Black Mesa. It is also said their souls roam the area in search of redemption. But that is not possible. They can never do anything equal in weight to the weight of their sins, so they continue to roam, and they will roam forever.

"By the way, the Tamoneeha tribe, my tribe, was descended from the Hachonee. So I must have some Hachonee blood—and probably Nopeka for that matter."

Finished with what she had to say, Loyola got up and moved back to sit with Sandy, who put his arm around her as she sat down.

They continued to talk for a while, but Alex was tired, and Doctor B, who had been drinking continuously throughout the evening, was now quite drunk.

Doctor B, using arms more than legs, pushed himself up and out of his chair. "Excuse me," he said, "I must visit the bathroom." The others watched as he walked unsteadily down the hall.

Alex took the opportunity to speak to Sandy. "I'm afraid I've got to leave soon. Was there something else you wanted to talk about?"

Loyola leaned over and kissed Sandy on the cheek. "Me too. I've got to pick up Sabrina."

"Yes, there was," Sandy said, "but it'll hold. I'm afraid Doctor B isn't in any condition to leave, so I'll either keep him here for the night or drive him home myself. Alex, mind taking Loyola back?"

"No, not at all."

"In the morning I need to tidy up some things at Riverside, but I should be in my office around ten. Why don't you stop by then and I'll tell you what it's all about."

They waited until Doctor B returned, then Alex and Loyola excused themselves, thanking Sandy for the dinner and Doctor B for sharing the results of the S-cubed work with them.

*       *       *

They were already off Barranca Mesa and heading past the small Los Alamos airport. "So what do you think?" Loyola asked.

"I don't know, but I guess it's what I've always hoped for—that some part of us would live on. Of course we don't know what that means, but the hope is there, for something like heaven, I mean. What about you?"

"I'm a little stunned, and I feel sick to my stomach. Like I'm suddenly closer to God, but I'm not sure I'm supposed to be there."

They were leaving Los Alamos proper now. "I feel the same way. You know, when Doctor B was telling us about the soul as an energy form, I got to wondering, how's that any better than just being any form of biological life—something that lives on this earth and then dies? So what if an energy form survives? Even if it is forever, it's meaningless unless there's some tie to God.

"And I can't explain it, but then I got to feeling that there was a connection, that somehow I knew it. Or maybe I extended myself out of this existence into the other fourteen dimensions of my soul and took a look. I don't know, but I felt it then…and I still feel it now. Of course it might just be wishful thinking, since I'd like to know for certain that somehow, somewhere I'll see my mom and my sister again. But," he said as Black Mesa appeared before them in the night, "with the S-cubed results, I'm beginning to believe that I will be with them again, and no matter what happens on this earth, that can't be taken away."

# Chapter 17

---

The next morning Alex was slowly awakened by sunlight slicing warmly through gaps in the otherwise dark curtains of his bedroom window. He hadn't slept much, and as he opened his eyes, shielding them from the light, he vaguely remembered dreaming. The dream had left dull impressions, like beach footprints washed once already by a gentle wave.

He could remember being frightened at the prospect of dying—nothing new to his dreams. But he was also somehow heartened, as if dying were not so bad, as if a heaven truly awaited him. But there was another fear that lingered, an uneasy one because it had no basis: a fear of the yet unknown. He yawned and rubbed his eyes, trying to focus his thoughts, then the evening came back to him, washing the rest of the footprints away.

Alex lay in bed waiting for the burst of energy that would get him started. He was physically and mentally tired, but it was Friday, so he could catch up on his rest over the weekend. If he wanted to. New Mexico gave him travel opportunities he didn't have on the East Coast, so weekends were not to be wasted.

Las Vegas sprang to mind. The airport at Albuquerque was a two-hour drive away, flights were always available, and flying time to Las Vegas was only an hour, so he could be on the Strip by ten o'clock that same evening. He'd done it before on the spur of the moment, and today some inner voice was urging him to make the trip. With the voice came the feeling that he was going to be lucky. But first there was a full day of work, including a meeting with John, and, of course, the business with Sandy, whatever that was.

Alex looked at the clock, groaned, and forced himself up and out of bed. He made his way to the bathroom and took a long, hot shower. He worked up a good lather, luxuriated in it, reflecting on the previous evening.

It was cold as he toweled off, so he slipped on a heavy cotton robe and his comfortable but well-worn brown leather slippers. Then Alex went upstairs to the kitchen and poured himself a cup of black coffee, brewed by the timer he'd set the evening before. After getting dressed and putting food and fresh water out for the cats, he fixed his break-fast—bran flakes covered with strawberries sliced half an inch thick, topped with milk.

Breakfast was how Alex fortified himself for the day ahead. More than nutrition, it meant relaxing, organizing, and settling his mind. He turned on the radio, already set to an "easy listening" station, and then sat at the kitchen table where he could gaze out the back window. Beyond the deck lay nothing but raw nature: Piñon Canyon, Deer Trap Mesa, and the Jemez Mountains far to the west. But this morning, it was the bird feed-er just outside the kitchen window that captured his attention.

The bird feeder was a large, simple tray on a six-foot pole. Alex kept it stocked with wild birdseed. Wrens and sparrows were frequent visi-tors, and an occasional cardinal added color to the otherwise drab gray and brown gathering.

Alex liked to watch the wrens. They were neighbors, having built nests in the canyon rocks beyond the back yard. They could be seen flit-ting to and fro among the rocks and from the canyon to the deck, either to the feeder or to the spillover of seed on the deck floor. Agile and live-ly birds, one second they'd be nowhere in sight, then suddenly they were at the tray of seed, then they'd be gone again at the slightest noise or movement.

This morning a single wren gorged himself at the feeder; he'd been there almost as long as Alex had been at the kitchen table with his bowl of cereal. Tail erect and constantly on alert, the wren ate, looked around, hopped from one edge to another, ate again, then repeated the defensive maneuvering.

What was he so afraid of? The cats could not climb the pole, and there were no other threats nearby. Even so, the wren did not relax his guard.

Alex looked at the mother cat, a large all-white mixed breed, curled up asleep in a far corner of the kitchen. The cat opened her eyes and looked back at Alex. How did she know? Then the cat must have spotted the bird at the feeder, because she rose straight up, lowered her head, and walked stealthily toward the small animal door in the lower half of the kitchen's back door that led out onto the deck.

Before the cat was halfway across the kitchen, the wren took off, dropping sunflower seeds to the deck as it fled.

On his way to work, Alex wondered how the wren knew the cat was coming. And why he, Alex, felt like the wren. Was he being watched? And by whom? No, that was silly.

After arriving at his office, Alex tackled his cluttered desk. He sorted papers and notes into several piles, picked up the largest pile, and dropped it into his trashcan. It was a routine he usually went through on Mondays, just before his weekly meeting with John, during which Alex brought John up-to-date on his work and John disseminated new information and guidance. The meeting was scheduled for this morning because John was leaving at noon for a well-earned, do-nothing vacation in the Caribbean. The meeting went well; John was pleased with what Alex had done so far and he said so.

Finished with John, Alex tried calling Sandy. No answer. Then he tried Loyola and had better luck.

"I'm thinking about going to Las Vegas for the weekend," he told her. "Do you suppose you and Sandy could come along?"

"I don't know about Sandy, but I can't, at least not this weekend. I've been spending so much time away from Sabrina, I promised her a weekend of activities, just the two of us. I thought we'd drive down to Albuquerque tomorrow morning and do some shopping, then stop and have dinner in Santa Fe on the way back. Sunday is still unsettled, but the day belongs to Sabrina. But you have a good time."

"I haven't decided for sure if I'm going, and I probably won't until I see how tired I am after work. I didn't sleep very well last night—kept dreaming about heaven and my beach ball of a soul."

"Wasn't that something?" Loyola answered. "I couldn't get it off my mind. I woke up thinking about it. Is Sandy in yet? I'd like to go with you, to find out what's bothering him. How could it be any more serious than discovery of the soul?"

"I tried Sandy a few minutes ago and he didn't answer, but it's nearly ten. He said he'd be there. Why don't I pick you up? Then we can grab some coffee and head over to his office."

They stopped at Otowi but carried their coffees with them as they left. The sunshine that had awakened Alex was gone, replaced by a thickening, ominous fog.

But the fog did nothing to dampen Alex's spirit, riding high, elevated by knowledge of a soul, of everlasting life, of a chance to someday be reunited with the people he had loved and lost. But Alex's analytical side would not rest either, would not allow him total euphoria. It reminded him that more questions had been raised than had been answered.

Who knew what continuation from this life into other dimensions was like? And why—*why*—was it possible to determine that a soul existed? Could any *real* God allow this to happen? *Was* God allowing this to happen? Yes, there were many questions yet to be answered.

# Chapter 18

Alex and Loyola approached Sandy's office. Alex saw him first, seated at his desk. His head was bowed, his hands propping up his forehead, as if he were deep in thought or poring over some technical paper. But there was no paper. The desktop was clean.

Alex followed Loyola through the door and into the office. Her "Hi, lover" was followed by Alex's cheerful "Good morning—so what's up?"

Sandy raised his head slowly. His eyes looked terrible, bloodshot and puffy. "Shut the door and lock it."

Alex did so.

With a haggard smile, Sandy quickly apologized. "I'm sorry if I was rude. Good morning—and please sit down. My nerves are shot. Didn't get more than a wink of sleep last night."

Loyola sat in the chair next to the desk but Alex remained standing. "Did you have to take Doctor B home?" he asked.

"Yes, but that wasn't it. I've got something on my mind, something terrible."

Loyola clearly felt uncomfortable. "Maybe you'd rather just talk to Alex." She started to get up.

"No, please stay," Sandy said as he moved behind her and put his hands on her shoulders. "You already know about the S-cubed project—what I have to say is related. Besides," he joked feebly, "Alex will be too analytical about this. I need a human response."

No one said anything, so Sandy continued. "I know I haven't told you much about the kind of work I'm doing here, the project I'm working on."

"Only that it has to do with some new kind of radiation," Alex offered in response. "And a weapon."

Loyola glanced sharply at Alex.

"That's right," Sandy said, "but let me explain. You know that fission produces nuclear energy—fission of uranium or plutonium nuclei. So does fusion, the combining of tritium and deuterium nuclei—in the process of forming helium. But the fission bomb is still the basic nuclear weapon, since a fission bomb has to be used to trigger a fusion reaction.

"There are only a handful of fissile materials—materials capable of being split. Uranium is one, but natural uranium is a mixture of several isotopes. Unfortunately, the fissile isotope uranium 235 forms less than one percent of natural uranium, with most of the rest being uranium 238, not ordinarily fissile. Before uranium is weapon-grade, the U-235 percentage has to be increased through an enriching process.

"A fissile form of uranium, uranium 233, can be produced by irradiating thorium, but gamma radiation hazards limit its use.

"Another fissile material is plutonium 239, but it doesn't exist in nature. It can only be produced in nuclear reactors.

"The point I'm trying to make is that both the uranium enrichment and plutonium production processes are a mite difficult and right expensive. So there are always experiments going on to try and produce new forms of fissile materials.

"A few months ago one of the lab teams created—by an accidental mixing of elements under very extreme conditions—what was hoped to be just that, a new material, highly radioactive. What they weren't expecting, though, was the kind of radiation it produced—different from any of the usual kinds."

"The usual kinds?" Alex asked.

"The usual kinds are alpha particles, beta particles, gamma rays, and neutrons. Only alpha particles are the result of normal—unfissioned—radioactive decay. Beta particles originate in radioactive fission products, gamma rays come from both the process of fission and fission products, and neutrons mainly from the fission reaction itself.

"What the research team discovered was something else, something between a particle and a gamma ray, which is a form of electromagnetic energy. They called the new material G-matter—I guess because it had this green glow about it—and also, for lack of anything better, the radiation from it was termed the Delta Effect—'delta' after alpha, beta, and gamma, and 'effect' because they knew it was there but they didn't really understand what it was."

Sandy was wringing his hands nervously. Alex could see the strain as it became increasingly more difficult for Sandy to continue. Alex wanted to help, but he didn't know how.

"Unfortunately," Sandy said, "—and that's about as big an understatement you can have—one of the technicians, think his name was Perkins, was accidentally exposed to the radiation. He died immediately. There was no apparent cause of death. The autopsy found initial signs of radiation exposure—but not enough to cause him to die.

"As a precaution, they sealed the G-matter in a single container, accessible only through another sealed chamber. Only about five pounds of the stuff exists, by the way. Then they started exposing animals to G-matter.

"What they observed was the normal effect of gamma-like radiation: progressive deterioration and eventual death, but no sudden death in any of the animals.

"They began to feel that Perkins' death was not from the Delta Effect, but from something else. I think they got careless. Anyway, another accidental exposure occurred, and there was another death, just like the first. The lab still didn't know what G-matter was, but they reckoned it was pretty unusual—and pretty deadly, so they stopped doing research while they jawed about how to proceed.

"This gave Colonel Hollis, who'd heard about the Delta Effect, time to maneuver. Under the guise of national security and with backing from his Washington friends, he grabbed the G-matter and all the notes and files dealing with its creation, and he got himself put in charge of testing. To Hollis, the Delta Effect was a potential super weapon, like the neutron bomb, but more lethal, and with no blast damage at all. And it didn't fall under any category of nerve gas, which is outlawed—supposedly.

"Once Hollis was in charge, he asked the military to find someone with a background in nuclear weapons and radioactivity to analyze the G-matter for him. It had to be somebody military, somebody Hollis could control. That's where I came in.

"Although my mission was supposed to be to explain what caused the Delta Effect, why it was so lethal, why it differed from, say, gamma rays, it became crystal clear that Hollis wanted something else. He was going to use the material to design a tactical weapon. So different questions were raised, like what was its lethal range, how could it be broadcast over large areas, and, since it appeared to have a lengthy half-life, how could it be cleaned up from the environment.

"In addition, since it caused death instantly but without any apparent cause, Hollis became interested in using it for covert activities, like assassinations. He wanted to know how it would be possible to expose someone to the radiation on command, like by remote control. I think he's working with two intelligence agents on this—on his own. I've seen them together, but he's never told me who they are. Word around the lab is CIA, but no one here knows for sure—except Hollis."

Alex recalled how Loyola had described the two as thugs on the way to Le Mistral. He looked at her, wondering what she was thinking, but her face showed only concern for Sandy.

"Anyhow," Sandy was saying, "I studied the scientific aspects of the radiation, and Hollis went to work designing, then building, a canister suited to his purposes. He was more successful than I was. He built the canister, and it works. It can be opened and closed by remote control, or by a self-contained timer, but I still don't know what the stuff is, or why it emits the radiation it does. They need a nuclear physicist for that, but Hollis won't allow it.

"I knew I was way out of bounds, but I got to thinking that since I probably wouldn't figure out the physics of the Delta Effect, maybe I could analyze its medical effects. After all, I had ready subjects available, patients literally on their deathbeds, and I had the equipment to monitor any energy effects or changes."

Sandy paused, swallowing uneasily. "You have to understand. I didn't want to be stuck here forever working for someone like Hollis. I was getting desperate to learn something about the radiation.

"So a couple of weeks ago, when I got a call right after work about a patient who had only a few hours to live—six to twelve at most—I retrieved Hollis's control box and canister, already loaded, and took it to the hospital. The patient was comatose but stable. I moved him to a spare X-ray area, where I hooked up our monitoring equipment. Then I arranged the canister close to the patient and set it to respond to Hollis's remote control unit. After that I went to the control room next door. It's heavily shielded, to protect from radiation leaks—and I prayed that included the Delta Effect. From there I could watch the patient and monitor our equipment.

"I started to think about what I was doing, then I stopped thinking…and I just did it. I remember being in a kind of stupor as I watched. The canister responded and everything worked perfectly, just like Hollis intended.

"As soon as the canister opened my equipment went wild—but only for a second—and I knew the old man was dead."

Sandy paused for composure. Alex and Loyola just sat there, not sure of what to say, waiting for Sandy to go on.

"I killed him. I didn't even know his name, and I killed him. But that's not the worst part." Sandy began to sob. Alex walked over to Sandy and put his right hand on Sandy's shoulder, while Loyola, still seated, took both Sandy's hands in hers. After a moment, Sandy went to a filing cabinet and found some tissue. Alex sat down as Sandy began again, leaning on the cabinet for support.

"I had the patient's death certified as being by natural causes, then I took all of the data home with me. I told the others on the S-cubed project that I didn't get the equipment hooked up in time.

"I knew that something incredible had happened, but I wasn't sure what it was—or maybe I was, but I didn't want to admit it to myself. So I went to Doctor B. I took with me only data from monitoring the patient's soul energy—nothing related to his condition or death. I told him the data was obtained in routine monitoring of a volunteer subject, not a dying patient. I also suggested that an electrical disturbance might have terminated the readings.

"I was sweating bullets while Doctor B looked at the dozen or so charts and graphs, then after about five minutes he laughed out loud. He said," and Sandy tried to sound like Doctor B, "'Of course it was an electrical disturbance! Do you know what this would mean if there were not? I will tell you what it would mean. It would mean that this subject's soul went POP, like the bursting of a balloon!'

"Right then I went sick, felt like I was going to faint. I had to sit down. I tried to hide what I was going through, and it probably worked since Doctor B was wrapped up in the data, very much amused by it.

"I asked him to explain, said I was interested in learning about the mathematical structure of the soul. Doctor B obliged. He said my data had to be erroneous. What it showed was that the portion of the patient's soul resident in our three-dimensional world had been destroyed. What he told me is that the soul, as we understand it in its energy form, is mathematically—topologically—like a hollow sphere. When a part of it is destroyed—and I will tell you Doctor B's exact words: 'which should not be able to happen if God is in his heaven and all is right with the world'—it literally collapses to nothing. The soul, in all of its dimensions, is destroyed.

"One form of energy—the Delta Effect—counters another—the soul, destroying it in the process, like matter and antimatter. That explains why the two researchers—and my patient—died. The Delta Effect destroyed their souls, and I guess human beings can't exist without them. Our bodies cease to function. Totally. Animals, without souls like ours, aren't affected. That's not to say they don't have their own form of energy that continues to exist somewhere after they die, but if they do, it's not the same as ours.

"I have no idea what havoc this might have wreaked beyond our world. Maybe conservation of energy still holds there, and the energy destroyed here became a nuclear holocaust on the other side. All I do know is that I not only killed a patient in our traditional sense, but I also obliterated him from *forever after*."

Sandy looked directly at Loyola, then at Alex. "Do you understand the enormity of this?" Each of them was beginning to. Alex nodded slightly, but neither he nor Loyola said anything, because they didn't know what to say.

"It's bad enough that three people have died, three souls have been destroyed, but Hollis is trying to develop the G-matter into a weapon!"

"Does he know?" Alex asked.

"He knows. The fucking asshole knows. I took him aside the other day and explained it to him. And do you know what? He says he doesn't care. Can you believe that?"

"So what are you going to do?" Loyola asked, breaking her long silence.

"I don't know yet. For now I just needed to tell someone. If Hollis were a reasonable person, he'd stop this work and find a way to destroy the G-matter and all the notes and files with it. I was hoping maybe he'd come around, but to be honest with you, I'm afraid of him. I think he's nuts."

"That makes two of us," Loyola said. "From what I've seen of him, he's cold-blooded, ruthless. I've seen him angry, really angry. The look in his eyes is like death itself. And those men he hangs around with, they're the same. I don't trust any of them."

Alex was beginning to worry. "So where *is* Hollis, by the way?"

"He flew down to White Sands this morning, to monitor a test of some missile under development. He won't be back until late this afternoon."

Sandy took a deep breath. "I reckon what's done is done. But I've got to find a way to stop this research and get rid of the G-matter. I'll figure something out over the weekend. Your listening to me has helped. I want you to know I appreciate it."

"No problem," Alex said. "Sure wish there was some other way I could help. Want to get away with me for the weekend? Say Las Vegas? Or the Grand Canyon? It might be just what you need."

"And I can change my plans with Sabrina. I can spend the weekend with you here, go to Las Vegas, or whatever."

"No, thanks. I've got to work this out, get straight what I've done, what I have to do. And I want to do this alone. If I need help later, I'll let you know."

Alex and Loyola rose as if to go.

"Wait," he said. "There is one thing you might do for me."

"Sure, Sandy, just name it," Alex said, and Loyola nodded, adding, "Yes, anything."

Sandy walked toward the filing cabinet. Standing next to it was a four-drawer government safe the bland color of wet sand. Out of habit more than anything else, Sandy shielded the combination from Alex and Loyola as he turned the heavy knob on the second drawer from the top to the left, right, left, and back to the right. He firmly twisted and pulled the metal handle just below the knob, and with a clank and a thud, the drawer opened wide.

Sandy reached to the back of the drawer and pulled out a small black notebook bound in leather, about five inches by seven, nearly an inch thick. He closed the drawer and locked the safe by turning the combination knob several times.

Although the door to his office was closed and locked, Sandy lowered his voice to a whisper. "This is a diary I've been keeping. Hollis won't let any of the G-matter files out of his possession for more than a few minutes, so I've been recording my own notes. Everything's in there—from how the G-matter was created to what happened to the patient at Riverside.

"Alex, I can trust you. Please hang onto this until I've decided what to do. I don't want to do anything rash. Besides, I'd want you to have it in case…well, just in case."

He handed the notebook to Alex, who accepted it reluctantly. "I'll hold it for the weekend, but I'd like to give it back to you on Monday. Then maybe we can put it someplace more secure—where Hollis wouldn't think of looking—like a safe deposit box."

"Thanks, Alex. I know if anything happens, you'll do the right thing with the information."

"Well, nothing's going to happen. You'll get it back on Monday."

Sandy walked Alex and Loyola to the door, unlocked it, and thanked them again for listening. After showing them out, he returned to his desk and resumed his pose of despair until he'd summoned enough energy to leave.

Alex escorted Loyola to the library and then headed back, retracing his steps past Sandy's office toward his own. He peeked in, but Sandy was already gone. Understandable, Alex thought. It was going to be difficult for Sandy to live with himself until he somehow righted things.

Alex turned a corner and suddenly went ice cold with fright, like the wren surprised by the white cat jumping from the house roof onto the bird feeder. There was Hollis, walking briskly down the hall.

On impulse, Alex stopped, went back to a doorway across from Sandy's and said to the secretary inside, "Excuse me. I was told Colonel Hollis was going to be gone today, but I thought I just saw him. Was I mistaken?"

"No," she answered, "his flight was canceled because of the fog. He's been here most of the morning. When I came back from my coffee break, he was standing outside Dr. Jeffers' door, reading a paper. I guess he was waiting for Dr. Jeffers. It's really none of my business—I don't like to mess with Colonel Hollis. But he stood there for a long time." She chuckled, "The hallway lights were reflecting off the sides of his head like it was a big light bulb."

Alarms screamed within Alex. He had to tell Sandy about Hollis. But the best he was able to do was leave a message for Sandy to call him as soon as possible.

# Chapter 19

Shortly after noon Alex drove home to pack for Las Vegas. During the drive he wondered if maybe he shouldn't stay in Los Alamos. But with Sandy probably already away, isolated somewhere thinking, and with Loyola busy with Sabrina, he'd just sit nervously waiting for Sandy to return. The most he could do was to keep trying to contact Sandy, and he could do that from anywhere. Besides, something inside was urging him to go.

He changed into a fresh sport shirt, then pulled an old leather suitcase down from the overhead shelf of his bedroom closet. The well-traveled overnighter was battered and scarred, but the quality Coach bag still had plenty of life in it.

He checked to make sure it contained a travel iron and a shave kit. Then he stocked the shave kit with toilet articles and pushed it and the travel iron over to make room for a pair of tennis shoes. He'd wear his western boots, dressy goatskin Luccheses he'd bought in Santa Fe his first summer at the lab.

He squeezed the tennis shoes in, finishing the bottom layer. Next he put in his underwear, socks, and a pair of swim trunks. Alex neatly folded two pairs of trousers, one a pair of blue jeans and the other dressy casual slacks, and gently stacked them on top of the underwear. Over the slacks he laid three short-sleeved shirts, each suitable for wear with his jeans or a sport coat, like everything else he had packed or was wearing. He would carry a sport coat, the only outer garment he need-ed, mainly to protect against the air-conditioned casinos and the always too-cold airplane cabins.

He wondered what to do with Sandy's diary. He could hide it some-where in his house, but that might not be safe—or wise. He'd have to take it along. He reopened the suitcase and removed the top two layers of clothes, careful not to wrinkle them. Then he placed the diary under his tennis shoes and repacked the rest.

Before returning to the lab he put extra food and water out for the cats and locked the house up tight. He figured if he were going to go, he might as well get a head start by leaving from the office.

Back at work, Alex tried phoning Sandy several times. Sandy's secre-tary had no idea of where he had gone or when he would be back. Alex had already left two messages on the answering machine at Sandy's house, the last one with what he knew about Hollis. Then he called Loyola.

"Why don't you bring Sabrina and join me in Las Vegas. Nowadays there's lots for kids to do. I think she'd have a great time."

"I'd love to, but she really wants to go to Albuquerque tomorrow. Maybe some other time. But put a quarter in a slot machine for me, and if I win a million dollars, call me and I'll come pick it up."

"I'll do it. Have a good time with Sabrina. And try calling Sandy to see if he's all right. He left right after we talked to him, and I'm a little concerned. If you reach him, tell him I'd like to get with him Sunday after I get back—just to relax over a beer."

Alex wondered if he should tell Loyola about Hollis being outside Sandy's office that morning, but he decided not to, afraid it might spoil her weekend.

"I'm worried about Sandy too," she said. "I'll call to see how he's doing—if he hasn't gone away for the weekend. But I'm also worried about you," she teased. "I'm worried you'll get with a sexy chorus girl and *relax with her* while you're in Las Vegas. Then get married in one of those chapels, and we've lost our most eligible bachelor. You wouldn't do that, would you?"

"Of course not, at least not without your blessing."

"You'd never get it, buster."

"Then it won't happen. Besides, I think the main reason I'm going is just to be alone. I'd like to have a chance to think about everything we've heard this week. First the soul, then this radiation. To learn about immortality, that's enough to blow your mind. You think about what it means, then a paradox creeps in. You're pondering what your soul already knows, searching for something already locked somewhere within you.

"Then to learn immortality can be snatched away. Another paradox. What does that say about God? And what would everybody else think if they knew about this? Like my father—he wouldn't understand. This conflicts with his view of God. If he did come to understand it, to believe some man-made substance could destroy your soul, he'd probably abandon his personal beliefs in God and in an afterlife, then who knows what would happen? Ever since my mother and sister died, he's needed that kind of hope to survive, and maybe I have too. Just a few days ago I was ecstatic with the promise of an afterlife. Now that's in jeopardy and I don't know what to think."

"I know what you're saying—and my mother's the same way. I hope she never finds out any of this. If it's true, it means there's no God, or that God's not as powerful as we thought. Wouldn't it be better not to know, so millions of people could go on believing as they do now? I think it would have been better if this soul energy had never been discovered, if Sandy had never learned about the Delta Effect. But then again, this could all be nonsense and we might be worrying for nothing."

"I know, and I agree with you—I wish none of this had ever happened. But in the meantime I need to sort it out for myself, and I've got to see if there's something I can do to help Sandy."

"Well, I'll call Sandy, and Sabrina and I will be thinking about you. But I'm going to try and keep the rest of this business out of my mind so I can enjoy the weekend. So you stay out of trouble, and keep your you-know-what out of you-know-where, but otherwise have a great time—and call me as soon as you get back."

"I will, and I hope you have a great weekend too. Take care."

"You too. See you Monday."

"Bye," Alex said, suddenly and inexplicably feeling very sad.

*        *        *

Alex tried Sandy one more time, then left for the airport. He debated turning around, staying in Los Alamos to help Sandy. But he didn't know where Sandy was, and besides, Sandy had asked to be left alone. Alex vowed to call again as soon as he reached Albuquerque.

He parked in the lot just outside the airport's main entrance, stopped to try Sandy again—no luck—and headed for the Southwest Airlines ticket counter.

The Departures Board told him that the next available flight didn't leave for another hour, and it stopped in Phoenix. He wouldn't get to Las Vegas until ten. He bought a ticket.

"But there's a nonstop flight about to leave Gate 16 right now," the agent said. "If you run, maybe you can catch it as a standby. It should have left fifteen minutes ago, but there was some kind of delay."

Alex grabbed his suitcase and took off running. If he did make it, he'd have an extra three hours in Las Vegas. Three hours: time to use or waste, time in which to win or lose, or time just to relax. Time was the one commodity you could not buy, and he was asking for a gift of three hours.

But what about the other three hours, the time he would spend if he did not make the connection? It was still there, obeying the conservation law that energy apparently did not: time could not be created or destroyed, just used. How to use it was his choice, and that's what really mattered. One thing was certain, though; he would rather spend the three hours in Las Vegas than in transit.

He reached the gate just as the attendants were about to close the door of the Boeing 737. A gregarious gate agent personally ushered him on board. He stowed his suitcase under the seat in front of him, settled back, and closed his eyes, thinking it must be his lucky day. "Maybe I'll win a fortune tonight, or," and he chuckled inside, "maybe I'll end up relaxing with a beautiful chorus girl."

*          *          *

Alex was lucky, all right, but it had nothing to do with money or chorus girls. While he was in the air, on his way to Nevada, two men waited for him to take his evening walk on Deer Trap Mesa.

# Chapter 20

Earlier that day, when Sandy left his office, the same two men had been waiting for him.

＊　　　　＊　　　　＊

The brawn of the duo was Hank, nearly six-and-a-half feet tall. His huge head was topped with a black crew cut and defined by large, bushy eyebrows and the mangled nose of a prizefighter. Surrounding his chiseled chin were broad shoulders from which hung long, hairy arms with large, powerful hands. His narrow waist and hips led to feet remarkably small for a big man. Thirty-one years old, Hank had never been married. His profession was his life, and professional women satisfied whatever needs his profession could not.

Eddie, on the other hand, was a family man. A wife, two sons, and a daughter waited in McLean, Virginia, for him to return from another of his many "business trips." Eddie was thirty-eight years old, ruggedly handsome and just under six feet tall with a medium build belying his strength and his deadly abilities. He looked like a businessman, but others in his profession knew him as "the Dispatcher."

As a minimum, Hank and Eddie carried identical long-barreled thirty-two caliber handguns equipped with silencers, and long, narrow-bladed, razor-sharp knives. Hank was the marksman, preferring the pistol. When close combat was necessary, his powerful hands usual-ly sufficed. But the long knife was Eddie's favorite weapon; up close it was as fast and as deadly as any bullet. Judging from the reactions of some of the Dispatcher's victims, it was the kind of weapon that could pierce one's soul.

*         *         *

Because Sandy had come to work late that morning, he'd had to park in an overflow lot well away from the main gate. It took him ten min-utes to walk to his car. He unlocked the door, opened it, and lowered his long frame through the doorway and into the bucket seat. Then he closed the door and locked it.

Before Sandy could put his key into the ignition, Eddie sprang from the floor of the back seat, in his hands a nylon cord with small hand-grips at each end. In one well-practiced motion, Eddie threw the cord over Sandy's head and, crisscrossing his hands, pulled tight when the cord reached neck level. Sandy thrashed wildly, but Eddie stood for leverage to pin Sandy down and keep him from kicking the front win-dow out. Eddie and Hank had plans for the car.

Outside the car, Hank stood nearby, watching for witnesses. There were none.

In less than a minute Sandy was dead. Eddie worked Sandy's lifeless body down onto the floor in front of the passenger seat before climbing behind the wheel. He looked for the car keys and found them still gripped tight in Sandy's right hand.

Eddie started the car and drove slowly and carefully out of the park-ing lot. Hank followed close behind in another car. They drove toward Santa Fe but didn't stop there, continuing east for several miles. When they were well past civilization, in the middle of desert-like wasteland, they left the highway for a seldom-used side road. After a while they stopped the cars.

Hank worked a lever under his seat, and Eddie opened Hank's now unlatched car trunk and pulled out two shovels. Moving quickly, they picked out a spot and began to dig. At first the digging was easy, mostly through sand, but then they hit rocks and clay. It took an hour longer than expected, but when they were finished, they had dug a hole three feet wide, five feet long, and four feet deep. They threw Sandy's body into the hole, refilled the hole, and scattered the extra dirt evenly around and away from the grave.

Then they drove both cars north into the Sangre de Christo Mountains. The road was paved, but it climbed and wound until the pavement stopped, leaving a narrow lane of gravel and dirt. They went as far as they could, until the dirt road stopped and only a narrow footpath continued up the mountain. They parked Sandy's car at the end of the road, locked it, and took the keys with them.

Hank drove them back toward Los Alamos. When they approached the Rio Grande, Eddie told him to slow down. In the middle of the new concrete bridge, Eddie flung Sandy's car keys out the window as far as he could into the river on the upstream side. When they got back to Los Alamos, after reporting to their boss, Colonel Billy Hollis the Third, they drove to Deer Trap Mesa, where they had expected Alex Feher to be taking his nightly walk.

# Chapter 21

---

After deplaning in Las Vegas, Alex walked to the bank of telephones connecting the airport to the hotel bureau. He lifted the receiver of the first available phone and heard a buzzing sound that was terminated abruptly by a velvety "Welcome to Las Vegas. How may I serve you?"

"I need a single room for the weekend. I'd prefer the Imperial Palace." The Imperial Palace was located on Las Vegas Boulevard, better known as the Strip, and although not as glamorous as some of the newer hotels, it offered one of the best government discounts in town. Alex qualified by working at the lab. All he had to do was show his badge.

"I'm sorry," purred the soft, sexy voice on the other end of the phone, as if she really were, "the Imperial Palace is completely booked—no, wait a minute," the voice came alive, accelerating its pace and raising its pitch half an octave. "There's been a cancellation. If I can get it before someone else does…yes, got it. Good room, too, overlooking the Strip. Maybe it's your lucky day."

"I'm beginning to think so." Alex gave the agent his American Express card number to hold the room, got a confirmation number in return, thanked her, and hung up. He threw his sport coat over his arm, grabbed the suitcase, and walked out of the airport terminal into the evening heat of Las Vegas in July; a taxi immediately pulled up to where he stood. Alex threw his bag into the back seat, dove in after it, and told the driver where he was going.

The taxi driver chomped on a half-smoked, unlit cigar. "Just make sure you don't play blackjack at any table where the dealer deals from his hand and not from a shoe."

"I thought gambling was pretty much on the up-and-up here."

"Not always. I got this friend, see, and he's a dealer. He's sort of a specialist. He can pull any card you want out of the deck, as long as he's got the deck in his hand. His job is to deal the right card at the right time. You know what I mean?"

The driver looked at Alex in his mirror. Alex shook his head.

"I mean he deals the right card for the House. Like, say it's early in the morning and there's too many tables going and they want to shut one down. The casino sends him in like a relief pitcher, and pretty soon everybody at that table is busted. Or sometimes they send him in when there's somebody at the table they want to lose. He can make it happen. But he's got to deal from his hand. So if you see a dealer not using a shoe, get away from that table."

"So your friend can play God? He can make people win or lose?"

"Nah, my friend—he just cheats 'em. God takes care of all the rest."

"Do you really think God can take care of everything—or can God be cheated, the way your friend cheats his customers?"

"What are you, atheist or something? God takes care of everything. Period. Maybe I don't go to church every Sunday, but I'm a good Catholic. I know what God can do."

"Yeah, so do I. Sorry I brought it up. And thanks for telling me about the dealers. I'll watch out."

Twenty minutes after his plane had landed, Alex was at the Imperial Palace. He checked in and went up to his room. He draped his sport coat over a desk chair and threw his suitcase on the nearer of the two queen-sized beds. He opened the suitcase, and after looking around for a place to hide Sandy's diary, chose the dresser.

Alex removed the bottom drawer. Underneath was concrete floor. The carpet did not extend under the dresser. Alex laid the diary on the floor, checked for clearance, then slid the drawer back in place.

After deciding he'd done the best he could to secure the diary, Alex opened the sliding glass door, stepped out onto the room's small balcony, and looked down at the bustling Strip.

Standing on the balcony, high above the glittering street where hundreds of people, most of them couples, strolled or scurried, Alex felt lonely. He wished Loyola and Sabrina had come with him. He looked up. Above him IMPERIAL PALACE was spelled out in bright lights, the four-foot letters made of large white light bulbs, each letter with a border of smaller blue bulbs. The balcony was located directly under the "L" in IMPERIAL. "L" for Luck, he thought. Or could it be for Lisa? *Lisa?*

After a quick shower, he slipped into clean clothes and went back down to the lobby, which merged indistinguishably into the casino. He'd been able to nap on the plane, so refreshed by the nap and the shower, Alex felt ready for a long night of easy gambling. He had no reason to leave the Imperial Palace, at least not tonight. Everything he could want was there: gambling, food, and should his mood change, women.

He headed first for the blackjack tables, remembering the taxi driver's advice. All of the tables, in the public part of the casino at least, had shoes for the cards, and the dealers seemed to be using them. Since Alex wasn't a "high roller," he waited for a chair to open up at a five-dollar minimum table. A middle-aged tourist stood up in disgust, grumbling at having lost a hundred dollars too quickly. Alex took the vacant seat and put five twenty dollar bills on the semicircular green felt table; the dealer passed him ten five dollar chips and two twenty-fives.

Alex started by betting the minimum at each hand. He was dead even after twenty minutes. His stack of chips dwindled as he gradually lost more than he won. He got impatient and decided to double or even triple his bets after each loss. If the hundred dollar investment wasn't going to return something, then he'd lose it quickly. Instead—as if he'd intimidated Lady Luck—his fortune seemed to change.

Alex was forty-five dollars ahead when he got tired of thinking and counting cards, so he cashed in his chips and walked around the casino to stretch his legs.

On his second pass by the roulette tables, he stopped to watch. He stood between an elegantly dressed fat lady with a German accent and an old man puffing and chewing on a powerful cigar with an ash as long and white as his mustache.

Some people play roulette with a system, but the fat lady had none, at least not that Alex could discern. She bet heavily, sprinkling five-dollar chips about the table at each turn, barking orders to the croupier when she could not reach the number she wanted, or when the chip she threw landed off-target. She lost steadily, but judging from her diamond-studded Rolex and the glut of gold jewelry around her wrists and neck, she could afford it.

The man with the cigar bet more conservatively, carefully placing chips on the same numbers at each turn: seven, seventeen, twenty-one and thirty-one—probably the grandchildren's birthdays, Alex thought. Occasionally the man put a chip on red or black, but mostly he stuck with his numbers, and since the wheel seemed to favor seventeen, his stack of chips had nearly tripled since Alex started watching.

When he left, and after the German lady had scattered the last of her chips around the table, Alex leaned over and placed a five-dollar bill on seventeen. The croupier smoothly exchanged it for a chip and spun the wheel. The ball finally settled into red, seventeen, as somehow Alex knew it would. The croupier placed his marker on Alex's chip, the only winner on the table, and the German lady complained good-naturedly to him, "What did you do, young man, steal my luck?" Alex laughed and walked away with his winnings.

From roulette he moved to slot machines, stopping briefly at a change booth for twenty dollars in quarters. He sat down on the wooden bar stool in front of the nearest vacant quarter machine, opened one of his rolls of quarters, and dumped them into the tray that collected the winnings. Priming the pump, he called it.

Seated to Alex's right was a buxom, strikingly beautiful Latin American woman. She squealed with delight each time she won and hurled Spanish curses at the slot machine when she lost. Long auburn hair accentuated flashing eyes the color of faded jade, and she wore a long, low-cut sequined dress of regal purple, split up the side facing Alex, exposing plenty of well-curved leg.

Her gyrations sent waves of sweet, exotic perfume his way, fanning the flame of passion she'd already aroused in him. There was something about that perfume. Alex was about to flirt with her when he saw her wedding band. A definite off-limits sign.

There were other attractive women in the casino, unattached women, and Alex enjoyed flirting, but tonight, the Los Alamos revelations still fresh in his mind, he decided the wedding band was a sign. He would gamble, relax, gamble some more, and in between try to understand what the revelations meant.

He sat at the slot machine, mindlessly feeding quarters and pulling the handle. Then it came to him. The Latin beauty wore the same perfume as Michelle.

*         *         *

Three years earlier Alex had been in the same casino, playing the slots and winning, when she strode brashly up to him. She gently nudged him with her shoulder, then whispered into his ear, "What's your secret? Clean living?"

"Hardly—dumb luck is more like it. How are you doing?"

"Can't win a thing. Maybe you should show me how. My name's Michelle, by the way," she said, raising her voice over the din of the casino.

"Hi, Michelle, I'm Alex. Why don't you try your luck on this machine?" He gave her a handful of his quarters.

Michelle was tall, almost as tall as Alex, mid-twenties, very blond. And very attractive. He learned while they played she was a graduate student in psychology at the University of Kentucky. She had developed a serious interest in Yoga and was on her way to study with the "masters" in California.

They hit it off and made the casino rounds from the slot machines to roulette to blackjack, where they played as a team, to Keno, where they selected their own numbers, laughingly competing against each other. Her numbers were based on numerological beliefs, while Alex's were blindly chosen. When his random choices outperformed hers, she ascribed it to their karmas.

They gambled together until two in the morning, when they broke for a late supper in the lobby-level restaurant. Michelle ran her hands through her long, blond hair. "Whew. It's nice to sit and relax." Michelle had a beautiful laugh but her tired smile was downright sexy. "I'm going up to my room, and I'm going to take a shower and go to bed. Want to join me?" She bit her lower lip, trying to look as seductive as she could.

Their lovemaking was a new experience for Alex, but it really didn't surprise him. When you think you've seen it all, only to learn otherwise repeatedly, you become accustomed to being surprised.

At the height of each orgasm, Michelle attempted to elevate the experience by humming deeply, apparently in tune with some cosmic force. For Alex the effect was more comic than cosmic, as she tried to suppress the audible gasping—her natural response—so she could sustain the humming. He got the impression later that she wanted him to ask about it, but he did not, and he certainly didn't let her know he was amused by it. But he thought it was hilarious—and contradictory. Why would someone hold back on what was natural to substitute something contrived? Why not just let go? Wasn't that what nature intended?

But what did he know? Maybe a harmony of nature did exist. Maybe she was in touch with it, or God, or both. Maybe he should have asked.

*  *  *

Alex played roulette until four in the morning when most of the tables had closed and the place was almost empty. Then, exhausted, he went to his room and collapsed into his bed. Too tired to think anymore, he quickly fell into a deep sleep, letting his subconscious mind wrestle with the question of immortality.

He slept until nine, showered, and went down to the lobby, where he ate a breakfast of toast, scrambled eggs, and coffee. After lounging in his room for a while reading the morning paper, he went for a walk on the Strip. The temperature had already soared to one hundred degrees, so he stopped at each casino to play a few slots, or sip a beer and relax. First one side of the street, then on his way back, the other.

When he returned, he exchanged his sweaty street clothes for a swimsuit and headed for the outdoor pool. After roasting at poolside for about an hour—he kept falling asleep—he went back to his room and tried to call Sandy. No answer. He tried Loyola. He did not expect an answer, and there wasn't one.

Sunday for him was a repeat of Saturday. But as he lounged by the hotel's pool he felt strangely uneasy, and the peculiar feeling stayed with him for the rest of his trip.

*  *  *

Meanwhile near Los Alamos, Loyola was at her mother's house. Eddie and Hank had positioned themselves nearby. They were waiting for her to leave.

*  *  *

Alex left for New Mexico around three that afternoon. His flight stopped in Phoenix, then continued on to Albuquerque. The Phoenix landing was marred by a blown tire, causing a short delay, so by the time he got into Los Alamos, it was nearly eight. He knocked at Sandy's house and was disappointed Sandy wasn't there. He tried phoning Loyola, but there was no answer. Probably at her mother's, he guessed.

There was barely enough evening light left for Alex to water the garden, and his walk along Deer Trap Mesa was an abridged one because of the darkness. He never reached the spot where Eddie and Hank were waiting, for a second time, to kill him. When he got back, he tried both Sandy and Loyola again but neither answered. No choice but to wait until tomorrow, he thought, and so he went to sleep.

# Chapter 22

During the night Alex dreamt that someone or something came and took him far away. A bright light engulfed him, and he felt warm and safe, like a baby in the womb. He could see nothing, yet he could see everything. He understood everything. The universe was as much a part of him as he was a part of it.

He floated; he flew. Effortlessly. He tasted; he drank. But he could not be sated, like the half-full jug of infinite capacity: no matter how much was poured in, there was always room for more (and no matter how much was poured out, there was always some left).

He laughed; he cried; he lived. He knew. He knew! *And it was so real.* But when he awoke, it was gone, all gone. Nothing remained, nothing of substance, only shadows on a wall. No, shadows on a mirror.

The experience left Alex vaguely depressed, a peculiar kind of depression. The last time he'd felt this way was when he was ten and his best friend, Ricky Simmons, had moved away.

He tried to break the mood by thinking of Las Vegas. He had come away nearly three hundred dollars ahead. Then he remembered the Latin American beauty and her perfume, which once again brought back Michelle. "Hmmmmmmmmm," he hummed out loud, then he burst out laughing.

Feeling a little better, Alex walked to Sandy's house and knocked sharply. No answer. He pushed the old-fashioned buzzer. Still no answer. Out of curiosity he checked the mailbox. It was full, mostly junk mail. He guessed it probably hadn't been emptied since Thursday. He opened the screen door, and the Saturday and Sunday newspapers fell out. Alex tried the gleaming brass handle of the large front door made of oak, but it was securely locked.

Alex walked back to his house very perplexed, and by the time he drove to the lab, he was more than a little concerned.

Loyola was not in yet, so he brought a cup of coffee back to his office. He propped his feet on the corner of his desk. In the center someone had left him a thin brown binder with a cover sheet entitled "A Report: Missile and Rocket Alloys." He picked it up and turned to page one. Alex got as far as page three, but either it was too technical or his mind was too preoccupied. He gave up the effort to read it. He scratched his initials on the routing slip and tossed the binder haphazardly into his out box. Sarah would pick it up later, look to see who was next on the routing scheme, and promptly deliver it to that person.

Alex brought his personal computer to life and logged on to the laboratory's electronic mail system. He hoped to see a message from Sandy. The system told him he had seven new messages waiting. Nothing from Sandy.

He went ahead and read the accumulated electronic mail, responding briefly to each message, before returning to the paperwork on his desk.

At eight-thirty an imposingly tall man in a gray uniform knocked at Alex's open door. He walked in without waiting for a response. The tall officer removed his hat.

"Excuse me. Dr. Alex Feher?"

Alex pushed his chair back away from the desk. "Yes?"

"I'm Deputy Martinez from the Los Alamos County Sheriff's Department." He displayed his identification card and badge to Alex, who rose to inspect them.

"Yes?" Alex's heart pounded.

"Dr. Feher, I'm sorry to have to tell you this, but there's been a death."

The deputy paused for a moment, less than a second, actually. He could have been waiting for the words to sink in, or he might have been looking for some reaction from Alex.

A stampede of thoughts raced through Alex's mind in that briefest of time. It must be his father, he thought, but why would a New Mexico police officer—

"Miss Loyola Sanchez. I believe she was a friend of yours?"

Alex's mouth dropped open, but he could not speak. Black dots filled his vision, and his body suddenly went limp. He collapsed backwards into his chair.

"Dr. Feher, are you all right?"

"Yes, just give me a moment."

After a few seconds more, Alex forced himself to speak. "What happened?"

"We're not sure. That's why we're investigating. Were you with her yesterday?"

Alex sat forward. "No, I spent the weekend in Las Vegas. I tried calling her last night when I got back, but there was no answer."

Tears began to form in Alex's eyes. "Please," he said, pausing to regain his composure, "tell me what happened."

"Well, we're not positive, but it looks like she was raped and strangled. Her body was found last night between the Zia Indian Reservation and the Santa Fe National Forest, about thirty-five miles southwest of here over in Sandoval County. That's not our jurisdiction, but we've been asked to assist in the investigation."

Alex could not believe it. She was too strong and too smart. She would never let that happen. Unless there were more than one, unless....

"Evidently she went to her mother's house yesterday morning, with her daughter, uh," and he looked at a small spiral notebook, "Sabrina."

"Yes, Sabrina," Alex said flatly.

"Apparently she went out around noon, by herself, to run an errand for her mother. She never came back. Her mother called our office later in the day to report Miss Sanchez missing, but we told her we couldn't do anything until she'd been gone for twenty-four hours. I understand her mother tried calling you, but got only a recording machine. She says she doesn't like machines, so she didn't leave a message."

Alex nodded blankly.

"Around nine last night a group of teenagers out to drink and blow off some steam stumbled on the body. Nude. Dumped in a ravine. They were parking and saw it in their headlights.

"Her clothes were found by her body, her purse not too far away. There was no money in it—her mother told us she usually carried at least twenty dollars—and all her credit cards were gone. According to her mother, the personal jewelry Miss Sanchez wore, two rings and a necklace, were also missing."

Alex knew the jewelry. A ring reset with the diamond from her engagement ring, a sterling silver and turquoise ring handmade by one of her tribesmen, and a gold chain with two small hearts. Alex had given her the chain.

"Preliminary indications are she was strangled with a rope of some kind, although we didn't find it. We're still looking for her car. That may have been stolen too. It looks like a case of robbery that turned into rape and murder."

While it sounded plausible to Alex, he kept thinking of Hollis's CIA-like friends, the ones Loyola had called "thugs." Then there was Hollis, listening outside of Sandy's door. But Alex was in too much of a stupor to know or decide anything. What really happened to Loyola? Where was Sandy?

Alex had to say something about Sandy. "I know there may not be a connection," he told the deputy, "but a friend of mine is missing. And he and Loyola—Miss Sanchez—were dating. I haven't seen him since Friday morning, when Miss Sanchez and I visited with him. His name is Sandy Jeffers, Lieutenant Colonel Sandy Jeffers. He's an Army doctor stationed here at the lab. Do you think you could look into it?"

"Well, first I have to finish interviewing people who knew Miss Sanchez. But I guess if there's a possibility of a connection to Miss Sanchez's death, I could ask a few questions. Where did this Jeffers work? Maybe we could talk to his boss."

"I think that's an excellent idea. Follow me."

Alex led the deputy to Hollis's office. The door was closed and locked, and Hollis answered the deputy's knock with an irritated "Who the hell is it?" before opening the door.

Hollis looked at Alex with contempt and eyed the deputy suspiciously, but he invited them in. Alex stood close by as Deputy Martinez told Hollis about Loyola. Hollis listened politely as if he had no interest at all in the matter.

"Too bad. Good worker," he said, "but why talk to me? I met her only once."

"Doctor Feher says that a Lieutenant Colonel Jeffers is missing, and he feels there may be some connection between his disappearance and the death of Miss Sanchez. Do you know where Jeffers is?"

"As a matter of fact I might, Deputy. Lieutenant Colonel Jeffers is an outdoorsman, likes to hike and camp. He told me Friday he wanted to get away for a few days, to go hiking up in the mountains. I told him to go, and not to worry about getting back today. He's been working long hours, and to be honest with you, he needed some R and R. I just hope he didn't get hurt. Some of the mountains around here are pretty rugged."

The deputy looked at Alex. "Dr. Feher?"

Alex knew Sandy wanted to be by himself. It was possible he'd gone off into the mountains. "Well, it could be, but I'll feel better when I see him again."

The deputy seemed satisfied, and he left after asking a few more questions about Loyola. Alex stayed behind.

"Hollis, do you really believe Sandy is away hiking?"

"That's where he said he was going. But Jeffers is a flake. He could be doing anything. Maybe he got himself lost. Who knows?"

"Something tells me you know," Alex said bitterly.

"You're just upset because that broad you used to bang is dead. Now get the hell out of here."

The crack about "that broad" exploded within Alex. He lunged at Hollis and used his left hand to grab Hollis's shirt. Alex swung at Hollis as hard as he could with his fisted right hand. The blow landed on Hollis's cheekbone, but he was already reeling backwards, and so no real damage was done.

Hollis wrestled hold of Alex's arms, pushed Alex away, sending him stumbling and reeling across the room. "Get the hell out of here while you still can."

Alex glared at Hollis, tried to decide what to do, how far to carry the confrontation. He clenched his fist, then extended his forefinger in Hollis's direction. "If you did this, Hollis, I'll kill you."

"Sure," was Hollis's reply, and Alex stormed out of the office.

*     *     *

Alex left the lab a short while later. He wanted to visit Sabrina and Loyola's mother, Maria. He had much to think about as he drove to the pueblo where Maria lived.

Maria and Loyola were spitting images of each other, like photographs of the same person taken twenty-five years apart. Alex had often remarked to Loyola how much she resembled her mother.

Maria was living proof that no one remains the same; physical beauty is transitory. Maria was once Loyola, and one day Loyola would be Maria. But not any more. Loyola was dead, murdered in her prime. Alex wondered if the soul aged like a person's flesh.

Now, at the pueblo and seeing Maria in her sorrow, Alex was struck by how old she looked, how much she had aged in the last twelve hours. Other family members were there lending support. Even Osbaldo had stopped. But Sabrina seemed to be the rock on which Maria steadied herself. Alex offered to help any way he could. Then, feeling the pain himself, too much to bear for very long, he excused himself. He intended to drive straight home.

# Chapter 23

---

Alex hurried to his car. He thought he might get caught in a thunder-shower, as heavy black clouds rolled swiftly over him. Lightning flashed and thunder sounded, but the rain never came. The dry storm passed quickly, leaving the sky a dreary, overcast gray.

From the pueblo, Alex took Route 4 toward Los Alamos. Almost immediately, Black Mesa loomed in front of him, then he was by it. But when the cutoff to Española approached, he slowed down and took the exit. Black Mesa once again sat in full view, slightly to the right of center. Why had he done that? He intended to explore the mesa sometime. But why now?

Somehow he knew to take the next dirt road to the right, and he drove until he was within a half mile of Black Mesa. The road continued, but away from the mesa, so Alex pulled off the road and parked the car.

He walked across flat, rocky land toward the mesa. The mesa walls seemed too steep to climb, but as Alex got closer, he noticed what seemed to be an old hand and footpath directly in front of him.

Using the well-worn holes carved into the mesa side, he began his ascent. The wall at this point along the mesa was not as steep as it appeared from the distance, so he was able to make his way up using leg power more than arm power.

Alex climbed for several minutes, feeling the work in his knees and in the leg muscles just above them. Finally the edge was in sight. As he reached the top, he could hear the wind howling above. He pulled himself up and over the edge, his shirt flapping in the brisk wind. He steadied himself and just stood there, but even after a minute his breathing still came hard and his chest pounded. Was it the climb? Or the elevation? Or could it be something else?

He walked to the center of the mesa, then to the far west end. The thunderstorm stood off in the distance, its lightning flickering softly and if he listened closely, its thunder booming gently. Soon the thunder no longer reached the mesa, but Alex stood and watched, mesmerized by flashes of quiet lightning.

After a while he returned to the center of the mesa, but only to be mysteriously drawn away again. He walked, as if he'd been aimed, toward a nondescript point near the southern edge. He walked, then trudged, heavy and tired, as if somewhere along the way he'd picked up additional weight. It was unnoticeable at first, but with each step the weight increased gradually until Alex felt its magnitude slowing him down to a slow-motion pace. He knew the point to stop, or rather it became known to him, when he could go no further. He sat there and rested.

Alex tried to get his bearings. He looked for his house and Deer Trap Mesa, but he couldn't find them. He tried to think about where he was and why he was there.

A single clear thought came through. Loyola. That was it. It had something to do with Loyola. Then a jumble of thoughts. No. Not Loyola. Somebody, something else. Then he was swamped in thought—too many thoughts, like a thousand voices all trying to tell him something.

Several minutes later, for no conscious reason, he stood up and knew it was time to leave. "Damn," he said to the closest yucca, "the climb and the elevation must have made me dizzy." No comment from the yucca.

He found the path where he'd come up the mesa, and slowly, carefully he worked his way back down, ignoring the echoes of the voices he'd heard on the mesa top.

Walking back to the car he was struck with the sense that he'd learned something up there—that he was a part of something. He had his role to play, just as they had. But what was this role and in what larger scheme did it belong? And who were *they* and what had *they* told him? The message wasn't clear, or maybe it just wasn't logical, so for the moment he pushed it out of his mind. He drove home.

# Chapter 24

About five o'clock that afternoon the telephone rang, shattering the peace Alex sought as he attempted to nap on his living room couch. It was Hollis.

"Hey, Feher, I'm sorry I got out of line before. I'm not a very emotional guy, but I should have understood your grief. I apologize. And I want you to know I'm worried about Sandy. I think I know where he went. Maybe we should drive up and take a look for him. What do you think?"

Alex was skeptical. He weighed the possibilities. "I appreciate your concern, Hollis, but the sheriff should be the one to look for Sandy. I suggest you call him and tell him what you know. Good-bye." Alex heard Hollis shout "Wait!" as he hung up on him.

The rest of the evening was a daze, and Alex operated on automatic pilot. He had no appetite, but he ate a light dinner anyway before readying himself for his walk along Deer Trap Mesa. He checked the weather conditions. The temperature had dropped slightly, but it was still comfortable. The air was heavy and damp, and rain was a good possibility. But if it did rain, it would not be hard. Alex grabbed a lightweight red windbreaker that had a hood rolled up in a zippered pouch. He might need it. He slipped the jacket on, zipped it half way, and headed out.

Alex was already outside the front door, having just locked the dead bolt, when the odd melancholy he'd been experiencing suddenly returned, and with it a notion that he should take something to read, something to get his mind off Loyola and Sandy. He unlocked the door and went back in and down the stairs to his bedroom. On his dresser he found a document he'd brought home from the lab his first day there this year. He'd intended to read it sooner but had never taken the time. Now seemed like the perfect time.

The weighty document, over two inches thick in a sturdy metal binder, was a condensed, unclassified intelligence report entitled "Russian Psychological Studies, Volume III—Personnel Who Work Around Nuclear Weapons and Reactors." Heavy reading. He tucked the report under his left arm, ran up the stairs two at a time, relocked the front door, then walked briskly around the street corner to the point where Deer Trap Mesa began.

Alex took the path along the left side of the mesa. The sun, hidden behind thick clouds, was still some fifteen degrees above the horizon, leaving enough light to read—if that's what he really wanted to do.

The horizon was the rim of the caldera left by the Jemez volcano. The only sign of civilization was at the base of the caldera, about a mile and a half away, the clubhouse of a private rifle club. Alex could barely make it out as a light mist fell now, obscuring his view. Appropriate weather for the day.

As the mist increased to a light but steady rain, Alex stuffed the report inside his windbreaker. He broke into a jog, holding the report firmly in place with his left arm. He headed for the deer trap and the nearby steps that would take him to the top of the mesa. His only plan was to climb the mesa, get to the end, then read or meditate for a while, depending on the rain.

Alex had jogged about thirty yards when the shot hit him. It was as if someone had smashed him in the chest with a sledgehammer. In the split second before he crashed to the ground, before the stunning blow took its effect, his mind registered two men with what looked like rifles off to his left. They were breaking into a run toward the rifle club.

He lost consciousness for about a minute, then the sweet smell of moist soil brought him to. He lay motionless on the ground for another minute, in shock and not at all sure how seriously he'd been injured. Then he realized that the report must have stopped the bullet.

He sat up gingerly, opened his windbreaker and looked at the binder. The bullet had passed through it, leaving a small hole at the top of the metal front cover where it entered, a gaping hole at the bottom of the metal back cover where it exited, and a diagonal path in between, through nearly seven inches of chewed-up paper. Alex's left side, at about heart level, was throbbing. He tore open his shirt and looked for a wound, but found only redness, some swelling, and a superficial cut. The bullet had not penetrated and must have fallen to the ground as he opened his shirt. He took a quick look for it on the path and on the mesa slope directly under the path, but he didn't see it.

Alex stood up and tested his overall condition. Satisfied he was all right and concerned that the men might come to check their target, he ran back to his house, barely conscious of the pain.

Alex was not much of a drinker, but he poured himself a large shot of whiskey. With shaking hands, he downed it in one gulp, just the way he'd seen his father and grandfather do so many times after coming home cold and tired from the steel mills. He shuddered, but the immediate warmth helped steady his hands and his nerves. He went to the telephone book, looked inside the front cover for the number he needed, and dialed the sheriff's office.

"Sheriff's office, Deputy Thomas."

"I'd like to speak to the sheriff."

"I'm sorry, sir. He's off duty. Can I help you?"

This time Alex wasn't interested in talking to any deputy. "Let me have the sheriff's home phone number. I want to speak to him personally."

"I'm sorry, sir, but I can't give that out—except in emergencies. If you give me your name and phone number, I can have him call you tomorrow, or if you tell me what the problem is, maybe I can help."

"The problem is," Alex shouted, "two guys took a shot at me and almost killed me. I know who's responsible—a murderous asshole named Hollis. Now what are you going to do?"

"Slow down, Mr.—what did you say your name was?"

"Feher, Alex Feher."

"O.K., Mr. Feher. Just tell me what happened."

"I was walking along the mesa behind my house, Deer Trap Mesa. You know the one?"

"Yes, go on."

"All of a sudden I'm hit in the chest by a rifle shot."

"Are you injured?"

"No, at least not seriously."

How do you know the shot came from a rifle?"

"I saw two men running away, carrying rifles."

"Did you recognize them? Where were they?"

"They were about a half mile or so away, maybe more—near the rifle club, and no, I couldn't see them well enough to identify, but I know who they were."

"A half mile or more is a long way off to try and kill someone."

"Not if you've got a scope and killing is your job."

"Look, Mr. Feher, I'll take your report, but more than likely you were hit by a stray bullet from the rifle club, or from someone hunting illegally who thought you were a deer."

"Deer, my ass," Alex mumbled to himself.

"I'll tell you what. I'll start patrolling that area to watch for hunters. But first I'd suggest you go to the hospital and get yourself checked out. There might be some injury you don't know about. Then if you still want to, come by here and I'll take your report."

Alex hung up angrily. He thought about what to do next, whom to call. John had left for the Caribbean. Someone else at the lab? Maybe lab security. His hand lay idly on the telephone as he tried to recall the telephone number. His mind was still dazed and fuzzy.

He got a dose of shock therapy when the phone came alive in his hand, its shrill ring sending a shock wave throughout his system. His hand leapt from the telephone as if the vibrating noise were a bolt of electricity. He was shaking as he regrasped the receiver and steadied it against his ear. At least his mind was in focus again.

"Hello."

"Hello?" Alex recognized the voice. Hollis.

"Feher?" He seemed surprised Alex was there.

"I think I know what happened to Jeffers." Hollis fumbled for his words. "We need to meet."

"Why? Where is Sandy?"

"You don't understand, but there's national security involved. It's bigger than you or me or Jeffers. I need to talk to you about it—right away." Hollis's tone grew angrier, more threatening with each syllable.

Alex stalled. "Look, I was just about to go out, to visit Loyola's mother. Maybe we can talk in the morning."

"The morning will be too late," Hollis almost shouted.

"Besides," Alex said to test Hollis's reaction, "I had a frightening experience earlier. Somebody took a shot at me while I was walking along the mesa. They missed but it was close enough. Sheriff thinks it was a stray bullet from the rifle club, but I'm not so sure."

Hollis must have been thinking, because he did not respond right away. "Hollis, you still there?"

"Yeah," he drawled, calmer now. "You know, you've got to be careful in this part of the country. All sorts of dangers."

"Yeah," replied Alex, "I know. Look, Hollis, I'm busy tonight, but you can catch me at the office tomorrow." Alex hung up without waiting for a reply. He took the phone off the hook so he could think without interruption.

Alex was certain Hollis was responsible for Loyola's death, probably Sandy's too. Still shaking from his own close call, Alex decided he'd leave Los Alamos. But first he needed a little sleep.

<h1 style="text-align:center">Chapter 25</h1>

---

About midnight Eddie and Hank arrived at Alex's home. Moonlight illuminated the street, but no one noticed the men dressed in black as they silently checked Alex's doors and windows. They did not attempt to open them or force their way in; that would be easy later. Their first task was to pinpoint Alex's location, so their other task could be carried out swiftly and easily.

The men were professionals. They knew their business and they followed orders meticulously. Their instructions had been brief and explicit, delivered to them in a military-style briefing, as if they were part of a military operation.

"You will go back there now!" Hollis had screamed, his small, beady eyes bulging. "But do not break into his house until oh-three-hundred—three a. m. Understand?"

They had understood; he need not have told them. Wait until the night is at its darkest and everyone is sure to be asleep, to minimize the chances of discovery.

"Until then, you will watch the house to make sure he does not leave. At precisely oh-three-hundred, you will enter the house. Feher will be there. Kill him, but make sure his death looks like a suicide. Under the circumstances," he said smiling obscenely, "that will be quite plausible.

"If Feher attempts to leave before then, you are to subdue him as silently as you can. If it's still possible, you will stage the suicide. Should that prove impossible, kill him quickly and silently, then dispose of the body.

"Call me when you are done. If all goes well—and I fully expect it to—you will ask for John Brown, then hang up when I say you have an incorrect—I repeat—*incorrect* number. If there are any problems, we will have to handle them as soon as possible. Questions, gentlemen?"

They had none. Any of these tasks would be easy for the men, and they left for Alex's house as soon as they had assembled their gear.

The house was completely dark inside, and the two men, in their quick, efficient inspection from the outside, had detected no movement or any other sign of life. Even so, they assumed Alex Feher was there. Hollis had said he would be. They would watch and wait.

The split-level house had three exits, two in the back and one in the front. The back door off the kitchen opened onto an elevated redwood deck with narrow wooden steps descending from the opposite end to the yard below. The other back door, on ground level, led out from a family room and into the small back yard. Beyond the back yard was a canyon, then the uninhabited Deer Trap Mesa. Hank stationed himself where he could watch both back doors, and Eddie positioned himself in front of the house.

At precisely two a. m., Hank crept to Alex's bedroom window. It was closed, and heavy drapes prevented him from seeing inside. He took what looked to be a one-eared stethoscope out of his pocket, put one end of it to the window, the other to his left ear. He heard nothing.

After forty-five minutes of fruitless eavesdropping, he re-pocketed the stethoscope and slowly, stealthily crept to his colleague, who lay prone along a hedge in the front yard. He lowered himself down beside the other and whispered. "Shit, Eddie, I think he must have skipped. I didn't get a sound from his room."

"Maybe so."

They lay quietly for a few minutes, then Eddie raised himself slightly, put his mouth near Hank's ear, and said, "Let's go."

They moved to the front door like two shadows, opened it silently and easily, and entered the house. They passed the utility room where the large white cat and her kitten slept peacefully. After quickly examining the upper floor, they headed for the lower level and Alex's bedroom.

They paused for a moment and then leaped through the open doorway. Silence and stillness greeted them; there was no sign of Alex, except for the rumpled bed. The intruders were disappointed, but they were not surprised.

After verifying that Alex was nowhere in the house, the two men began a careful search for clues to his whereabouts. They couldn't find anything. But they weren't worried about finding Alex; they had many resources available to them. What they did have to worry about was the man they worked for.

Before leaving, Eddie used Alex's telephone to report their findings. The voice at the other end of the line was angry, just as Eddie had expected. But as the shrill voice grew in pitch and volume, Eddie thought he detected something else—just a touch, but it was something he had never imagined possible in the man: hysteria.

# Chapter 26

---

After a couple of hours of bad sleep, Alex knew where he had to go: Ohio.

Before leaving, Alex telephoned the lab. It was nearly midnight, so he waited for the beep at the end of Sarah's voice mail message. "Mrs. Hall, this is Alex. I've got to be away from the lab for a few days. I'll call you again with details as soon as I can. Thanks."

He threw a few things into his overnighter, put it and Sandy's diary into his trunk, and quietly headed out of Los Alamos only minutes before Eddie and Hank arrived at his house.

*   *   *

Alex's Mercedes hurried cautiously along the twisting two-lane road from Santa Fe to Clines Corners. There he'd pick up Interstate 40. He wondered at the horror that had eclipsed his calm life. He peered nervously into the night, wondering what lay ahead of him, dreading the evils behind him. He monitored the rearview mirror for any sign of headlights. But there were none, at least not yet. He breathed half a sigh of relief.

In fact there was nothing in the mirror, nothing but darkness. No car lights, no streetlights, no house lights. Desolation under cover of darkness. But it wasn't pitch black. The full moon softly illuminated the countryside. And, on closer inspection, the rearview mirror picked up a dim red glow from his taillights. But compared to the wedge of land ahead bathed eerily white by his headlamps, the rest was dark. There was absolutely no sign of civilization anywhere around him.

Alex had driven this stretch of New Mexico more than a dozen times before, but only in the daytime, and it was bad enough then. But now, should he swerve to miss an animal, or blow a tire, or take a curve too fast, should he have an accident, he was sure no one would find him—no one except maybe the wrong people. He shuddered. But perhaps, he decided, it was better that he had to drive so carefully. He would watch for animals and potholes, rock slides and curves—the natural dangers. Then he would be too busy to think about the other kinds.

He glanced at his watch. The large, stainless steel Rolex was special; Alex had scrimped and saved for it during his first year in graduate school and then had held the money hostage until he'd earned his degree. But more than accomplishment, the watch was a portal to the past, to any event when time had been critical, and to the unknown future, when time was the only measure along the way.

The Rolex's luminescent green hands and hour markers told him it was one o'clock in the morning, so he was only an hour out of Los Alamos, and twenty-five hours of driving time remained before he'd reach his father's home in Ohio. Twenty-five hours: a span of time that could be agonizingly long, or cruelly short.

Time had been very much on Alex's mind. Time and life. And death. The three foundation stones of God's pyramid. Alex's mind had been grappling with them individually and collectively in relation to each other, like a juggler struggling to handle three weighty and awkwardly shaped objects, all the time wondering if the stage were about to be pulled out from under him.

Maybe what he was gradually learning—coming to understand—was that God could not possibly exist—at least not the way we'd want Him to. Yes, maybe that was it. Maybe God was dead. Or if not dead, then on His deathbed, exposed as a pretender. So, Alex asked himself for the umpteenth time, how can anything ever be right again? And for the umpteenth time: it couldn't.

The stuff was already created, and the secret was out. No fixing this one, no going back.

If that was true, why didn't he give up on it and protect himself? Because, damn it, you can't just give up. Despite the gloomy outlook and the paradoxical problem with no possible solution, hope was alive within Alex. After all, didn't he have a reputation for solving problems thought to be unsolvable? He laughed. Black humor. They had been academic problems. So why was he proceeding as if he could fix the unfixable? Because, he reminded himself, there's got to be a way.

So maybe there could be a way out of this mess. He'd just have to assume there was. He'd have to persist until, well, until it was done. And he did have a plan. Well, at least the outline of a plan. His mind was too weary right now from trying to sort everything out. It had been weary ever since he learned about G-matter.

But even if he could forget G-matter and put aside all the philosophical speculation and all of the supernatural unknowns, he faced a time-life-death issue more mundane and more immediate: how much time did he have left to live?

Alex had fled from Los Alamos in fear of his life. Now, as his headlights cut wedges of light into the darkness all around, he wondered if he could be wrong. He had no hard evidence that he was a target. Still, he wasn't going to wait to find out. Like the deer that doesn't wait to find out what snapped the twig, Alex was running away from Los Alamos, running to Ohio, his boyhood home, where he hoped to find cover and safety until he could catch his breath: the first step in the sketchiest of plans.

Yet a safe haven—by itself—would not be enough. What Alex needed as much as any sanctuary was someone else, someone he could talk to, someone who would listen to him and maybe understand, someone who might even be able to help.

The secrets he knew were a burden too immense to handle alone, even if he were to survive whatever, whoever, was after him. But that was a piece of the paradox: he needed help, yet sharing what he knew only increased the problem. Finding the right person to share it with seemed as impossible as the problem itself. Alex was confused and scared, but he refused to give up. He was going home to his father.

At last the highway flattened out, and he increased his speed, but not *too* fast, he reminded himself. He didn't need the police right now. Or maybe he did. He just didn't know. And when the sign for Interstate 40 finally appeared, he accelerated with jubilation, stepping up his speed even more when the lights of the freeway came into view. He felt that he was leaving a world dark with fear, entering another, bright with promise. He nearly lost control on the entrance ramp, but recovered nicely, and soon his was just one of many cars traveling cross-country in July.

# Chapter 27

*A mild earth tremor, not unusual for New Mexico, gently rocked the area between Los Alamos and Santa Fe. A narrow but deep fissure formed in the soft volcanic rock that lay in the belly of the canyon beneath Route 4. It was the middle of the night, so no one noticed, except for a few far away and unimpressed geologists, and a dozen or so startled coyotes who howled their displeasure at the moon above. Black Mesa watched stoically and unaffected.*

*  　　　*　　　　*

Alex had already crossed the Pecos River and was more than halfway to Amarillo. Three hours later, as he was approaching Oklahoma, the sun came up fast and bright, right in front of him. In another three hours, fighting the sun all the way, he reached Oklahoma City.

He marked one more leg of his journey completed by turning the well-worn page of his Triptik, courtesy of the Roanoke branch of the AAA. Alex had used the same strip map for the past three years, traveling between Virginia and New Mexico.

Oklahoma City was as far as Alex could get using the Triptik. Instead of following the next page and continuing east on I40, he took the I44 exit, northeastward toward St. Louis.

By this time, after more than nine hours on the road, Alex had had plenty of opportunity to think. He did not dwell on what had happened, what was behind him; he tried to sort out what he should do next. It was all so complex—so terrible—so important.

The way he saw it, he faced three problems. First and most immediate, Hollis and his friends were almost certainly trying to kill him. They weren't amateurs with a personal vendetta he might outrun, outlast, or outfight, but professional killers who would stop at nothing to finish their job. His task was to survive. He might be able to do that, although it was least important in the larger scheme of things.

The second and larger problem was one of national security: a madman had fashioned the most devastating weapon imaginable. Hollis intended to use as a weapon a substance that not only kills, but also destroys the soul and terminates an eternal afterlife. Alex might be able to stop Hollis, but could he stop the others that would follow, and for how long?

The third problem, as Alex had put it to himself, was bigger than a breadbox and not your usual can of worms. It was one he knew he couldn't solve, but he had to push on anyway, as if, somehow, there were a solution. This problem was devastating knowledge, knowledge about human existence and God and life after death, knowledge that could shatter the beliefs of most of the people on the face of the earth, knowledge that could cause worldwide panic and devastation.

Alex's "plan" for dealing with the first two problems was simple: escape, survive, and contact the media, which for him meant his old college fraternity brother and friend, Frank Minsanto. Frank was a reporter at *The Washington Post*. But Alex wasn't sure how much he could tell Frank, how much he could count on Frank's friendship above his loyalty to *The Post*, and alerting the media was exactly the wrong thing to do for the third problem.

For the time being, all Alex knew for certain was that he was going home. There he'd regroup, catch his breath, try to decide what to do next and how to do it. He didn't know—hadn't decided—whether he would involve his father in this mess, but since Alex had never married, there was no one else close to him, and right now he needed someone, something to guide him to do what was right, what was best.

The thought that he had never married flashed across his mind again, like a meteor, burning itself out in disappointment. It always happened when he thought about home. He had only one regret about Ohio, and that was Lisa. He should have married her.

*          *          *

About two-thirds of the way between Oklahoma City and Tulsa, after ten full hours of driving, Alex was tired and hungry. Coffee and a good breakfast were what he needed, and the blue road sign with a white fork and knife meant that the next exit had a restaurant. He decided to stop at whatever source of food there was in the middle of this nowhere. After something to eat and an hour's rest, he'd be able to drive until well into the evening. And while he was there he'd call his father, to let him know he was coming. After all, he couldn't just "drop in" from New Mexico.

For some time the Oklahoma countryside had been devoid of civilization. The truck stop was like an oasis in the desert, although it consisted only of a restaurant, an adjoining store selling Indian artifacts, and a dozen gas and diesel pumps. A solitary battered red phone booth stood in a corner of the parking lot, away from the buildings. Alex parked near that corner, where he could keep an eye on his car from inside the restaurant. He did not want to carry the diary in with him. The diary—what to do with it—was another complication.

Alex entered through the gift shop and made a pretense of browsing, though he felt conspicuous as the old wooden floorboards squeaked under his tennis shoes. He passed into the restaurant through a pair of authentic swinging doors. The restaurant, he guessed, must have once been a saloon. What was probably the original bar was now a long counter, and small tables and booths filled the rest of the dining area. A faded handwritten sign posted above the counter told him to seat himself.

Only two of the ten counter stools were taken, but Alex opted for a booth by the window overlooking the parking lot. Several used morning newspapers lay in a heap by the cash register, and Alex yawned as he stopped to pick up a copy of *The Tulsa Gazette*. He used the paper to shade his eyes from sunlight filtering its way through particles of dust.

He yawned again as he reached his table. There, waiting for him, stood a perky blond waitress holding a pot of coffee in one hand and a large brown mug and several thimble-sized containers of cream in the other. A laminated menu, peeling at the corners, was tucked under the arm with the coffee pot. Without asking, she poured him a cup of coffee.

"Thanks. You must be a mind reader."

"Nah. It's just that I could tell. Cream?"

"No, this is fine."

She put the pot down, dumped the containers of cream into her apron pocket, and offered Alex the menu.

"No, thank you. I know what I want. Three eggs over easy with sausage—patties if you've got 'em—and whole-wheat toast. And more coffee soon."

"Sure thing, honey. Be back in a sec."

Alex picked up the newspaper and was still on the first page when she returned with his order. She refilled his coffee cup and left him to his breakfast.

The food was gone in less time than it took to arrive, and Alex turned his attention again to the paper. He sipped the rest of his coffee while reading every headline. Nothing about Los Alamos. Was that good? If the media knew what he knew, there would be headlines! MAN DEFEATS GOD! GOD IS DEAD! ETERNAL LIFE A SHAM! And after the headlines what? Panic? Mass suicides? Revolution? But if it were up to Alex—and maybe it was—they would never know. Nobody would.

The waitress came back with a fresh pot of coffee and a clean mug. She removed his nearly empty cup and poured steaming, rich brown coffee into the new one.

"Where you headin', hon?" she asked, clearing off the rest of the table.

Can't be too careful, he thought, but he also knew he wasn't a good liar so he bent away from her to re-tie a tennis shoe. "New Mexico. Going to visit my brother in Albuquerque."

"Never been there. In fact, never been west of Oklahoma City."

She used a damp rag to wipe the crumbs of toast off the table and onto his dirty plate.

Alex waited until she had disappeared into the kitchen. Then he left money for the tab and a generous tip and headed for the phone booth.

The folding door was old and squeaky, and Alex had trouble closing it. Despite the stifling heat, he made sure it was shut tight. As he worked the antiquated rotary dial, he thought of all the B movies he'd seen where some poor sap got riddled with bullets, trapped in a phone booth just like this one. His eyes nervously swept the parking lot until the operator answered. Alex gave his charge card number from memory, and the call went through. After five rings, his father answered.

"Hello?"

"Hi, Dad?"

"Alex. It's good to hear from you. How are things out West?"

"Fine, fine. How would you like some company for a day or two?"

"Sure. What's up?"

"Nothing special. But I have a couple of days free, and I thought I might stop by. Sure it's no problem?"

"Of course not. It'll be great to have you here. When will you fly in?"

"Well, actually, I'm driving."

"Oh?"

"Yeah. A great way to get some thinking done."

"Do you need anything? Anything special you want to eat?"

Alex laughed. "No, nothing special. Listen, Dad, I've got to get going. I should be there sometime tomorrow. We can talk more then."

"Great, great. Oh, by the way—someone asked about you."

Alex's defense system sent shivers through his body. His grip tightened on the phone. The black plastic instrument felt cold and clammy in his sweaty hand. He clamped it more firmly against his ear before forcing his mouth to move. "Really?" squeaked out. He waited for his father to give him the rest of it.

"I ran into Lisa—Lisa Martin. She asked how you were doing."

Alex was braced for another cold chill, but this news—when it finally registered—flooded him with warmth. "You saw her? She's there?"

"Yes. Staying with her mother. Anyway, I told her you were fine, but that you wouldn't be back this way 'til maybe Christmas. She said you should call her sometime."

"I'll do that—if she's still in town."

"She will be. She's spending the whole summer here."

Alex hung up in a daze. Lisa. After all this time. He got in his car, refreshed by his break, alive with thoughts of Lisa. He was ready for another shift of driving.

# Chapter 28

---

After Tulsa came miles of rolling hills and cattle croplands. Oil rigs dotted the countryside, some methodically pumping up and down, others sitting unused and wasted. In Missouri, Interstate 44 barely touched Joplin, wound past Carthage, birthplace of George Washington Carver, and then shot smack through the middle of Springfield.

The miles eastward were uneventful but hot; the middle of the country was mired in a midsummer heat wave, and, like every other driver on the road that day, Alex shut his windows and turned his air conditioner on full blast. Being boxed in made him feel somehow secure. For the time being, his only fear was of the air conditioner giving out from overwork.

For a long time Alex concentrated on the highway, suppressing thoughts of Lisa. But they lingered on the periphery of his mind like hounds kept at bay, waiting to be released.

Midway between Springfield and St. Louis, Alex relented and opened the gate. Memories of Lisa rushed in, scrambling, competing for attention. Each one was a trigger; each one evoked some feeling, set free some long-repressed emotional response. His heart hardened, drawing blood from a well-hidden pool of cold reserve that past hurt had taught him to maintain. He took a deep breath and let everything come back to him, from beginning to end.

The end was easy. Nothing happened. But the beginning…ah, that was different. The beginning was magic—powerful, instantaneous magic. It was love at first sight.

He had always been a believer in love at first sight. But since Alex was Alex, his belief had to have a logical, scientific basis: love at first sight was chemically induced, a theory reinforced when pheromones were discovered in humans. But after his recent Los Alamos experiences and revelations, after all that had happened, Alex knew there was more to it than chemistry. Much more.

Alex and Lisa met for the first time when they were only fourteen. Nearly twenty years later, Alex remembered it as if it were only the day before. A Saturday. Morristown Junior College. They were finalists in Ohio's annual scholastic examinations. From the same hometown, they attended different schools, had heard of each other, but had never met.

School by school, students formed into clusters in the hallway outside the auditorium. They waited anxiously for the doors to open. Alex and Lisa were at opposite ends of the throng when the milling crowd adjusted itself minutely, allowing a narrow but clear line of sight between them. To Alex it was something akin to the parting of the Red Sea.

They saw each other at the same time, and their gazes met and held. It lasted for just an instant, but something passed between them, as if some grand and complex electrical circuit had been completed. Alex's heart beat faster and harder. He smiled what felt like a Mona Lisa smile and suppressed gasping at the extraordinary, ticklish sensation.

Usually shy, Alex summoned all his nerve and walked stiffly over to her. He felt as if some guardian angel were prodding him along. He didn't know what he'd say, but he had to say something.

"Hi," was all he could muster.

"Hi." Lisa smiled warmly.

"I'm Alex Feher."

"I'm Lisa, Lisa Martin."

She extended her hand, and he took it. He didn't shake it; he just held it for a moment. Her touch excited him, and he knew they were being pulled together like magnets. He was North to her South.

Something else about her excited Alex. An indefinable something in her look. Not the sexy smile, but the warm, strong, confident eyes. She was a competitor. So was he. And since they were both accustomed to winning, in this respect he was North to her North.

Romance and competition. Hepburn and Tracy. She had been willing, even at fourteen, but it was much too soon for Alex, still fighting adolescent insecurities.

Their hometown had only one high school, where they continued a spirited but friendly academic rivalry. Lisa became a cheerleader, later homecoming queen. Alex starred on the baseball team. Lisa began dating when she was sixteen and a junior, but Alex still felt awkward and "ugly"—too ugly for someone like Lisa—so while they were good friends, he never asked her out. Their friends were baffled and so was Lisa, because the strong mutual attraction was obvious.

So the strangest part of the relationship between Alex and Lisa was romance; there had never been any. They had never become lovers, never even dated. What evolved between them was friendly, even close, but the emotional ties that might have been were suppressed, supplanted instead by a competition of sorts.

Alex, who was pretty demanding, didn't earn his self-esteem until he was in college. Lisa never had such a problem. She was always cute and the center of attention. Athletic, energetic, she had freckles and a natural smile that turned into a laugh with ease. She was bright, confident, and even as a flat-chested adolescent in baggy jeans and tattered tennis shoes she had a femininity that radiated through.

Lisa was a born leader. She was popular with her teachers and with both boys and girls. Not that she sought popularity—other kids just followed her style of good-natured enthusiasm surrounded by intelligence and an alluring, devilish attractiveness.

Was she beautiful? If you analyzed each piece, probably not; her small, button-like nose was not symmetric, off just a shade—cute was the word for it, and so with her mouth, not what you'd call sensuous, but wide, the lower lip protruding just a bit more than the upper, so that when she wanted to be playful, she could easily pretend a pout, but the twinkle in her hazel eyes would give her away. Her hair was an ordinary brown, short to medium in length, yet it sparkled with the rest of her.

Lisa had her pick of colleges and chose Purdue. Alex turned down baseball scholarship offers to accept an academic scholarship at Notre Dame, where he overcame his earlier insecurities, joined a fraternity, and enjoyed a full and balanced social life.

While Alex studied mathematics, Lisa majored in economics. Each was elected to Phi Beta Kappa. They both earned doctorates, Alex at Ohio State and Lisa at Indiana. Alex was hired by Virginia Tech, and Lisa took a position at Ohio State, where they missed overlapping by a couple of weeks. The parallels ended, however, when Lisa married her college sweetheart, Bert Nestor.

Bert had been captain of the Purdue football team in Lisa's senior year. He stayed close to her while she was at Indiana by coaching high school football near Bloomington. Bert wanted to marry Lisa then, but she insisted she had to finish her degree first. When Lisa took the job at Ohio State, he accepted a position as assistant football coach and physical education instructor at nearby Columbus Wesleyan College.

Alex stayed at Virginia Tech and built his reputation early by tackling tough problems others wouldn't touch and then solving them. He earned his tenure and professorship by concentrating on research in the summers and on his students and teaching duties the rest of the year. He dated but never got seriously involved. For a while he kept track of Lisa, and like old and dear friends, they occasionally wrote to each other and even called once or twice a year.

Just before she and Bert were married, Lisa had confided to Alex she had misgivings about Bert. When she agreed to marry him, after all his coaxing and cajoling, she never really said yes—she simply stopped saying no. Alex was in no position to advise her, bearing the pain of what he felt was rejection while concealing his true feelings. After she was married, the notes and calls to Alex stopped, even news of her stopped—or maybe it was Alex who stopped paying attention.

Yet after all these years, the deep, mystical attraction remained for Alex, and it was the one he compared all others to. That was surely why he had never married.

# Chapter 29

---

Around nine p. m., now on Interstate 70 approaching Effingham, Illinois, Alex knew it was time to stop. He was dog-tired and seat-sore. He needed to sleep. About six hours should do it, he thought, and then he could be on the road again before four in the morning. It would be good to get an early start on the remaining 420 miles.

It was dark, but not dark enough to call night. Alex took the second exit ramp and sailed without slowing past the yield sign, north and away from Effingham. On his left was the Midwest Motor Inn. Alex had imagined it larger, misled by the huge sign towering above the motel proclaiming its location.

Alex swung the Mercedes across the highway and onto the motel's gravel drive. He continued past the lobby, beyond the last of the motel's rooms. The motel property jutted up against a wooded area of medium-sized Scotch pines. Alex backed his car into a space on the wooded side of the parking lot.

Alex stepped out of the car and stretched. The pine trees sheltered the parking area from the highway's sounds. It was quiet, almost eerie. The spell was broken by the slamming of his car door and the crunch of gravel as he made his way across the parking lot and to the sidewalk alongside the motel.

Suddenly Alex remembered the diary. Instead of wheeling around, inviting attention, he nonchalantly circled the lot and made his way back to the car. Alex opened the trunk and removed his suitcase. He lifted the vinyl cover hiding the spare tire. There, wedged under the spare, was the black notebook. Alex looked around. Seeing no one, he dislodged the notebook from its hiding place but left it in the trunk until he had returned the spare's cover and the suitcase to their original positions. With a secure grip on the notebook, Alex quietly shut the trunk and headed back across the parking lot.

The sidewalk took him around to the lobby. The doors were locked. A sign hanging on the inside of one of the doors instructed him to a night window, where he pushed an old-fashioned, tit-shaped buzzer. He shifted the diary behind him, tucking it under his belt at the small of his back.

Inside, a hefty middle-aged woman waddled from around a corner and into view. A brown and white print dress, sleeveless and faded to the color of oatmeal in milk, hung around her like a tent. "Yeah?"

"I need a room for tonight."

"Just you?"

"Yes."

"That'll be $34.00, cash—includes the tax. If you want to use a credit card, it'll cost you five bucks more."

"I'll pay cash."

"Here, fill this out."

She shoved a registration card through an opening under the window, and Alex hunted in his pockets for a pen. He wondered what name to use, discarding Smith and Jones as too obvious, though he guessed this woman wouldn't care. Last name: he invented Hilberg, penned it carefully in the space. First name, don't hesitate, Larry—no—Lawrence. For automobile, he used Ford, and he fabricated a Kentucky license plate number.

He fished $35.00 out of his wallet and passed it and the form together, figuring that with money in hand, the lady wouldn't much care who he was or what he was driving.

She accepted the form without looking at it and slipped Alex a room key and a dollar bill in change. "Room 212—second floor, around to your right." She used her thumb to point over her left shoulder in the general direction of the room.

"Thanks." Alex pocketed the key, deftly switched the diary back into his hand, and hurried off.

He went to the car and retrieved his suitcase. He could see his room, on the upper floor of the two-story motel, midway between staircases. He did not see an elevator, but that didn't matter. He dashed up the nearer stairs and walked quickly to his room.

Room 212 was like so many cheap motel rooms Alex had stayed in on his cross-country trips. A double bed, color TV secured to the wall with a cable, clock radio bolted onto a nightstand, and a combination air conditioner and heater on the floor next to the door and under a large picture window. The hollow metal door had no dead bolt, just a lock in the handle and a flimsy chain lock at about eye level.

Alex tossed his suitcase and the diary on the bed, closed the curtains, and secured the chain lock. A light switch on the wall just inside the door controlled the lamp by his bed, and he turned it on.

He took a quick shower, put on clean underwear, and set the clock radio's alarm for three a.m. He thought about reading the diary, but he knew that would be a mistake. Besides, he was just too tired. However, he did want to relax for a few minutes, so he got a glass from the bathroom and poured himself two ounces of gin from the flask he carried in his suitcase. Alex's usual routine included a nightcap of four parts gin and one part Rose's lime juice—a strong gin gimlet. He didn't have any lime juice with him, but the gin was Tanqueray, a quality "sipping" gin.

After fifteen minutes of rambling thoughts, he downed the last of the Tanqueray. He walked to the door and, feeling somewhat paranoid, double-checked that it was locked and the chain in place. Alex flicked the light switch, and settled into bed and the darkness.

The sheets were cold, so he curled himself up into a ball and pulled the covers tight all around. The rapid, snuggling warmth took him back to his childhood, when his mother used to sit at the end of his bed for a moment after tucking him in. "Remember to say your prayers," she would tell him. The simple words came back to him in her soft, soothing voice:

*"Now I lay me down to sleep;*
*I pray the Lord my soul to keep.*
*If I should die before I wake,*
*I pray the Lord my soul to take."*

Now, full of confusion and anger and clouded by the gin, his mind kept going, pulling the words from some hidden place, putting them in the harsh voice of a stranger, or maybe it was his own voice:

*"And if my soul should die as well,*
*I pray that God may burn in Hell."*

He was asleep in less than a minute.

Alex slept well, the monotonous drone of the nearby interstate highway and the humming and blowing of the air conditioner drowning out most other noises. But when the lock on the door handle clicked open at two a. m., he awoke instantly, knowing something was wrong.

He rolled out of bed, away from the door, on the side by the nightstand. He hoped the air conditioner would cover the thud as he hit the floor. Alex quietly shifted his body, still lying on the floor, but now his head was at the bottom of the bed where he could watch the door to the room.

The handle turned and the door opened about three inches, until the chain tightened. A pistol was thrust through the opening, well under the chain. One large human eye, reflecting light from somewhere outside the room, tried to peer into the darkness. The eye squinted; the gloved hand below extended the pistol farther.

Thwap-Thwap. Pause. Thwap. A silencer reduced the noise to burps. The bullets tore harmlessly into the center of the bed.

Alex stayed where he was. The hand withdrew, then returned without the pistol. It felt along the wall until it found the light switch. The hand flicked the switch up, and the light above Alex came on. The eye widened at the empty bed.

Certain he had to act, Alex raised himself up and knocked the lamp from the table, sending the room once again into darkness. He dove back to the floor.

The man outside the room threw his shoulder into the door. The chain held, but the doorframe burst apart, and a tall, lean body crashed into the room.

Alex desperately felt for the glass on the nightstand, the one he had used for gin. As soon as he touched it, his fingers curled around it. He knelt, whirled, and threw all in one motion.

The man was only a few feet away, and despite the darkness, Alex knew he would hit his target somewhere. As it turned out, the glass could not have been thrown any better. It struck the half-upright man squarely between the eyes. The glass shattered as it hit, and the man howled in pain.

Alex saw the outline of the man silhouetted against the open door. What was this? The silhouette of a skin-diver? The face appeared to wear a diver's mask with a snorkel attached to the right side, sticking up into the air. Then Alex understood. The man clutched his face with both hands, but he still held the pistol flush to the side of his head, the long barrel aimed at the ceiling.

Alex's only escape was through the open door, blocked by the injured gunman. Alex didn't know how much time he would have before his assailant recovered. He pushed himself up and hurled his body toward the doorway, expecting the impact of a gunshot, holding his breath, praying not to be hit.

The gunman fired once. The shot narrowly missed the onrushing Alex. Before the man could get off another shot, Alex hit him head on, sending him crashing backwards into the frame of the doorway, the gun flying into the air. Stunned momentarily, the gunman collapsed in a heap, half in and half out of the room.

The gun lay on the concrete balcony just outside Alex's room. The other man stirred, and they both dove for the pistol. In their struggle neither was able to grab it, and the gun slid toward the edge of the balcony. Alex watched as it passed under the wrought iron railing and sailed over the balcony edge, falling to the parking lot below.

Alex was first on his feet. He scrambled down the stairs and reached the pistol just ahead of his attacker. Alex grabbed the gun and ran for the pine trees across the parking lot.

Just as he reached the woods, his pursuer caught him with a flying tackle, and they both went down on a bed of pine needles. Alex kicked himself free momentarily, and using both hands, firmly gripped the pistol. He controlled his panic long enough to slide his right middle finger under the trigger guard and over the trigger. Then he rolled onto his back as the other man once again lunged at him. Alex closed his eyes and squeezed the trigger.

The bullet struck Alex's attacker in the chest at pointblank range. The man collapsed onto Alex and died a few seconds later, draped around Alex's waist.

Alex pushed the lifeless body away and looked around to see if anyone had witnessed the fight. At two in the morning no one was about, and the silenced shots apparently hadn't awakened anyone.

It wasn't the fight that worried him—certainly no one would charge him with any crime—but he couldn't stop now. There was too much to be done before he could go public—if he could go public.

Well, he'd see if he could buy some time. He grabbed the feet of the dead man and pulled the body deep into the woods. He covered it with what leaves and branches he could find. Alex never did get a good look at the man's face, but he didn't have to. He knew it was the Major.

Alex took one final look around to make sure he hadn't missed anything. Then he retrieved the pistol and, still in his underwear, streaked back to his motel room.

After he had packed, Alex fished three spent bullets out of the mattress and dug the fourth out of the wall. He wrapped them in toilet tissue, threw the wad in the toilet, pressed the handle, and watched as they moved slowly but completely out of the bowl.

He left the sheets in a disheveled mess, hoping the rips in the mattress would not be noticeable. He filled the hole in the wall with toothpaste. He repaired the doorframe by fitting it back into place, again using toothpaste to fill the cracks. Then he went around the room with a towel, wiping away fingerprints.

Alex left the motel room and walked silently to his car with some new piece of knowledge gnawing inside his head, like a rat trying to get out. As he looked toward the woods where the Major's body lay hidden, he realized—with a perverse kind of relief—he didn't have to wonder anymore. They really were trying to kill him. At least that much had been verified.

Then the other feeling returned, or maybe it just made its presence known again, the sensation that had been with him all summer. That he had some kind of role to play, a mysterious part, small yet significant, in some much grander scheme. He now felt more certain, as certain as he could feel not understanding much, that he wasn't just filling the role, but he was playing the part—ad-libbing it—exactly right, though blind to what it was.

Alex replaced the diary in its spot by the spare tire, added the pistol next to it, loaded the suitcase, and drove quietly out of the motel's parking lot. It was three a. m. in Illinois. Almost immediately he was back on Interstate 70. Seven more hours and he would be at his father's house.

# Chapter 30

---

Air. Warm, fresh, and earthy—the Ohio country air Alex had known as a boy. Off the main highway now, he opened his car window the rest of the way to bathe himself in that air, the first really fresh air he had driven in since getting on the interstate. It was morning in Ohio, and there were no other cars in sight. He slowed the car down to look and smell, and he almost cried.

He made his way past wooded fields and rambling farms. Farms with corn, farms with cows, and as the grass was losing its morning dew, farms with children playing. Occasionally the children stopped what they were doing to watch him pass, as did a few cows. Cornstalks bent to and fro with the gentle morning breeze. Everything was a lush green. He could taste it: the air, the soil, the growth, the life, and he savored the experience.

Alex was only thirty minutes from his father's house, yet he was more like thirty years removed. He didn't get back often enough. Even for the funerals, he just flew in and out. Still, he had the feeling that some part of him had never left, or maybe it was that his Ohio boyhood was with him everywhere he went. The events of the past week had given him a profound respect for whatever the feeling was, and for all the other *deja vu* experiences he had felt, or would feel, for however long he lived.

The closer Alex got to home, the fewer farms he passed. Houses now lined the road where farms used to be, and traffic thickened, seemed more rushed than he remembered. But his mind was no longer on the scenery or the traffic, but mostly on what he would tell his father.

Bela Feher was sixty-five. His mind was still sharp and his heart was strong, but his body suffered the effects of a life of hard labor. Like his father before him, he had retired from the local steel mill after working there—mostly shift work—for more than forty years.

Alex was both surprised and pleased that his father had adjusted so quickly to the death of his wife and then his only daughter, and now he seemed at peace with the world. He would be more than willing to help Alex with his problems; Alex knew that. But Alex wasn't sure he should put his father's life in jeopardy with so little of it left. Nor did he want to upset his father's life, because—and this was probably the most important consideration for Alex—his father was also at peace with his notion of God.

For Alex, God was now a shuffled deck of cards that would have to be resorted. Alex's own beliefs had centered firmly on the existence of a God, on being a part of that God, for always, even after death—especially after death. It wasn't that he *had* to believe in God, the way some people did. He just did, and that belief had been revitalized after the death of his mother, and even more so after Margaret's.

Once when he was a little boy in church with his parents, he asked them about a man seated in the very front pew.

"Who's that, Daddy?" and he pointed toward the thin, middle-aged man. "He's sitting where Mrs. Novak likes to sit. I don't remember ever seeing him before."

"No, but I imagine you'll be seeing more of him, at least for a while. That's Steven Szabo, old Ernie Szabo's son. He works in the mill—or he used to. The doctors just told him he's got cancer. He may not have much longer to live, so I guess he's trying to get straight with God."

Alex came to believe that all people have a need beyond food, shelter, and clothing. A need for something to sustain them at the worst of times, something to help overcome their fears, especially the fear of death. And it doesn't matter what you call it: faith, hope, or God, maybe love. Alex wondered over the years why people like Steven Szabo waited so long to look for it, like trying to cram for a final exam. Wasn't it something you should have had all along? And why should you have to go to a church to find it? Shouldn't it be self-evident, self-motivating, self-sustaining?

Now Alex wondered more whether *it* really had to exist in order to work for you. He thought not—as long as you believed that it did. What a paradox! Belief in God seemed to be more important than the existence of God. Like the Tin Man's heart in *The Wizard of Oz*.

Once secure in his own beliefs, simple as they were, Alex had just had his world turned topsy-turvy by the most wonderful and the most terrifying week in his thirty-three years, a week in which he learned a secret about life. And death.

His own brushes with death were bad enough, but the sudden and unexpected death of a friend and lover was devastating. And to cause the death of another human being—"living soul" as he reminded himself—even in self-defense, brought him nothing but anguish.

Death, the universal certainty. Or so Alex used to think. In the space of a week, Alex had come to know death. But more than that, he had gleaned something of the secret of the universe, of immortal life, only to learn that man had progressed one step too far. Now the prospect of death could be more chilling and more horrifying than it ever was before. Not even Ohio could fix that for Alex.

# Chapter 31

A small sign announced that Alex was passing under the Ohio Turnpike, the first real signpost of home. He turned left at the next light, and now he was on completely familiar terrain: the main highway into his hometown.

He maneuvered the Mercedes around recent potholes not yet patched, and gingerly over mounds and bumps from the older ones that were. Everything was just as he remembered it: run down. He laughed at the joke, but it was true. Economic downturns and foreign competition had punished northern Ohio. His Mercedes, like any other foreign car, would not be popular in these parts.

Tall oak trees ahead on his left marked the edge of the park where Alex played his childhood baseball. His father's street was next, a turn to the right where an old Buick approached the stop sign. Alex, with more than a thousand miles of freeway driving still inside him, had to brake hard and veer sharply to avoid hitting the Buick.

Two-story wooden homes built after World War II lined the street. Each one looked like the rest. He eased his way to his father's house and turned left into the driveway. The crab apple trees, one in each half of a front yard split by a sidewalk running from the street to the front door, were twice as tall as Alex remembered. The concrete driveway, with Alex's initials carved in the corner by the street, was marked with cracks, and the small white house with green shutters would soon need to be painted.

The house had belonged to Alex's grandparents. After they passed away, Alex's parents bought it from the estate and sold the one where Alex had been raised. Alex was in college at the time, so the change didn't bother him, and he was pleased that his parents could move into a larger home.

Besides, his grandparents' house had been a second home to him. He ate and played there, and sometimes he spent the night when his parents went away or were out late. Later, when his grandparents were older, he used to visit just to ease their loneliness.

Alex drove slowly past the side door and up to the garage, which sat well behind the house. He knew his father would be watching, waiting for him to arrive. Before he could unbuckle his seat belt, his father was barreling out the side door. He seemed much smaller to Alex, and in truth he had shrunk a bit and was stooped with age, but Alex was thinking about those days when as a little boy his father seemed enormous. They shook hands first, and on an impulse Alex hugged his father. Then they proceeded in the side door, up the three steps, and into the kitchen.

"Want a beer?"

"Too early. Any coffee left?"

"I'll make fresh. Only take a minute."

The kitchen table where he now sat had once towered over him. Made of sturdy oak, it had endured the Depression, a world war or two, and too many children, grandchildren, and great-grandchildren to count. The table was glossy white, a fresh coat of paint added to all those beneath it, with a rectangular top and thick, hand-carved legs. Still rock solid and level, only the collection of nicks and the simplicity of design indicated its age.

The table was the scene of a nightly ritual in his grandparents' house. Just before going to bed, Alex's grandfather would read aloud in Hungarian from an old, leather-bound Bible that he'd brought with him from the old country. He would sit in his chair, the one nearest the sink, and Alex's grandmother would sit at the opposite end, hands folded, a serene look on her face. She would listen as if hearing the words for the first time.

On those occasions when he slept there, when he was so very young and still uneasy about night's mysteries, when strange lights and shadows were cast on unfamiliar walls by passing cars, Alex could hear from his bed, and he would fall asleep to his grandfather's readings: foreign words of a familiar yet foreign voice, usually deep and resonating, now cracking with emotion. The experience had always affected him, always left him with a hollow, empty feeling, and yet he felt strangely in tune with the house and his grandparents as he drifted asleep. Even as he grew older, he ascribed the feeling, a kind of excitement that easily came back to him when he thought about it, to the combination of his fears countered by the security and protection his grandparents provided. Now as he sat opposite his father at that same table, he wondered if there wasn't more to it.

"So what brings you here?"

"I just wanted to take a break, to get away from the grind for a while—you know." Alex was still undecided about what to do and whether to tell his father. "I may go to Washington for a couple of days. I haven't been to D. C. in years."

"Seems like a long way to come when most of the year you live only a few hours away." His father knew something wasn't right.

Alex changed the subject, asking his father how he was getting along with his new neighbors, the ones on the left. Then they caught up on local news: who had died, or divorced, or remarried, and who still asked about Alex (though such inquiries were fewer now).

"That reminds me, someone called for you a while ago, just before you got here. Didn't say who he was or if he'd call back. In fact, he was kind of rude."

Panic flashed through Alex like lightning from a summer thunderstorm, and he struggled to keep his father from noticing. No one at the lab knew he was coming. He hadn't told Sarah where he was going. Only the men chasing him would be making inquiries this soon.

If there had been any uncertainty before, it was gone now. Alex could not involve his father in this mess, at least not until he felt safe again. He'd leave for Washington as soon as possible.

"If he calls again, tell him you think I've gone back to Los Alamos. Probably a vendor or contractor trying to sell me something, and I could do without that now. Besides, if it were someone from the lab who really needed to get in touch with me, they'd know how."

The last part was a lie, but it made his story more plausible. It was also the sort of thing a father wants to hear. Anyone who could be contacted anywhere in the United States had to be important.

Alex's father went down to the cellar to fetch some pickled cauliflower he knew Alex liked.

Alex got up and moved to the top of the stairway. He yelled loud enough for his voice to penetrate the cold cellar where his father was rummaging among the jars of pickled food. "Dad, I'm going to try and call Lisa. Do you think she's still here?"

His father opened the cold cellar door—Alex heard the squeak of the door's spring—before calling back. "Yeah, she told me she wasn't teaching this summer. She'll be staying with her mother 'til the middle of August."

Alex wondered about Lisa's husband, but he didn't want to ask his father. He looked up the phone number and dialed nervously.

"Hello." The same voice that he remembered, except it sounded weak, or maybe disinterested.

"Lisa, is that you?"

A pause. "Yes."

"This is Alex. Alex Feher. How are you?"

"Fine, just fine. How are you? It's been ages."

"Yes, I know. I'm fine." He wondered if she could tell by his voice that he was not.

"Are you at your father's?"

"Yes, but I'll be leaving tomorrow. I just wanted to say hello. It's really good to hear your voice."

"Yes, yours too. And, Alex, I was really sorry to hear about your mother—and then Maggie."

"Thanks, Lisa. I'm just grateful that Dad's holding up O.K."

"I know. I had a nice talk with him the other day." She hesitated for a split second, as if thinking. "Alex, I imagine you're probably busy, but would you like to have dinner with us? I know Mom would love to have you."

"I have a better idea. Let's go out to dinner, my treat. Is your husband with you?"

"I thought you knew, Alex. Bert died about a year ago."

"Oh, I'm sorry, Lisa. No, I didn't know. I guess I always put my foot in it."

"That's O.K., and you're still sweet. Let's go out to dinner, it'll be fun—like old times. How about the Castle? It's still the best restaurant around here. And we'll arm wrestle for the check."

"Great. I'll pick you up about six, so we'll have plenty of time to reminisce. God, it's good to talk to you." His voice carried a twinge more emotion than he cared to show, and he wondered if Lisa could tell.

Alex made two more phone calls. The first, to George Mills, an old friend, was to say hello, but also to ask about Lisa's husband. All George could tell him was that Bert had killed himself, apparently in some kind of accident.

The second phone call was to Frank Minsanto at *The Washington Post*. Frank wasn't in, so Alex left a message saying he needed to talk to him and would be in touch soon. He did not say where he was.

# Chapter 32

In Los Alamos it was early afternoon and hotter than normal. Eddie and Hank had spent most of the morning on the telephone with their contacts trying to locate Alex. They had a number of sources available to them, in fact a network of sources—automated and manual, federal and local, even underworld—spread across the country and around much of the world.

They already knew Alex had set out by car and was traveling east, possibly to his father's home in Ohio. There had not been time to put a tap on Bela Feher's phone, but the line could be monitored for the phone number of any long distance calls placed in or out. So when someone called the Feher home from a truck stop in Oklahoma, Eddie figured it had to be Alex.

Hollis had sent the Major to intercept Alex, under the assumption he was on his way to Ohio. But the Major hadn't reported back, so Eddie and Hank could only presume he had failed at his mission, that Alex was still alive and now alerted to their efforts.

When word reached them that someone—likely to be Alex—had telephoned *The Washington Post* from the Feher home, a decision had to be made about what to do.

Because the call to *The Post* had been brief, their instincts told them Alex was not interested in reporting anything over the phone; it was more likely he would travel to Washington. They arranged for surveillance of the Feher home to begin the next day. Then, gambling on their instincts, Eddie and Hank drove to Albuquerque and caught the next plane to Washington.

*       *       *

Lisa's mother, Elizabeth Martin, a schoolteacher for some forty years and a widow for ten, greeted Alex at the front door. "Alex, I thought that would be you. Please come in."

"Thank you, Mrs. Martin. How've you been?"

"Oh, pretty good. But teaching gets harder every year. I'm going to retire after this next one, though." She had been saying the same thing every year since becoming eligible for her pension, but the truth was she loved teaching too much to ever quit.

"Excuse me, Alex," she said, then she turned and called up the stairs, "Lisa, Alex is here."

"O.K., Mom. Be down in a minute," came back like a song, sending a wave of anticipation through Alex.

Mrs. Martin escorted him into the living room, where they sat and waited for Lisa.

"You know, Alex, I'm glad you're here. Your phone call—" Lisa was coming down the stairs.

Alex stood and Lisa walked directly to him and took both his hands in hers.

"Alex, it's so good to see you."

"Yes," was all Alex could muster in response.

As Alex looked at Lisa, he was struck by the change in her appearance. The physical changes were unimportant; he could ignore the tiny wrinkles around her eyes, and the fact that her hair was a different shade of brown, maybe hiding some gray. But the other change, the one he had noticed immediately, saddened him: the sparkle in her eyes, once so exciting, vibrant, and contagious, was nearly gone.

Mrs. Martin led them out a side door onto the veranda, where they sat for a while, sipping wine and chatting about hometown personalities and events. Brief as it was, for Alex it was a time to cherish, to be with Lisa as if he hadn't a care in the world. Above, the sky was a faded blue. A few clouds, half silver to the east and half pink to the west, drifted slowly overhead. The moon, nearly full but waning slightly, was climbing to meet the stars and join the nighttime sky.

By the time they left, the stars were shining above, not nearly as bright as those in the thin air of the Los Alamos sky, but no less effective. Lisa seemed genuinely happy, and Alex was as euphoric as he could be under the circumstances. They were fulfilling an old promise, one neither of them had made, but one there nonetheless. And by the time they pulled into the Castle parking lot, much of the sparkle had returned to Lisa's eyes.

# Chapter 33

Its real name was St. Morris Castle, but most people knew it as just "the Castle." The Castle was situated about a quarter of a mile north of the main lakeshore drive, on a bluff overlooking Lake Erie. The Castle had been a restaurant for about twenty-five years, although the building itself was much older than that. It was, in fact, a reconstructed castle brought piecemeal from Scotland in the 1920's, when easy wealth and extravagant lifestyles abounded.

But the stock market crash in the fall of 1929 ended that for many, including the original owner, one Henry St. Morris. Poor Henry saw death as the only way out of his monetary predicaments and embarrassments.

After fortifying himself with a large glass of Scotch whiskey, Henry tied one end of a rope to a chandelier in the upper portion of the castle tower and fashioned the other end into a noose, which he placed around his neck. Full of the dramatic, Henry appeared in the window, standing on the ledge where he beckoned the servants he could no longer afford to gather on the grounds below and witness his last deed. He made a short speech full of bluster and bravado, and then he flung himself off the ledge.

Unfortunately for Henry, his bulk was too much for the chandelier. At first yank it came out of the ceiling and crashed onto a table below. Then one of the chandelier arms snared a table leg. The chandelier and table sailed across the floor toward the window, where they crashed into the wall and parted. The chandelier moved up and snared the windowsill, but then it stopped, wedged firmly into place like an anchor.

Henry dropped a few feet with each movement of the chandelier, but not with enough force to break his neck. Instead, the noose was slowly strangling him as he hung along the castle wall.

Apparently the bravado disappeared, because according to the witnesses, he began to flail and scream, at least raspingly, until finally the rope broke from cutting against the rough granite ledge below the window. Then Henry fell, screaming all the way down to the rocks below on the Lake Erie shore.

Henry's children were forced to sell most of their interest in the castle estate, but Henry's portrait still hangs in what today is the main dining room. And of course there are stories about Henry's ghost being seen from time to time, sometimes walking along the shore, sometimes in the yard, and at times floating outside the tower window. But the most common belief is that he's inside, guarding his portrait, making sure it remains hung.

✶        ✶        ✶

The maitre d' escorted Alex and Lisa to a table by the huge master fireplace, where he seated them directly under the watching eyes of Henry St. Morris. A few logs were burning in the fireplace, mainly for effect, although the small fire helped combat the chill of the air-conditioned castle.

The small talk they'd begun at Lisa's house continued over cocktails, and by the time their salads arrived, Alex and Lisa were again fully in tune with each other. Some fifteen years had been erased.

Over entrees of Lake Erie perch, the conversation turned more serious as each of them summarized the past fifteen years. Alex told Lisa about the few serious involvements he'd had, intimating that some key ingredient was always missing but not going any further than that. The only one Alex omitted was Loyola, because she was part of Los Alamos, and his story had not yet caught up to the past few weeks.

Lisa was talking about Bert.

"I was finally ready to have children. I wanted a child. But Bert began drinking, and about that same time he stopped making love to me. When I tried to talk about it, he said I'd waited too long, that his time to be a father was past. Then he accused me of having an affair. He thought I would try to get someone else to father a child, so if he abstained, it would prove I was unfaithful.

"There was more to his unhappiness, though. Much more. He'd been trying to get a head coach's job anywhere, or at least an assistant's job at a bigger school. He said he was going nowhere as an assistant coach at a small college, while I…" and she paused.

"I was fairly successful—in my career, I mean. And Bert couldn't seem to match me. He thought he was going to be hired at Ohio State, and when they turned him down, his frustration turned to anger, and he began to drink even more.

"Then last year, one day in the spring, he came to see me at my office. He'd probably been to the athletic department first. He was always hanging around there. Well, I wasn't in, and who knows where he thought I was. So he went over to the Ohio State football stadium, somehow climbed to the roof, and either fell or jumped off. There was no note, there were no witnesses, and Bert's blood alcohol was so high, the coroner gave him the benefit of the doubt, listing the death as accidental.

"When I heard about it, I didn't even cry. I guess I knew it was coming. I feel bad, but not bad enough. I know it's a terrible thing to say, but maybe I didn't love Bert. Maybe I don't want to know."

She paused for a moment, her eyes sad but dry. "But life goes on and so did I. I've been as busy as I could be. I added a basic econ course to my teaching load to get back in touch with younger students, and I stepped up my research activities. Guess who's been invited to address the Society of International Economists next year in Paris?"

"That's great. What's the topic?"

"Unification of micro- and macroeconomic theories. I wrote two papers right after Bert died, and both were accepted for publication."

"Social life?"

"I haven't gone out yet, but I've been asked, mostly by other staff—and one very cute sophomore. I spend my Saturdays helping inner-city kids with basic math and business skills."

"Sounds like you've got a very full life."

"Full, yes, but not complete. Something's missing, and I'm not sure what. Maybe just peace. I haven't really been at peace with myself since Bert died."

For all her life she had had things easy; she was the best, the prettiest, the brightest, and she was accustomed to having her way. Alex guessed that the real impact of Bert's death came from the sudden realization someone so close could be removed so quickly and completely—and she had been powerless to prevent it. Her emotional turmoil would be compounded by the haunting thought that she was to blame for Bert's suicide. Alex suspected that Bert had been trying to compete with Lisa and couldn't live with—at least in his mind—failing.

Alex desperately wanted to reassure her.

"Lisa," he said, "look at me," and she did, lifting her gaze to meet his. "I know you too well. You loved Bert, but you're too much of a thinker to let it be. Stop analyzing it and start living again. And if I can do anything to help, you know I will."

"Thank you, Alex," she said, and she patted his hand.

Lisa seemed to cheer up, and the conversation turned back to Alex, partly to get off the topic of Bert's death, and partly to get to the events of Los Alamos, about which Alex had decided that he wanted—he needed—to tell Lisa.

"You know I spend my summers at Los Alamos."

She nodded.

"Well, this year I reported there as usual, expecting another routine summer." He stopped. Remembering brought him pain, and his face showed it, as if he might burst out in tears at any moment. From his eyes alone Lisa could read the anguish.

"This isn't going to be easy," he said, responding to the look of concern that Lisa now wore.

Not sure where to start his story, he hesitated again, thinking. Then he began: "Do you believe in eternal life? In a soul?"

# Chapter 34

Alex's voice was barely audible over the restaurant clatter as he finished his story. His eyes stared at the empty coffee cup in front of him, but his thoughts were of Loyola and Sandy. He knew Sandy was dead.

Lisa's hand rested on his. He had no idea when she'd put it there, but it was comforting. He looked up, into warm, understanding eyes. She had not spoken since he began telling her about Los Alamos.

"Shiii-it."

This utterance, so uncharacteristic of Lisa, caught Alex off guard, and he laughed, his first real laugh in days. But right behind the laugh were the pain, the sorrow, and the fear that filled his emotional cup. He stopped laughing so he would not cry. Lisa squeezed his hand.

"I'm sorry," she said, laughing herself. "I just didn't know what else to say."

"That's O.K. It was an honest reaction. Besides, I needed to laugh."

"Maybe Sandy's still alive, being held somewhere. Or maybe he escaped like you did. You never know. Don't give up hope."

Alex had, but he could not tell Lisa that. "No, I'll hope for the best."

"I'm sorry about your friend, Loyola."

"She was a fine person. I feel badly for her daughter." Lisa squeezed his hand again.

St. Morris Castle was now nearly empty, but the waiter had just tossed another log on the fire burning in the fireplace under the portrait of Henry St. Morris.

"Must be trying to keep old Henry warm," Alex said to Lisa as he beckoned the waiter to their table.

"Could we have more coffee, please?"

"Certainly, sir. Would you care to see the dessert cart?"

Alex looked at Lisa who shook her head.

"No, thanks. Just the coffee. No—wait. Bring us each a glass of Harveys Bristol Cream." He looked with raised eyebrows at Lisa. Her smile said yes.

"Up or on the rocks?"

"Up."

"Yessir, be right back."

On his way to the bar the waiter caught a busboy and sent him back to refill their coffee cups. A moment later the waiter returned carrying a tray with two glasses of Harveys Bristol Cream. He put one down in front of Lisa, to the left of her coffee cup, and then did the same for Alex.

"Thank you. Looks like we're the last ones here—except old Henry there." Alex raised his glass of sherry, indicating the portrait.

"Yes, it's been a slow night." The waiter glanced at the painting. "Do you know the story of Henry St. Morris? I mean about his death?"

"Yes, we're both from around here," Alex replied. "I can remember as a child, I was probably no more than six, sitting around with other kids trading ghost stories in the dark. I think we made most of them up, but the one about Henry, especially how he died, that was one of the first ones we learned."

The waiter set his tray down on their table and leaned on an empty chair. "Well, his grandson owns this place now, and he talks about Henry quite a bit. Says he was always happy, you know, cheerful, with a

'Good day, Laddie' to everyone he saw." The waiter gestured with an animated wave and a broad smile.

"Ever see his ghost?"

"Interesting you should ask. The answer is yes and no." The waiter stopped, obviously waiting for Alex or Lisa to coax him into continuing.

It was Lisa. "Yes and no?"

"By that I mean I've seen him, but I couldn't really look at him. The only way I can describe it is to say it was like seeing something in the dark."

"Oh?"

"Yes. See, your peripheral vision is sharper than your central vision. You have rods on the outside of your eye and cones in the center of your eye. The rods are more sensitive to dim light than cones." His left hand had formed an "O" with thumb and forefinger, to represent the retina, and his right hand was pointing to where the cones and rods would be.

"So if you catch a glimpse of something out of the corner of your eye in the dark, when you go to look at it straight on, you might not be able to see it. But look away a little bit, and it can appear again.

"That's how it was with Henry. I saw him when I wasn't looking, but when I tried to focus on him, he was gone. It happened each time."

"Each time?" This time it was Alex.

"Yeah, I've seen him three times."

"Where? In here?"

"One time, yes. Once I saw him outside, like he was looking at the lake. The other time he was in our banquet room. He's not scary, you know. Most people see him around happy times, like at wedding receptions or anniversary parties. I think he misses the fun."

"Still sounds kind of spooky to me," Lisa said.

"Not really, and it gives the restaurant a kind of mystique." The waiter picked up his tray. "Can I get you folks anything else?"

"No, you can bring the check."

"Very good, sir."

"Well," Alex said after the waiter had gone, "maybe we should drink to old Henry St. Morris. What do you think?"

"I think we should drink to Loyola and Sandy, and to you getting out of this alive."

"You're right," he said. "Here's to Loyola and Sandy," and he added softly, "wherever they might be." Alex and Lisa lifted their glasses, touched them lightly together, and then drank to Alex's friends.

"Now here's to ol' Henry, wherever he may be tonight." They drank to Henry St. Morris.

Their coffee had cooled, so Alex asked the busboy to bring them two fresh cups. After they arrived, Lisa stirred her coffee slowly, her eyes lowered; something was obviously on her mind. She put down her spoon and looked somberly at Alex.

"I can tell you really believe everything, I mean about the soul."

"Yes. I do believe it."

"Well, I have to admit I'm a little bit puzzled. You were always cynical about things that couldn't be proven—like religious beliefs. But you're convinced about this?"

"Yes, I am. I don't have a complete grasp of it, but I believe it anyway. It's like a lot of mathematics. You get into subject areas beyond your own, and the theory can get too deep to comprehend easily. But if you really understand mathematics, someone who does know that other subject area can describe methods and results to you, and you can *feel* that they make sense, even if you haven't followed all the details.

"The S-cubed work is like that. I follow most of the mathematics, but while I don't understand everything, I have a feeling for understanding it. To this theoretical mathematician, it makes sense, it's logical, and it feels right.

"And it explains connections that we seem to know exist but can't explain. Like ESP, like connections—special ones—between certain people, like our connection to God, or to nature, or to eternity and whatever exists beyond our life, in terms of other dimensions and in terms of time, before and after our life.

"Then again," Alex said with a resigned smile and a shrug of his shoulders, "maybe I just *want* to believe it, or maybe I *need* to believe it. But I do, and according to Dr. Bershinski, so do others more intelligent than I—and also less religious than I. In fact, he told me that religion doesn't enter into it for some of them. The soul is just a multidimensional energy form that happens to intersect our corporeal existence.

"So yes, I believe it. And maybe it's my imagination, but ever since I learned about it, I've felt differently. I see more, taste more, feel more. I'm more alive, more receptive to everything that's around me. But also I feel like there's more I could do, if only I knew the right trick. Can you understand what I'm saying?"

"I think so," Lisa said, "and I get goose bumps thinking about it. But I don't know if I believe it all yet. It's too much for me to comprehend without some thought. But I would like to believe it."

"When you do, like I did," said Alex, "you'll realize how horrible this Delta Effect is—not just death, but eternal annihilation. Maybe equally horrible are the implications. Can this be God's will? If the answer to that question is yes, what does that mean? And if the answer is no, what does *that* mean?"

"I'd say it would mean there is no real God. But I don't believe that. I mean even if this Delta Effect does destroy the soul, if it wasn't part of God's plan, then I believe somehow She would rectify it."

"She?"

"Yes, She."

"O.K., She. But how? Let's assume I somehow survive this, and let's go so far as to assume Hollis is somehow stopped. The fact will remain that God has a chink in His—in Her armor. Millions of people will probably know about it before all is said and done. How do you repair that? It's like the atomic bomb. You might wish it was never built, but there's no going back, no way of changing that fact. It's here to stay, and so is the Delta Effect."

"Logically speaking, you're probably right, but I hope not. It's so mind-boggling. I'll have to think about it more when I'm not under the influence of Harveys Bristol Cream."

Lisa studied her glass for some moments, then looked up and met his gaze again. "Your friend, Loyola. Did you love her?"

Alex held the glass of sherry a couple of inches off the table and looked into the dark red liquid. He would, of course, tell Lisa the truth. But first he had to make sure he would not be lying to himself. Above all, he had to be fair to Loyola.

"I liked her very much. And we had a very good relationship—as lovers and friends. But no, I never loved her."

He downed the rest of his sherry and took her hand again. "Now I'll tell you something you should have guessed years ago. I have been in love with you since the day we met. Only problem was, back then I was too insecure—too stupid—to let you know. I like the way you are, the way you look, *who* you are, but there's an attraction beyond that, and I can't explain it—at least I couldn't until now."

Her cheeks flushed warm and red and she avoided his eyes as he continued. "Loyola and every other woman in my life was competing against the feeling I had for you, and it was never topped—not even equaled. I guess—to put it simply, the way we used to say it—I had it for you bad."

She brought her gaze back to his and took both his hands in hers. "The first time we met I melted inside. It's funny, but you still have that effect on me. Like that special kind of connection you mentioned. I just wish we could have gotten together years ago. Of course, maybe it wouldn't have worked out; we still might have gone our separate ways. But it would have been worth finding out."

Alex caressed her hands. "Maybe it's not too late. If I can take care of my problem with Hollis."

"It's not too late. And I want to help you. What are you going to do?"

"I'm flying to Washington, D. C., to see an old friend of mine. His name is Frank Minsanto. We were fraternity brothers—pledged together, and now he's a reporter with *The Post*. I want to tell him everything—well, almost everything. I think he'll be willing to help."

"Why don't you just go to the police?"

"They probably wouldn't believe me."

"You've got Sandy's diary."

"I know. But I'm not sure the police wouldn't just turn everything back over to the Army or to the lab. If the police knew, then word would get out, and I'm not sure the general public could handle this."

"What do you think Frank can do?"

"I don't know. But I don't want him to publicize anything; I just want to be armed. Maybe if Frank and the threat of *The Post* are brought into it, Hollis will back off. Maybe with Frank's help we can figure out how to initiate some kind of investigation into Loyola and Sandy's—into Loyola's death and Sandy's disappearance, connect them to Hollis. I'm not sure yet, but that's all I can come up with.

"I've got to keep moving before they find me, and I've got to get away from my father, so he's not associated with any of this. There's a United Airlines flight tomorrow morning around six out of Cleveland. It gets into Dulles at seven-thirty. I plan to be on it."

"I'd like to go along, if you'll let me."

"I don't know," Alex said, "it could be dangerous, and I don't want to lose you just when I've found you again."

"Well, since I'm *found*, as you put it, I want to stay found. I'd like to be with you. You're the one in danger, not me. Besides, I could use some excitement in my life, and I haven't been to Washington in a while."

"I'd love to have you come with me. Is there any problem leaving your mother now?"

"No, she'll be fine. But I may tell her we'll have separate rooms."

"Will we?"

"I think it might be dangerous to be with you." She was teasing him now. "Isn't it true in the Army they tell their troops not to stay too close together, to disperse, so one bomb can't kill them all?"

"You might be right, but I'd throw my body on yours to protect you."

"That's the danger I was talking about. I might not let you up. And about my mother, well, a daughter has to ease her mother's mind."

Lisa could see the waiter making out their bill. "I'll make a deal with you," she said, squinting mischievously at Alex. "I'll get the dinner check, and you decide the sleeping arrangements, or you can get the check, and I'll decide the sleeping arrangements. O.K.?"

"That's dirty." But Alex did not take long to decide. "O.K.," he said, "dinner's on you."

The waiter arrived with the check in a red leather folder on a small silver tray.

"Will there be anything else?" he asked.

"No, thank you," Alex replied.

Without hesitating, the waiter placed the little tray in front of Alex.

"I'll be back shortly, sir."

Alex slid the tray to Lisa, and she quickly scanned the check, then placed her American Express card half in and half out of the leather folder. The waiter came for the tray, raised his eyebrows a fraction of an inch at the sight of it in front of Lisa, but without saying a word smoothly whisked it away. He returned in a matter of seconds with the folder and a pen. Lisa signed the statement, adding a generous tip to match her mood, and then they left.

As they walked along the stone path leading away from the castle's huge front doors, Alex put his arm around Lisa.

"Would you like to look at the lake before we go back?"

"Uh huh," she said lazily.

The back of St. Morris Castle sits flush along the southern shore of Lake Erie. The path they were on led east along the front of the castle, then split south to the parking lot and north toward the lake.

Walking slowly, Alex and Lisa took the northbound path that brought them to a small stone wall and the cliff overlooking the lake. The wall was connected to the castle, so the path could only turn right, where it ran due east, parallel to the shoreline for about fifty yards, before curving gently to the northeast. After the path curved, Alex and Lisa could see the back of the castle and the window where Henry St. Morris tried to hang himself.

They kept walking until the path ended in an oblong oval of stone. Terminating the path, like the dot at the bottom of an exclamation point, was a well-shaped, full Cockspur hawthorn tree, the only lakeshore tree still blooming in July; clusters of fragile white flowers glistened in the moonlight.

Just to the right and towering above the hawthorn was a large Ohio buckeye tree; its spiny pods contained the brown and white seeds that resembled the eye of a deer and gave the buckeye tree its name. The two trees marked the spot where Henry's household staff gathered to watch his suicide attempt, the same spot where Alex and Lisa now stood.

The moon was directly overhead, and its light was reflected in the waves lapping at the shore on the far side of the castle. Alex was mesmerized momentarily by the dancing moonlight, and for a second he pictured Henry St. Morris bouncing and squirming at the end of his noose.

Directly north, on the lake's far horizon, were the lights of some large eastbound ship, more than likely an ore carrier bound for one of Ohio's industrial ports.

The lake breeze blew warm and friendly, quiet concert to the wip-wap clapping of the waves over the low, steady murmur of the giant lake. An occasional gull, most of them asleep now, chimed in with its staccato offering, and a foghorn from some distant lighthouse kept time with the slow symphony of the northern Ohio lakefront night.

The breeze picked up, rustling the shiny, dark green leaves of the hawthorn tree, and even though the wind was warm, Alex held Lisa tighter. A sudden gust—or was it Henry St. Morris adding his blessing?—showered them with hundreds of white blossoms, and for the first time ever, they kissed.

# Chapter 35

The moon had set, allowing the light from a thousand stars to boldly pierce the black night sky.

Alex pulled the Mercedes into Lisa's driveway. The house was dark, but he thought he could see Lisa watching for him from the living room window.

She switched on the porch light and opened the door. Her bags sat behind her in the hallway. She carried them out and placed them on the front steps. Alex left the motor running but cut the lights as he went for her luggage.

"Good morning," she whispered.

"Good morning. Sure you want to go?"

"Positive."

"Then here's to a good day." He took her into his arms and kissed her for a long time.

Alex carried Lisa's bags to the car while she switched off the porch light and locked the door. He held the car door open for her and, before she got in, he kissed her again.

After Alex had joined her in the car she said, "I wasn't sure how much to pack, so I just threw a few things into a suitcase. Slacks, jeans, a couple of sweaters and blouses. I hope you're not taking me anywhere formal."

"I have no idea where we're going, except to talk to Frank. But you'll look great in whatever you have. If we need anything else, we'll buy it there. I don't have much myself."

"What did you tell your father?"

"He already knew I might be going to D. C., just not so soon. I promised I'd stop here for a few days on my way back to New Mexico. That made him feel better, but he was downright tickled pink when I told him you were coming with me to Washington."

"He didn't ask any questions?"

"No, he's great about that."

The drive to Cleveland Hopkins International Airport would take about an hour, so Alex suggested that Lisa rest on the way.

It was well after midnight when he took her home the evening before. After leaving the restaurant, they stopped for soft drinks at Greenwood Tavern, a place where Alex's parents used to take the family on Friday evenings for fresh Lake Erie fish. The neighborhood bar and grill was empty except for the bartender and a few steelworkers who had just come off the three-to-eleven shift. Tucked away in a dark corner, Alex and Lisa reminisced about high school days, and they talked about a future together, but they avoided the present. Tomorrow would come soon enough.

Lisa drifted in and out of sleep as they neared the airport. Alex spotted a Marriott Hotel, and Lisa was jolted awake when he veered the car sharply to the right, from the center highway lane across to the exit ramp.

"Can't be too careful," he said. "My car—especially with its Virginia tags—sticks out like a sore thumb. If it's the CIA we're dealing with, they'd find it fast enough at the airport. Leaving the car here won't make it much tougher, but it might help."

He parked the car in the middle of the hotel's street-level lot. They carried their luggage to a spot near the hotel's entrance, where a single orange-and-black taxicab was parked. The driver had been sleeping, but he wakened at their approaching footsteps.

"Good morning," Alex said.

"Mornin.'"

"We need to get to the airport terminal."

"Well that's too short a trip for me, but the hotel has a shuttle bus leaving in a little while." The cab driver pulled his short-brimmed black leather cap back down over his eyes.

"We need to get there now. We'll pay you twenty dollars, regardless of what the meter says, and you can be back here before somebody else gets your spot."

The cabby pushed his hat back and forced his eyes wide open. "O.K., I guess. Throw your things in the trunk," he said, and he released the trunk latch by pulling on a small lever at his feet.

Alex opened the taxi's back door for Lisa and put their luggage in the trunk then slammed it shut. He slid into the back, next to Lisa; he took her hand in his. "The hotel may tow my car," he whispered, "but that's a chance I'm willing to take."

"I don't think so," she said. "The hotel doesn't look busy enough to worry about one extra car."

In two minutes they were at the airport. They had the cab driver let them off near the entrance for TWA and Northwest Airlines. Then they walked back to the United Airlines ticket counter.

The counter had not opened yet, so they went to an isolated section nearby, where they could watch for the United Airlines agent without attracting attention. He arrived a few minutes later. They waited for someone else to be his first customer, and then they got in line.

Lisa's ticket was issued in her name, but Alex misspelled his when the agent asked ("Fehrer"), and the agent didn't notice the difference on his driver's license. Lisa paid for the tickets with her American Express card.

"Do you have any luggage to check?"

"Is the flight crowded?"

"Not particularly."

"Would there be any problem carrying these on board?" Lisa pointed to their luggage.

Sandy's diary was in Alex's suitcase, but he would hand-carry it if they had to check the luggage. He'd left the Major's pistol in his car trunk, afraid that he might be caught with it if he tried to bring it along.

The agent peered over the counter and shook his head. "No, shouldn't be any problem at all."

They thought it prudent not to wait in the gate area, so they found a coffee shop and sat down at a table in the rear. After two cups of coffee and day-old Danish pastry, they walked back to the gate, where boarding was already under way. They joined the short line and marched onto the plane, feeling and acting like newlyweds.

An hour and a half later they were on the ground at Dulles International Airport in suburban Virginia, about twenty miles outside of Washington, D. C. The plane taxied to a gate at the mid-field terminal. From there Alex and Lisa boarded a shuttle bus that took them to the main terminal building. With luggage already in hand, they headed straight for the Hertz counter.

"You'd better get it," Alex said to Lisa. "A small car. Parking can be tight around D. C."

"I'm sorry," the young woman in the golden Hertz uniform said, "we have nothing below midsize. But I can give you a Lincoln Town Car at an economy rate." Alex stood nearby, listening to the exchange. Lisa looked at him, raising her eyebrows.

What real difference could it make, he thought.

His facial expression and shrug conveyed, "Sure. Why not?"

Lisa passed her driver's license and American Express card to the Hertz agent.

"Will there be any other drivers?"

"My husband. " Lisa gestured toward Alex.

"I'll need his driver's license too."

In a flash, because she realized Alex's name shouldn't be on the rental agreement and in Hertz's nationwide computer system, she lowered her voice and leaned closer to the agent. "Never mind. Let's just let Mr. Men-Are-Better-Drivers-Than-Women ride in the passenger seat for a while."

The agent smiled conspiratorially and whispered, "I understand."

As Lisa waited for the computer to process and spit out the rental agreement, Alex walked to a pay phone and tried to call Frank at his home. Frank's wife, Cynthia, answered the phone. Alex knew Cynthia from their college days, when she and Frank were dating.

"Sorry, Alex. Frank's out of town on assignment, but he should be back this afternoon. I can have him call you. Where will you be?"

"I don't know yet, Cynthia. When I find out, I'll call and let you know. Will you be at home?"

"No, I'll be at work, but the answering machine will be on. Or you can call *The Post*. Frank will probably stop there before coming home, or at least call in to see if he has any messages. Is it something important?"

"Not that important. Thanks, Cynthia. Tell Frank I'll be in touch." Alex rejoined Lisa, and they went out of the terminal to wait for the Hertz shuttle bus. The large yellow and black van picked them up a few minutes later and delivered them to a white, full-sized luxury car in the Hertz lot adjacent to one of the satellite parking areas.

Alex stowed their luggage in the Lincoln's trunk, opened the passenger door for Lisa, and disregarding the rental agreement, got behind the wheel. In a moment he was past the rental car area gate and onto the Dulles Access Road, a twelve-mile stretch of freeway connecting the airport to the Capital Beltway.

Alex's only real plan had been to contact Frank. Now he had to avoid being seen until Frank was available. He glanced at Lisa, who had closed her eyes and was resting in the luxurious Lincoln seat.

"I think we should get a room somewhere and stay there until I can reach Frank. What do you think?"

"Sounds reasonable to me. Do you know of a good place?"

"I think we should find a small motel, something inconspicuous. There're quite a few along Route 50. Years ago that was the main route from the west into Washington, and it still has its share of motels, but not like the old days. Now the traffic comes in from Interstate 66 to the Beltway, bypassing Route 50."

Still on the Dulles Access Road, about halfway between the airport and the Beltway, Alex looked into the rearview mirror. What he saw disturbed him. The car that had appeared behind them when they left the rental car lot was still there.

"Oh, oh," he said, glancing again at the mirror. "Maybe it's my imagination, but I think there could be someone following us."

"Shit." Lisa's rest period was over.

"Let's find out."

The other car was small and shiny black. Alex guessed Porsche. He slowed the Lincoln from sixty-five to forty-five. The Porsche slowed too, remaining about a quarter mile behind them. Alex sped up, and the Porsche sped up.

Alex switched the emergency flasher on and pulled his car off the road and onto the right shoulder, but he kept the engine running. The Porsche slowed at first, then sped up as it passed the Lincoln. Two silhouettes were visible in the Porsche—both men. Alex could not see them well enough to be positive, but he felt they had to be the two from Los Alamos, Hollis's friends.

Alex and Lisa watched the Porsche until it was out of sight. Then Alex pulled the big Lincoln back onto the road. When they were within a mile of the Beltway, the Porsche popped back into the rearview mirror.

"Shit." Alex spat the word. "They're back. They must have stopped and hidden between the bushes."

Alex kept going and took the exit south onto the Beltway toward Richmond. He merged into the morning rush hour traffic without a hitch. The Porsche stayed with them.

Alex drove about five miles, past the Route 50 exit he had planned on taking. He was watching the road carefully. "Hang on," he told Lisa, "I'm going to try and lose them."

He slowed the car down on the crowded highway. Four lanes of heavy traffic moved steadily in each direction, separated by a concrete median barrier. Alex gradually moved the Lincoln into the left-center lane. The Porsche was still in the right-center lane. Alex finally spotted what he had been looking for about a half mile ahead: a break in the median, put there to allow emergency vehicles access to either side of the Beltway. It was slotted, with the right side overlapping the left, so that to get through you either had to be going in the wrong direction, or you had to be backing up.

When the opening was less than a quarter of a mile away, Alex maneuvered the Lincoln into the left-most lane. He slowed as he neared the break in the barrier, provoking the ire of the driver behind him, who leaned on his horn. The Porsche pulled even with the Lincoln and began to pass.

As he reached the barrier, Alex hit his brakes, forcing the driver behind to do the same. Then Alex suddenly accelerated, pulling as close to the barrier as he could. He jammed the automatic transmission into reverse, then held his breath as he hit the gas pedal. The Lincoln shot through the opening doing about thirty—in reverse. They came out on the other side of the barrier going with the flow of traffic, in the left-most shoulder lane, but with the Lincoln pointed in the wrong direction.

Alex watched the Porsche, trapped in heavy traffic, sail on down the Beltway as he brought his own car to a stop. He inched forward— against the traffic flow, bringing traffic to a halt. Then, as the traffic spurted in its effort to keep moving, Alex maneuvered the Lincoln into a choppy U-turn, much to the disbelief and anger of the other motorists.

Alex and Lisa each expected to hear police sirens, but all they heard was the honking of angry rush-hour drivers. Alex took the first exit, Route 50 East, toward Washington.

"I don't believe it—not a scratch. That was some piece of driving."

"It was pure luck we didn't hit something or get hit, but I would have traded a fender-bender for getting rid of the Porsche."

Lisa laughed. "Sure you would. This car is rented in my name."

Alex steered the car onto the first side street and into a residential housing area. He took the next side street, which was lined on both sides with parked cars. He turned around in a driveway and parked in the only spot available, next to a fire hydrant.

"Well, what now?" Lisa asked.

"We just wait, I guess—until we're not likely to run into the Porsche. Then we'll find a motel. Do you have any other ideas?"

"No, I just want to get where it's safe."

They sat there for about twenty minutes, hoping the Porsche would give up trying to find them. Alex did not tell Lisa, but he was also waiting for his hands to stop shaking.

When Alex was ready, he headed back to Route 50. He turned left, west toward the city of Fairfax. They passed under the Beltway, and Alex kept going until Lisa noticed a small motel set well back from the highway next to a Burger King.

"That looks like a good place," she said. "You can park in the back, and if we're hungry, I can walk next door and pick something up."

The motel had a small white brick building for an office, connected, as an afterthought it appeared, by a covered walkway to the two-story collection of some thirty motel rooms behind it. There was one parking space per room, but only three cars sat in the parking lot.

"I know the place," Alex said. "In its heyday it was called the Isle of White Motel. But when tourists began to find other routes into Washington, the owners looked for new clientele—local lovers in need of a rendezvous spot—so they renamed it the Isle of Love Motel."

Alex waited for an opening in the traffic, then he swung the big car left, across the highway and into the motel's driveway. He pulled past the white brick building and parked beyond the three tenant cars and out of sight of the highway.

Lisa went in to register while Alex stayed in the car. She asked for a single room, paying in advance with cash Alex had given her. She signed the register as Lisa Quincy. Quincy, she told Alex later, was the name of a mutt she'd had as a child.

Once they were in the room, located on the first floor facing the Burger King, it was Alex's turn to tease. "I thought you were getting separate rooms. So where's mine?"

"You gave me only enough money for one."

He moved over to her, next to the bed, and put his arms around her. "What about your mother?"

"What my mother doesn't know,…"

# Chapter 36

Alex and Lisa made love, and all thoughts of Hollis and the Delta Effect were forgotten, like weeds in the winter that lie dormant under a blanket of new-fallen snow. It was their honeymoon. The fact that there had been no marriage ceremony did not matter. And even if it had been delayed these many years, they did not rush anything. Each kiss, each caress, was savored, as if to be remembered and to be treasured for years to come.

When their energies had been spent, after the last caresses and after the holding and the talking, reality began to intrude; they were hungry. Lisa volunteered to get some food, and Alex said he'd try calling Frank again.

It was still early afternoon when she went out. Alex locked the door, then watched her through the motel room curtains.

She walked to the Burger King and ordered sandwiches, French fries, and soft drinks. As she was leaving, she noticed a liquor store on the other side of the highway. In high spirits, she dashed across the street, clutching her bags of food. Lisa picked out a bottle of fine sauvignon blanc and an equally expensive bottle of champagne. She nearly forgot her change in her rush to get back to Alex.

As Lisa returned, she did not notice the black Porsche cruising slowly down the highway, nor did the men in the Porsche notice her; she was too far away.

Eddie and Hank knew Alex had a female companion, and they had a good description of her, but they were more intent on spotting the rental car. By the time they drove past again, Lisa was back inside the motel room.

*　　　　　*　　　　　*

"I brought some champagne—for when we can really celebrate. Also some good white, for relaxing. I hope the food didn't get cold. Better eat it now."

Alex got out of bed and moved to pick through the bag of food. "I'm starved. What's it like outside? Hot?"

"Must be ninety." She looked in the mirror; fine beads of sweat covered her brow. "And humid—I thought Ohio summers were bad, but I'm soaked from walking next door and back. Did you have any luck reaching Frank?"

"Not yet. His office expects him around four. I'll try again before that, though." He picked out a hamburger and a bag of fries, then looked at the wine. "This is good stuff. Why don't we open the white now? Maybe we can have the champagne after we've seen Frank."

"Fine. Pour me a glass while I take a quick shower." Lisa stripped tantalizingly and went into the bathroom.

Alex wolfed the burger down, took the cellophane off two plastic motel glasses, and opened the sauvignon blanc with the corkscrew of an old Swiss army knife. He heard Lisa get into the shower as he poured the wine. He undressed quickly and, stark naked, carried the two glasses of wine into the bathroom.

Lisa was already lathered, and she'd clamped her eyes shut against the soap; she was singing softly as he slipped open the shower curtain.

"Oh—you startled me."

"Sorry. Maybe this will relax you." He stepped into the shower and handed her the glass. Doing a poor imitation of Bogart, he said, "Here's looking at you—and more—kid."

"To us," she responded.

"To us, and thank you for being here."

*      *      *

Alex tried calling Frank twice more before finally reaching him at his office around five.

"I've been trying to get you all day. What are you working on?"

"A story about fraud and waste in the government—nothing new. But we've got the goods on somebody this time. I was in Texas doing some last-minute interviews to reconfirm what we already had. You can read about it Sunday. So what's so urgent?"

Alex knew he had to be careful on the phone, but something also told him not to say too much to Frank, to hold out and hold off as much as he could. It was a curious sort of reluctance, based on some knowledge that he couldn't quite put his finger on—a feeling not unlike the one he'd come away with as he left Black Mesa.

But he had to tell Frank something. After all, that's why he had come to Washington.

"I'm involved in something that's pretty big—and dangerous, for me and for a lot of people. I wanted to let you know what's happening. Maybe get your help. But I don't want to discuss it over the phone. Can we meet somewhere tonight?"

"Well, I just got in, and my editors are waiting for my stories, so I'll be tied up until late tonight. Could we make it first thing tomorrow morning?"

"I guess I can survive until then. At least I hope so." Frank probably assumed Alex was joking, or at worst, exaggerating. "But if something should happen to me—if I get hit by a bus or something, there's an

Army colonel named Hollis, Billy Hollis, from Los Alamos who should be investigated. I don't want to say any more than that, but take my word for it."

Frank was curious now. "What's this all about, Alex?"

"It's hard to explain, but I'll try tomorrow. For right now you need to know that Hollis is dangerous. I'm certain he ordered the killings of two people in Los Alamos, and he's sent two—no, three—men after me. All of this revolves around a new kind of weapon. I'll tell you the rest— what I can—when I see you."

But how much should he tell Frank? Why not everything? Of course Alex already knew the answer to that—the public might be better off not knowing. But wouldn't Frank need to know if he was going to help?

"Can we meet privately someplace?" Alex asked.

"Sure. I know I'll be at the office past midnight trying to satisfy my boss, but we could meet around eight tomorrow morning. Let's make it then, say in the Pentagon South Parking Lot. We can go somewhere from there. Do you know where that is?"

"Yes, I've been by there before. I'll be driving a white Lincoln Town Car."

"Since it'll be Saturday, the lot should be fairly empty, but let's say Lane—what should we make it?—Lane 13."

"Fine, eight o'clock, Lane 13, Pentagon South Parking. Oh, and there'll be someone with me—the lady I'm going to marry when this is over."

Lisa blushed, and she put her arms through Alex's. She could hear Frank's voice on the other end of the phone.

"Congratulations! Thought you'd never find anyone—wasn't there someone—"

"Yes. This is the one."

"That's great. Maybe we can celebrate tomorrow night—your engagement and my story. And I'll do whatever I can to help you out with this Colonel Hollis. After all, when a brother is in need and all that. Listen, I've got to get to work. Take care and I'll see you in the morning."

"See you then."

Lisa disengaged her arms from Alex's and moved as if to encircle his waist. He relaxed, his eyes closed, and waited for her hug. Instead she tickled him, poking and squeezing until he couldn't take any more.

"Heh, what gives?" he said as he trapped her arms under his and wrestled her down onto the bed.

"What do you mean, *the lady you're going to marry*? You haven't even asked me."

"You're right, and I'm sorry. Lisa, I love you. Will you marry me?"

"No."

"What?" Alex was panicking inside. How could he have misjudged things so badly?

"No, I won't marry you, just like you won't marry me. Just like you don't make love to me, and I don't make love to you. We make love together, and we're going to get married together, but I won't be marrying you any more than you will be marrying me. Understand?"

"Yes," he said, laughing now. "I think I do. And I do love you. That is, if that's allowed. I mean for me to love you without saying simultaneously that it's with the understanding that you love me, and—"

"Shut up," she said, hitting him with a pillow. Then she fell on him and kissed him hard.

# Chapter 37

___

Alex was living on two times. Time with Lisa was precious but passing too quickly. The time it was taking to see Frank, to somehow get the whole ordeal over with—that time seemed to be dragging on forever. Forever. What this was all about.

It was evening and they were both tired, although Alex was more weary than tired. Lisa had been able to nap, but Alex's mind would not let him sleep. He tried to remember the last good sleep he'd had. Los Alamos, a long time ago.

Now he was beset with anxiety, troubled by what he knew. How in heaven's name could all this be happening? He was sorry he had ever learned about the soul, its existence, its destruction. He wished he could forget.

He wondered what he would do when he saw Frank. He tried to play it out in his mind. He would tell Frank about Hollis and the G-matter, that it was a new weapon, very deadly. He'd tell Frank about Sandy and Loyola. That Hollis was trying to kill him too. But not about the soul. Frank—the public—shouldn't know about that. But was that for Alex to determine? Yes, somehow he felt it was.

Or maybe he could tell Frank about the soul and depend on Frank not to disclose that part of the story. But Frank would say the public should know, the public has a right to know. That was part of Frank's job.

And what about Sandy's diary? What should he do with it? He could turn it over to the government, but whom could he trust? Los Alamos, the Army, the police, Hollis—they were all government.

Could he give it to the church? If so, which one? What would they do with the knowledge? What would they do with the diary? They'd probably denounce him as crazy, and they could make a convincing case for it. Then they'd destroy the diary or lock it up where no one could ever get at it.

He could destroy the diary himself, but would that help anything? Hollis still had the master documents. Maybe the diary could help someone find a way to counter Hollis's weapon. But that didn't solve the other problem—how the public would react to this new and most terrible knowledge, knowledge of the Delta Effect, knowledge of the complete and utter destruction of what was supposed to be an eternal life force.

*     *     *

Lisa was awake now. She reached for Alex, and when she found him, she pulled herself closer and rested her head on his chest, her arm and shoulder across his stomach.

"I'm hungry," she told him. He was too; it had been a long time since lunch.

But worse than hunger, worse than fatigue, was the feeling of being cooped up. It was getting to both of them. Even honeymooners needed to get out, to breath fresh air once in a while.

They talked it over; they would go out for dinner, but not while it was still light outside. So they watched television and chatted while twilight passed to dusk and finally to darkness.

At nine o'clock they peered carefully through the curtains. The parking lot was empty. The only people in sight were at the Burger King. They opened the motel door slowly then walked quickly to the Lincoln.

For fear of attracting attention, they did not say anything until they were safely in the car.

Alex brought the diary with him. He reached down and stuck it on the floor under his seat, out of sight.

"What a waste," he told Lisa. "So many fine restaurants around Washington, but we're not free to enjoy any of them. I'd love to find a good restaurant, sit down and relax, but it's too risky. The smart thing is probably to pick something up and bring it back. Like Chinese, or a pizza. What do you think?"

Lisa put her left hand over his right. "It doesn't matter to me. It would be nice to relax and get waited on, but you're right, it's probably too risky. Chinese is fine. Do you know a good place?"

"Hang on just a second." Alex started the car and pulled past the motel's white registration building toward the street. He waited for an opening in the traffic, then turned right onto Route 50, heading east and toward the Beltway. He was already checking the rearview mirror.

"There used to be a good Chinese restaurant nearby, Hunan something. We can see—Oh, no! They're behind us!"

The Porsche was gaining fast. Alex gunned the engine and the Lincoln responded.

The traffic light ahead changed from amber to red, leaving the Lincoln some one hundred feet short of the intersection, leaving Alex with an appreciation of just how long a second really is as he decided to run the red light. In that second, they sailed up to and through the busy intersection, through the red light. The Porsche also ignored the signal and stayed right behind them.

They approached the Beltway. Alex decided it would be better than Route 50 because there were no lights or intersections to slow him down. He had no plan except to drive as fast as he could. The large green highway signs told him he could either take the Beltway north toward Frederick, Maryland, or south to Richmond. He chose north.

As soon as they entered the Beltway, exit signs for Interstate Route 66 popped up. There were two I-66 exits on the right: one westbound and one eastbound—a second westbound exit on the left. Alex stayed right to keep his options open. The Porsche stayed in the same lane, right behind the Lincoln.

Alex took the first I-66 exit, eastbound toward Washington. He recalled hearing that Route 66 was heavily patrolled by State Police, but then he remembered he was only half right. During rush hours they were out in force watching for violators of the High Occupancy Vehicle (HOV) law. Route 66 was HOV-2: only vehicles with two or more occupants could travel it during the rush-hour period. The rest of the time, when traffic was unrestricted, the highway received only moderate attention, and it was now after rush hour on a Friday evening.

*            *            *

Eddie was at the wheel of the Porsche, looking trendy in a blue blazer over a white knit sport shirt with light gray golf slacks. He wore tight brown driving gloves with holes over the knuckles. He calmly fastened each one shut with the snap at the back. "O.K.," he said to Hank, who sat in the passenger seat. "Time to end this cat-and-mouse game."

"Right. See if you can get closer." Hank was dressed more casually, in a loud Hawaiian shirt and khaki slacks, and deck shoes without socks. A cold black gun rested in his lap; he picked up the nine millimeter German-made pistol without a serial number, checked the seventeen-round clip for ammunition, and with a flick of his thumb slid the safety switch off.

Eddie's gun was still in its holster under his left armpit. His attention was focused on Alex's car just ahead of them. Out of the corner of his mouth he told Hank, "Hit Feher, then we can take care of the woman. We'll clean up before anyone knows what's happened."

Hank began to roll his window down.

# Chapter 38

Alex was doing about eighty in the Lincoln. The Porsche was right behind him. They reached the Potomac River in only a few minutes and were about to cross into the District of Columbia when the passenger in the Porsche began firing his pistol at them.

The first shot ricocheted harmlessly off the trunk, but the second shattered the rear window, ending up just above Alex's head in the car roof. When the glass broke, Lisa screamed and instinctively covered her ears with her hands. Alex held tightly onto the wheel, fighting off panic.

Route 66 ended, turning into Constitution Avenue as they crossed the Theodore Roosevelt Bridge into D. C. The Porsche tried to pull even with the Lincoln, but Alex used the other cars on the road to keep distance between them. There was no stopping, however.

At 23rd and Constitution they reached a line of cars waiting for the traffic light. The Lincoln and the Porsche swung around the cars and through the light, narrowly missing collisions with the 23rd Street traffic.

They roared past the White House, the Washington Monument, and the Smithsonian museums, heading at a deadly speed in the general direction of the United States Capitol Building. The road was becoming more narrow and less familiar to Alex.

Traffic forced Alex into the right-hand lane, where he had to take the Pennsylvania Avenue fork, past the Reflecting Pool and straight toward the Capitol. The Porsche remained with him.

Directly in front of him, to the left of the Capitol, was a small traffic circle. He chose to go straight, passing in front of the Capitol and ending up at a second traffic circle; the obelisk in its center had been erected to the memory of President James A. Garfield.

"Garfield," Alex said.

"What?" Lisa shouted, panic in her voice.

"President Garfield—from Ohio—that monument." But his eyes were intent on the road ahead and on the car following them.

"Jesus," Lisa said in a loud sigh.

With the Porsche right behind him, Alex swung completely around the second traffic circle, back to the first. Then he headed past it, in the wrong direction, and back onto Pennsylvania Avenue. He stayed on the wrong wide of the road long enough to pass a line of cars waiting for the light to turn green where Pennsylvania Avenue intersects Constitution Avenue. The Porsche did the same.

With the Porsche gaining on him, Alex retraced his path along Constitution Avenue, toward Route 66 and out of Washington.

When they neared the Lincoln Memorial, Alex screeched the car to the left onto a road giving him the option of staying in the District or continuing back into Virginia. All this time Alex kept asking himself, "How could they have found us? And where are the cops?"

In front of the Lincoln Memorial, where he had to decide which direction to take, he turned hard right, intending to stay in Washington. He lost control momentarily, veering wildly to the right, then back to the left, causing one of the other cars making the turn to sideswipe another, sending both of them into the wall abutting the Arlington Memorial Bridge.

"Too bad, but got to take care of us first," Alex said to Lisa. "Hope nobody got hurt. Also too bad the Porsche didn't get tangled up with them."

He found himself driving northwest along the Potomac River, then under the Kennedy Center overhang, past the Watergate Hotel, and, as the Potomac River curved off to the west, north onto the Rock Creek Parkway.

Alex knew Rock Creek Parkway as a twisting, sometimes two-lane, sometimes four-lane road running from the Watergate Hotel north through the District of Columbia all the way into Maryland.

The Porsche had caught up and was now pulling even. Alex swerved to force it back. He was having a hard time staying ahead because the Lincoln could not maneuver like the Porsche. At one hairpin curve Alex nearly turned the Lincoln over. When he regained control, the Porsche was even again, but on the right side.

Alex could see the gunman leaning across the driver of the Porsche. He fired as Alex attempted to brake and swerve at the same time to throw the gunman's aim off. But his aim was good enough; this shot was a hit.

Lisa gasped as the bullet struck, entering right of center, high in the chest. She slumped forward, restrained only by the car's shoulder harness. Blood seemed to pour out of her.

"Lisa!" Alex's mind was racing, spinning, crashing. What was happening? Was Lisa dead? Was he going to die? What chance did they have?

He slammed the Lincoln sideways into the Porsche, forcing it off the road and into a line of shrubs. The Lincoln pulled well ahead while the Porsche struggled to get back onto the road. But in just a few seconds it was squarely in the middle of Alex's rearview mirror and growing larger. Another shot crashed into the rear window, this time exiting just behind Alex's head through the side window.

Alex had had enough. He was tired of running, tired of being scared. For all he knew, Lisa was dead or dying, and he seemed powerless to prevent the Porsche from overtaking him again. He gave up any thought of living and instead thought of killing.

He let the Porsche get close, on the passenger side, and once again he slammed the Lincoln into the Porsche's left front side, forcing it off the road. As before, the Porsche was several hundred yards behind by the time it recovered.

This time Alex knew what he had to do. Twisting the wheel slightly to the left, he braked as hard as he could, throwing the Lincoln into a controlled skid. The car turned nearly one hundred and eighty degrees, counterclockwise. Alex gunned the motor. The Porsche and the Lincoln were now headed straight for each other, a game of chicken. To Alex's left small trees and brush lined the parkway. To his right and well below the level of the road was Rock Creek.

Eddie, the driver of the sleek little Porsche, was suddenly terrified to see Alex's big Lincoln coming straight at him. "Shoot him!" he yelled to Hank, who sat frozen in the passenger seat. Hank stuck the pistol out of his window and fired rapidly, but the bullets would not hit Alex. The explosions turned to clicks. Now utterly helpless, Hank held the empty gun out the window, training it meaninglessly on the Lincoln.

When they were only fifty yards apart, Alex feinted left, turning the Lincoln's wheels ever so slightly. Eddie saw this, taking it for an opportunity to pass to Alex's right. He steered the Porsche a few degrees to the left, speeding up to try and get through the narrow opening.

Alex was so sure the Porsche would take the feint, he had already begun to steer back, directly at the Porsche, which was now pointed slightly toward Rock Creek. Alex had shut off any escape for the Porsche to its right. To avoid a head-on collision, Eddie had no choice but to jerk the Porsche's wheel to the left.

The small black car passed a few feet in front of Alex. He could see the faces of the two men. Sheer terror on the passenger's face.

The Porsche hit the small brick retaining wall separating the parkway from a bicycle path, and the shiny black car hurtled, end-over-end, over the wall and down onto the rocks after which Rock Creek was named. The Porsche landed on its roof with a loud crunch-bang. Almost immediately flames burst from the undercarriage, and with a "whoosh" they spread throughout the car.

Alex stopped his car and threw it into reverse. He backed to where he could see the Porsche below, burning on the rocks. He was satisfied the two men inside had to be dead. Even if they had survived the impact of the crash, there would be no surviving the inferno now engulfing the car.

He looked at Lisa. She was losing a lot of blood. Alex felt her neck. Nothing. Then, yes, he detected a pulse. "Thank you," he said as he accelerated away from the Porsche, in search of a hospital.

He seemed to remember that the Walter Reed Army Medical Center was somewhere off Rock Creek Parkway, so he took the next exit he saw, Sherrill Drive. Amazingly, or maybe not, considering all he had learned, the exit led to 16th Street and the back gate of the Walter Reed complex. Alex didn't know if military hospitals were allowed to treat nonmilitary patients, but he knew they could not turn away an emergency.

He approached the guard station by the gate. A young man in uniform motioned for Alex to stop.

"Hey," Alex shouted to the guard through the hole in his window, "this woman's been shot, and I need to get her to the hospital. Where is it?"

The guard, an Army corporal, could see Lisa in the front seat, bleeding profusely. "Straight ahead, sir, then bear left—big new building. You'll see the Emergency Entrance signs." He waved Alex through the gate while halting cross traffic.

*         *         *

Less than a minute later, two enlisted medics put Lisa on a stretcher and carried her into the Army's largest and most modern medical center. Another medic told Alex he would have to move his car into the underground parking garage.

Alex drove into the garage, tires squealing as he took the down ramp at high speed. He parked in the first place he saw, bumping the wall harmlessly in his hurry. Then he pulled the diary from under his seat, and clutching it securely, he ran into the hospital in search of Lisa.

The medics had taken her to one of the rooms off the emergency entrance sign-in area where, Alex was told, a doctor was with her. Alex went to the doorway of the examining room and waited. In a few minutes the doctor came out. Alex could see an Army uniform under the white lab coat, but he could not see the rank.

"I'm Doctor Emerick. Are you the one who brought in the young woman with the gunshot wound?"

"Yes, I'm Alex Feher." They shook hands. "How is she?"

"She's lost a lot of blood, and I'm not sure what internal damage has been done. She's on her way to surgery now. Can you tell me what happened?"

"It's a long story, but someone from another car shot her. I don't know who it was, but they had an accident themselves. You may be hearing about it. Right now what can you tell me about Lisa's chances?"

"To be honest, I can't say yet. She's stable at the moment, but until we know the extent of damage, I wouldn't venture a prognosis. We'll do our best. I'll be assisting Dr. Maxwell. He's our chief of surgery, and he happened to pull duty tonight, so your friend will be getting the best."

Alex suddenly remembered that Sandy had been stationed at Forest Glen, a place he referred to as part of the Walter Reed complex. Alex took a shot in the dark.

"Doctor Emerick, by chance do you happen to know an Army physician named Sandy Jeffers?"

"Sandy? Sure. We did our residencies together. Great tennis player—nice guy, too. He's out west somewhere right now. Friend of yours?"

"Yes, as a matter of fact, a good friend. Later, when we have a chance, I'll tell you how he fits into all of this."

"Look, I'm on my way up to the surgical suite right now. Why don't you come along? I'll show you where you can rest. It may be a long night."

Dr. Emerick took Alex to his office. An olive drab Army cot sat against one wall. Doctor Emerick pointed to it.

"There it is. Circa 1942. It may not be very comfortable, but it works."

With nothing else to do but wait, Alex thanked the doctor, stretched out, closed his eyes. He said a prayer for Lisa, hoping there was a God to hear it, then exhausted, he fell asleep.

# Chapter 39

*Johnny Whitefeather was nearly ninety but still stood erect and proud. He was working in the cornfield with his grandchildren when he stopped and looked up. "Do you see them? Do you see them? Too many to count, but all warriors! Do you see them?" The children looked hard, but all they could see was Black Mesa off in the distance. By the time they turned back, Johnny Whitefeather was dead, and the warriors were attributed to the stroke that killed him.*

⋆          ⋆          ⋆

In Los Alamos, Colonel Billy Hollis III waited anxiously to hear from his associates in Washington. The mission he had given them was clear enough: find Alex Feher and kill him. If they failed, and Alex was allowed to get to someone who might believe his story, Hollis would have to take matters into his own hands.

It should not come to that, he told himself. But if it did, he wanted to be prepared. He was already contemplating his options, not that he was ready to select a particular one. It was reassuring to know he had several available to him. In any event, and regardless of what long-term options existed, he had begun to formulate an escape plan.

He spent that Friday afternoon in his office, retrieving all the G-matter files and data. The canister itself was located in one of the lab's research buildings, just a couple of miles from his office. It could be picked up quickly in case Hollis had to leave. He was certain that any number of countries would be interested in purchasing the G-matter as well as providing him safe passage, should it come to that.

Of course he would prefer to stay in the United States and had not given up hope of making general, but that depended on his associates getting to Alex Feher. It should be easy enough. The last time he'd checked with them, around noon, they had told him they were zeroing in on Feher's location. It was just a matter of time.

Hollis remained in his office into the evening, waiting for the phone to ring. He did not dare go out, for fear of missing his call.

He used a phone in an adjacent office—so his own line would remain open—to order dinner. He called Steak Heaven, a restaurant located in "downtown" Los Alamos, meaning it was on one of the two four-block long business streets. Steak Heaven did not routinely deliver, but Hollis had been a regular customer, so they made an exception in his case and the night manager personally brought his food: salad, a T-bone steak—medium rare, mashed potatoes, and hard rolls.

The meal was Hollis's favorite, his standard fare at Steak Heaven. But like a condemned man presented with his last meal, Hollis had little appetite. He ate half the steak and barely touched the rest.

Hollis's associates, Eddie and Hank, were usually reliable and efficient. Their organization, known as The Alexandria Group, Ltd., was an offshoot of the Central Intelligence Agency, and it enjoyed the same reputation for being able to deliver results quickly and discreetly. When Eddie and Hank had not called by nine o'clock to confirm the kill, Hollis began to worry in earnest.

The phone finally rang around ten, midnight Washington time. Hollis grabbed the receiver before the first ring had ended.

"Yes?"

"Colonel Hollis?"

The voice was low and clear, not accented, yet stiff and unnaturally stilted. It was a voice Hollis recognized, but it was not Eddie. He should have been the one calling. Nor was it Hank's voice. Hank could fill in for Eddie, but only if, for some reason, Eddie was unable to call.

Hollis was irritated; he was expecting Eddie—and only Eddie—to be calling. This did not bode well.

"Go ahead."

"Colonel, I understand you asked two mutual friends of ours to do a favor for you."

"Yes?"

"I'm sorry to say that our friends are dead. They died in an automobile accident." There was a pause.

"Go on."

"I do not know what they were supposed to do for you, but I am afraid they may not have been successful."

"Shit," Hollis muttered.

"Say again?"

"Worthless bastards!"

"Is there something I can do?"

Hollis spat on the floor. His trust of the CIA and its sister organizations went only so far. "No, I'll have to take care of it myself. Thank you for calling." He slammed the receiver down. "Shit," he said again.

For the next hour, Hollis agonized over just what to do. Chain-smoking all the while, he alternated pacing and sitting at his desk, where he madly scribbled notes of possibilities. He listed, scrutinized, and boiled down his options until he had come up with several rough plans, some contingent upon the success or failure of others. But the central plan was for him to go to Washington and to kill Feher himself, before it was too late. If he did not succeed, then he would reevaluate his options, playing it by ear. If necessary, he would stash the G-matter and make the best deal he could.

He might be able to lie his way out of trouble, even deny the existence of G-matter. He had complete control of the project, and as far as he knew, he possessed the only written record of its existence. Now that Eddie and Hank were dead, there was no direct link between him and the deaths of Loyola Sanchez and Lieutenant Colonel Jeffers, whose body would probably never be found anyway.

As a last resort, he could go to one of the foreign embassies located in Washington and offer to exchange the G-matter for safe harbor and a comfortable existence. Even without the G-matter, he knew enough military secrets to be quite useful to an enemy country for a long time.

And there were a few friendly countries that would be interested in the wealth of information he either possessed himself or could get easily enough from other sources. He knew if he showed up on their doorstep asking for asylum, it would be awkward for them to accept him, but given the additional prize he could offer, he was certain safe passage and a haven could be arranged.

Enough thinking. He had to get back to work.

Hollis emptied his briefcase by pouring its contents on the floor and then cleared his desk with one long sweep of his arm. He put the open briefcase on one end, stacking all the G-matter files and data in the middle. Then he began to sort through the pile of papers. Those he would keep, he tossed haphazardly toward his briefcase. He selected a relatively small part of the whole—only what he thought was essential for his purposes. The most important item would be the G-matter itself. He threw what he did not want in the opposite direction, onto the office floor.

When he had finished sorting, Hollis scooped up the material on the floor and carried it to his shredder, which sat in a corner behind his desk. There he carefully fed each document into the machine, watching as it came out like some kind of thin paper pasta.

Before leaving the office he packed his briefcase with the files he was going to keep. Then he forced it closed and locked it. He put the shredded mess in a cardboard box and carried it down to the basement of the office building where, for good measure, he burned the box and its contents in an incinerator specially designed to leave no residue.

From his office Hollis drove straight to his apartment. The three-room flat was located just across Diamond Drive Bridge, which spanned the far-western portion of Los Alamos Canyon and connected the laboratory to the town of Los Alamos proper.

Hollis was not at his apartment long. First to his bedroom closet, he found an extra uniform and placed it neatly into a garment bag. Next he reached up and to the back of the top shelf and pulled down his Army-issue 45-caliber pistol. From another shelf he grabbed an Army blanket made of heavy wool. In the kitchen he retrieved a hunting knife from a drawer containing otherwise ordinary dinner cutlery. He packed the rest of his clothes, along with the pistol and the knife, into a battered olive drab suitcase.

The briefcase was already in the trunk of his car. Hollis added the suitcase, then he carefully laid the garment bag over them. He slammed the trunk door shut, put the blanket on the seat next to him, and drove back to the laboratory to retrieve the G-matter.

The silver canister containing the G-matter was locked up tight in the most restricted and secure research facility at the laboratory, Building Lambda. Located in the laboratory's remote Technical Area 17, Building Lambda was where many of the lab's radioactive materials—for the most part plutonium—were tested, processed, and stored.

The road to Building Lambda wound down from the main plateau. An armed guard was posted at the building's only entrance, but three more guards watched the entrance from a machine gun nest hidden in the canyon wall opposite and high above Building Lambda. They knew Hollis was coming long before the guard at the door did.

Hollis parked his car in the small parking lot that terminated the road about fifty yards short of the building. Large concrete barriers kept vehicles from getting any closer, but they were not high enough to obscure the machine gunners' line of fire.

The guard recognized Hollis immediately. Hollis had the blanket tucked under his arm.

"Good evening, sir. Kind of late to be testing materials, isn't it?"

"None of your goddam business. Just let me by."

"I'll need to see your pass, sir."

Hollis stuck his identification badge in the face of the guard, who examined it, then said, "Go ahead, Colonel. And have a nice evening."

"Hrrmmpff," said Hollis as he stormed past the guard and into the building. About ten minutes later he came out, carrying the G-matter canister and the remote control device wrapped in the blanket.

Hollis had complete and unrestricted access to the facility, and the guard had no right to know what the blanket hid, but Hollis was obviously removing something from the building. The guard was suspicious, but there was nothing he could do except make a mental note of the event. As Hollis walked past, the guard said, "Good night, sir," with sarcastic emphasis on the "sir." Hollis said nothing.

It was after midnight. Albuquerque was the nearest airport providing service to Washington, but the first scheduled flight did not depart until seven in the morning. Even so, Hollis wanted to leave for Albuquerque immediately.

Located adjacent to Albuquerque International Airport was Kirtland Air Force Base. Hollis thought he might be able to bully someone there into providing him with a ride to Washington. He had done it before. This time he would cite urgent national security reasons. If that did not work, he would just have to wait for the first commercial flight.

Hollis retrieved the briefcase containing the G-matter information from the trunk of his car, placing it and the G-matter canister on the passenger side of the front seat. He wanted them close to him, within sight. The less important remote control device went into the back seat with the blanket.

The full moon was at its apex, illuminating the countryside. Everything was still and quiet. The town of Los Alamos had gone to sleep, to dream, but also to awaken. Hollis's car was the only one on the road, the only noise in the night.

Ignoring the beauty and solitude, Hollis raced away from the laboratory and out of Los Alamos. Down the main street and past the last traffic light, past the small airport, past the original guard tower, built to protect the atomic bomb scientists in the 1940's and still standing.

His headlights and the moonlight lit the way. The road was climbing rapidly now, Los Alamos Canyon opening to Hollis's left. He braced for the two sharp right turns he knew were ahead.

At the first turn, Black Mesa came fully into view. The moonlight gave it an eerie glow, a bronzed look.

"Looks like a damned Buddha, squatting there, grinning at me," Hollis muttered out loud.

And as he approached the next turn, he thought he could hear shouting. His window was open, catching the cool night air. He cocked his head and trained his ear on the sound.

He could hear an ill-matched chorus of voices, ranging from high-pitched screaming to low-pitched chanting. Before he could sort the sounds and make sense of it all, he saw them. Hundreds of Indian warriors suddenly stood in front of him. They stretched from one side of the road to the other, back down the road as far as he could see.

They were arranged with one in the front, a few right behind him, then more and more until they filled the road. The leading brave was on horseback. A headdress trailed down his back, almost reaching the ground. (Had he been on foot, he would have walked with a noticeable limp, favoring his right leg.) Hollis could see that the Indian brave was young, much younger than himself.

Closest to the leader, to his right but just behind him and also on horseback, was a tall, lanky Indian. What caught Hollis's attention in that briefest of time spans was the Indian's white hair and unusually light complexion.

Others were on horseback, but most were on foot. Faces painted with war paint, they menacingly displayed spears, tomahawks, and bows and arrows. Armed and dressed for war, yes, but to Hollis there was something much worse. He could see their eyes. Each brave had a crazed look, one Hollis knew well. The look of a man intent on killing.

Hollis was frozen with fear. They could not be real, he told himself, but they were.

There was no way he could avoid hitting the first Indian. Hollis had come around the curve at maximum speed. Any faster and he would not have been able to hold the road. At his speed and with so little warning, he could not possibly stop in time.

All his life Hollis had acted and reacted aggressively. Striking the first Indian—and probably several more—was inevitable, but allowing himself to be caught among this mass of Indians after killing their leader would certainly be fatal. The collisions would slow the car, but he had to make it through. Instinctively, defensively, Hollis closed his eyes and accelerated, waiting for impact.

There was none.

His car left the road, smashed through the weak wooden guardrail, and sailed over the edge of the cliff. He opened his eyes as the car began its hundred-foot plummet to the canyon floor below.

Hollis did not understand what was happening, but one thing was certain: he was going to die. He knew it. There was no reason for him to panic; there was nothing he could do. He held onto the steering wheel and relaxed.

Then, as if by remote control, the canister began to open.

Hollis had wedged it between the car seat and seat back to keep it from rolling around. Out of the corner of his eye he could see it twisting apart. "Oh my God, no!" he screamed, as he made a desperate lunge for the cylinder containing the G-matter. But before he could reach it, the canister opened.

The energy known as Colonel Billy Hollis III was gone. Forever.

His body, so suddenly and so totally lifeless, as if someone had thrown an "off" switch, sagged across the front seat. His arms still reached out. His hands touched the canister. His mouth hung open but slack-jawed in mid-scream. His eyes, just a moment before bulging with rage and fear, still watched the canister, but now they were dim and vacant orbs.

The canister closed just before the car hit the base of the canyon wall.

The car tumbled the remaining distance to the flat canyon bottom before exploding into flames. In the first half-second the pressure of the explosion spread Hollis's face into a smile. Then, as the bristles on his head burst into flame, his flesh melted with the heat, and finally all of Hollis was ablaze.

The G-matter files, trapped in the car with Hollis, were completely destroyed in the fire. The canister, however, was thrown free when the car exploded.

It sailed through the air and landed on the rock-hard canyon floor. It rolled, at first like a wobbly football, then like a golf ball on a hard, bumpy green. The canister rolled straight for the fissure made by the recent earthquake. Like a Jack Nicklaus putt, it stopped rolling at the hole, hesitated over the lip, and dropped in.

It fell deep—past dirt and stone and clay, past molten rock; it fell deeper than man should ever go. When at last it stopped falling, the earth rumbled gently, and the hole was closed.

The Hachonee watched solemnly, then they were allowed to leave. They had done their part. They had finally atoned for their sins.

Black Mesa was a silent witness left alone to guard the secret.

# Chapter 40

---

Friday night in the nation's capital had come and gone like a good fire-place blaze. With no stoking necessary, the nightlife had built itself into a roaring fire, lasting well past midnight. But when it began to die, it succumbed quickly, flames turning to embers, and embers to cold ashes.

Late-night revelers departing Georgetown via Rock Creek Parkway saw nothing of the Porsche. Its charred remains and those of its two passengers had already been removed.

Park police had been the first to arrive at the scene of the accident, and after summoning the fire department and determining that the two persons trapped inside the still-burning shell could not be alive, they followed standard practice and radioed the Porsche's license plate number to their headquarters for identification.

The police didn't know it, but any computer query of the Porsche's registration was automatically and simultaneously passed to the agency for which Eddie and Hank worked. Within minutes of the police call, three agents from The Alexandria Group, Ltd., arrived in Rock Creek Park. Their job was to influence the investigation, unless they could control it outright. They were also there for any cleaning up required. In this case they had to remove the weapons, still white-hot from the fire, then find and dispose of several spent shells, without alerting Park and District of Columbia police as to the questionable activities of the individuals in the Porsche.

Although the police had long ago learned to tolerate the many intelligence agencies in the Washington area and how they operated, still they bristled at interference in local police matters. But late on a Friday night and apparently with only the one car involved, the Washington police quietly deferred to the agency's investigation.

Meanwhile, at the bottom of Los Alamos Canyon, Colonel Billy Hollis's car was still ablaze. Rescue personnel and vehicles were making their way to the accident site, but judging from the inferno engulfing the car and the fall it must have taken, they had faint hope for anyone in the car when its plummet began. Little did they know.

# Chapter 41

In a small office on the fifth floor of the Walter Reed Army Medical Center, Alex Feher dozed quietly. He had fallen into a deep sleep, taken there by a mind ignoring its own fears and its body's hunger. It went willingly, escorted by exhaustion. The journey to sleep was rapid, and Alex had the subconscious sensation of purposeful movement, like an animal responding to the call of a mate.

When he was as far away from consciousness as he could get, he began to dream. He dreamt he was in a two-dimensional plane, a pane of glass. He was stretched out, reaching high with his hands but confined to the plane.

Something was happening. He was growing, expanding outward, as if his arms and legs were still in the pane of glass, but his torso was inflating and becoming three-dimensional. He was backing out, hands and feet still attached, and now he could see it in front of him, the pane of glass. No. There was a reflection. A mirror.

His face was too close to the mirror to focus, but he knew he was watching himself change, materialize if you will, hands still touching hands, feet touching feet, slowly backing out. But as his vision came into focus, it was not his reflection that he saw but Loyola, joined to him at hands and feet, moving opposite him, moving with him.

He tried to speak but could not; he did not know how. She seemed to understand this, and she spoke to him slowly and carefully.

"Alex, don't be afraid."

And he was not, at least not of her.

"There is nothing to fear anymore. Hollis is dead." She stopped momentarily, as if to let Alex comprehend. He still could not speak. His eyes asked her to continue.

"Hollis is dead, and the G-matter is gone. Buried. Forever." She paused again. "The files have been destroyed. Nothing remains." Another pause. "An accident produced the G-matter. It will not happen again."

Alex seemed to understand, but he had no idea why. He wanted to ask about Lisa.

"Alex, I once loved you, but not with the kind of love Lisa has for you and you have for her. She will be fine." Pause. "You two will marry soon, and she will have your child—next summer—in Los Alamos."

And Sandy?

"Sandy is dead, but he does not want you to be sad. He asks that you remember the name Knielson—with a 'K'—and mention it to Dr. Emerick."

Alex felt like he was nodding assent.

"One last thing. You and Lisa can have several children if you want. But the child to be born in Los Alamos next summer will be a daughter." Then Loyola got this smile, her smile, not malicious or evil, but a confident, knowing smile. "You will name her Loyola." It was not a command, just a statement of fact.

Alex was still looking at Loyola, their hands and their feet merged together at the mirror. Her smile faded, and he felt his hands being gripped tightly by hers. The two of them began to move together, back into the glass. Alex held her gaze one last time before she vanished.

He was sleeping soundly, peacefully. Something was shaking him, gently at first, then more vigorously.

"Mr. Feher. Mr. Feher."

"Huh?"

"Wake up, Alex. It's Dr. Emerick."

"Oh, sorry. I was really out of it. How's Lisa?" Somehow he already knew the answer to that.

"Lisa's doing fine. We've listed her in serious condition, but everything looks good. The bullet shattered a rib about here." Dr. Emerick snatched a pen from his desk and used it to point out where the bullet struck and its trajectory. "Then it passed through the right lung, behind the heart, and lodged against the back of the rib cage, here. We were able to repair the damage and remove the bullet without much trouble. All in all, she's mighty lucky. She should be as good as new in a few weeks."

Doctor Emerick began to change into his street clothes. "It's after three, and I need to get home and get some sleep. I was supposed to be off duty at midnight. You're welcome to stay here for the night. There's a shower through that door if you need one."

"Thanks, Doctor. When can I see Lisa?"

"She'll be in recovery for a while, then she'll sleep until mid-morning. After that you can see her. Oh, I'm sure the MP's will want to talk to you about the circumstances of the shooting. Not to mention our administrator. He'll want to know who's paying the bills. Now," he said, pulling on a pair of sweatpants, "how did you say you knew Sandy Jeffers?"

"We were at Los Alamos together—got to be pretty good friends. I just came from there. Two men were chasing me, the ones who shot Lisa. Before that they killed a friend of ours and tried to kill me. It's a long story, but Sandy was involved, and when I left Los Alamos he'd disappeared. He may have turned up by now." But Alex knew he had not and probably would not.

"Sounds like you've been through a lot. Sure hope Sandy's O.K. What was it?" Dr. Emerick asked, looking up while tying his shoes. "Some kind of espionage thing?"

"Something like that."

Alex decided to check on the message Sandy had sent him. "By the way, doc, does the name Knielson—with a 'K'—mean anything to you?" Dr. Emerick's face turned pale.

*                 *                 *

Knielson was a name Dr. Thomas Emerick had hoped he'd never hear again. It took him back more than ten years, to when he and Sandy were residents together.

They shared an apartment then, and sometimes they had trouble making ends meet. Once, when times were really tough, especially for young doctors living in anticipation of their future salary but well beyond their current means, they were forced to come up with a large amount of cash quickly.

About the same time, they were approached by an acquaintance of theirs—married—who was trying to arrange an illegal abortion for a woman he had been seeing. He offered them more than enough money to cover their debt, and they agreed, albeit reluctantly, to perform the abortion. The patient's name was Judy Knielson.

The abortion went smoothly and there were no complications, but they vowed never again to put themselves in that kind of position, nor ever to tell anyone what they had done. There was too much at stake for each of them.

*                 *                 *

"Where did you hear that? Sandy wouldn't have said anything."

"You won't believe this, but he passed it to me in a dream. I guess it means something to you. I don't care what it is—I just needed to know if it was a silly dream or something more. I think I know for sure now."

Alex stuck out his hand. "I want to thank you for taking care of Lisa and for letting me use your office."

Dr. Emerick shook Alex's hand firmly. "For a friend of Sandy, any-time. Just fill me in later. It sounds like you've got quite a story to tell. But right now I've got to get some sleep." He slipped a sweatshirt over his head and opened the door. "I'll be checking on Lisa in the afternoon, so I'll see you tomorrow." He looked at his watch. "No, I guess I mean later today."

"Thanks again, doctor."

Alex went back to sleep, setting a mental alarm clock to wake up at six. He did not want to be late for his appointment with Frank. He was not sure now what to tell him; that would depend on how certain he was that everything in his dream was true. As he drifted off, he thought he might dream again; maybe Loyola would help him decide how much Frank should know, what to do with the diary.

But Alex slept without dreaming—as far as he could tell. When he awoke at six, he felt refreshed and invigorated.

He showered, slipped back into the clothes he had worn the evening before, and with Sandy's diary firmly in his left hand, he went to the nurse's station to ask about Lisa.

"She's doing just fine," the young military nurse told him.

"I'd like to see her. Can you tell me which room she's in?"

"She's in 522, but you can't visit her yet. She's still sleeping, and she really shouldn't be disturbed."

When the nurse turned her back, Alex quickly walked down the hall and found Room 522. He peeked his head into the room. Lisa appeared to be sleeping peacefully. He left for his meeting with Frank.

Chapter 42

---

Alex's trip to the Pentagon, using Rock Creek Parkway, would take about twenty minutes. There were only a few cars on the road early that Saturday morning, so out of curiosity, when he approached the area where he thought the Porsche had overturned, he slowed down, searching for the exact spot and any remnants of the accident. The Porsche had been removed. The morning dew helped disguise the telltale scorch marks, so he could only guess at where it had been. Funny how different things looked in the light of day.

Alex exited the Parkway near Georgetown, its downtown famous for nightspots now quiet and empty. He crossed Key Bridge into Virginia and passed quickly through Rosslyn, a community of condominiums and high-rise office buildings full of contractors and consultants ready to do the federal government's bidding.

He reached the Marine Corps War Memorial, more popularly known as the Iwo Jima Memorial. Just past it, Arlington National Cemetery appeared on the right, its white stones all dressed and covered, gleaming in the morning sunlight. Alex thought about the soldiers they represented, their bodies, what war had left of them, interred and decaying beneath the Virginia sod, their deeds, mostly long-forgotten, but their souls—their souls were intact, somewhere, presumably forever.

The Pentagon exit was next. Then the huge office building itself was in sight, on Alex's left, the west side looking gray in the morning shadows. The east side, in contrast, looked a bright tan in the sunshine. Alex drove past the Pentagon and its helipad to take the exit for the Pentagon South Parking Lot.

The winding exit ramp took him alongside a drainage ditch partially filled with litter and garbage. Something caught his eye and he stopped the car. Then he backed up, pulled off the roadway and put on the emergency flashers. Alex got out of the car and walked over to the pile of trash. There, in the middle, was a small metal box, about twelve inches square and ten inches deep. It was the kind he'd seen outside doors of medical offices, and on the side in large red letters was "CAUTION! RADIOACTIVE MEDICAL SPECIMENS." The lid had been torn off.

Alex carried the box back to his car, set it on the passenger seat, and continued down the ramp and into the Pentagon parking lot. He turned left at Lane 13 and drove halfway down the row before parking. He looked for Frank although it was only seven forty-five. Frank wasn't there yet, and Alex was betting he'd be late. Old habits were hard to break.

He scanned the parking lot again but saw no one. Alex knew it was time to use the metal box. When he'd spotted it on the side of the road, he had decided—then and there—he was going to destroy the diary.

Alex bent down, reached under his front seat and pulled out the small black book with its dreadful secrets. He looked at it as if for the first time. He was mildly surprised to notice Sandy's initials, in gold, in the lower right hand corner of the cover.

"You could be worth millions," he told it, "millions of dollars, millions of lives—millions of souls." Then he opened the cover and looked at the first page. Sandy's handwriting filled the page and stared at him chillingly. Sandy had used red ink—thin red lines of script on cold white pages. Alex thumbed through the diary. Red ink everywhere. Alex stopped abruptly and slammed the diary shut. Should he—should he scan it first?

After a few seconds, he opened his car door and placed the metal box on the ground just outside the car. Then he reopened the diary and tore out the first few pages. His hand trembled as he fumbled for a pack of matches in his pants pocket. "Isle of Love Motel" was written in red script across the white cover. He lit a match and held it at the edge of the pages he had torn from the diary. He thought they were not going to catch fire, but they did. He held them until the flames reached his hand, singeing the hair on his forefinger and thumb. He dropped the flaming pages into the metal box and then tore several more pages out of the diary.

Alex added these pages to those already burning and repeated the procedure until every page from the diary was aflame in the box. After he had thrown the last page in, he tossed the diary cover into the back seat of the Lincoln. He wanted to keep it, a remembrance of Sandy.

The small fire burned for several minutes. When it died out, when the secrets had been consumed, Alex got out of the car and kicked the box over. Hot ashes spilled onto the asphalt parking lot. A few blackened pieces of the diary, about the size of quarters, remained intact. With his shoe, Alex ground them to nothing.

He looked at his work. Inexplicably, his visit to Black Mesa and the uneasy feeling he had left with came back to him. But the feeling was different; it was as if the itch that he couldn't reach before had now been scratched. He looked again at the residue from the diary and felt a sense of having done what he was supposed to do. He had done his part.

Of what?

He still didn't know. And now, after everything that had happened and everything that he had learned, he wasn't sure he cared. As long as it was over.

Alex used his shoe to scatter the small pile of ashes into a circle a couple of feet in diameter. Then he placed the still warm box in his trunk, intending to dispose of it properly somewhere. He drove away from the ashes to the far end of Lane 13, where he waited for Frank to arrive.

Sitting there, just outside the huge five-sided headquarters of the Department of Defense, Alex wondered about the Pentagon brass: the Secretary of Defense, the Chairman of the Joint Chiefs of Staff, the Service secretaries and chiefs of staff, and all the other generals, admirals, and bureaucrats. How many Hollises were there among them?

Alex was standing comfortably against the Lincoln when Frank arrived at eight-fifteen. Alex got into Frank's car and they shook hands warmly.

"Good morning, Frank. You're looking good."

"Good morning to you, brother. You sound a lot better than on the phone yesterday. How are you?"

Before Alex could answer, Frank said, "Holy cow, what happened to your car? It looks like it's been in a war!"

Alex had not even thought about its appearance. The front door windows on both sides of the car were shattered, as was the rear window, and the right side was scraped and dented from his collisions with the Porsche.

He chuckled. "It was kind of a war. I guess I got used to the car looking like that. It runs fine. To answer your other question, I am much better. But Lisa isn't. She was shot last night and she's in Walter Reed. The doc says she's going to be all right. And the two men who were after me are dead. Killed in a car accident—Rock Creek Park—also last night."

Frank started driving out of the parking lot, heading for Interstate 395, south toward Richmond.

"Were those the two? I heard about the accident—Porsche flipped over, then caught fire. But that's not all. Your Colonel Hollis is dead, too."

Alex felt ecstatic, more of his *dream* confirmed.

"What happened? How do you know?"

"I had to drop some papers off at my office on the way over here. The Hollis story had just come in, and his name caught my eye. It said his car went over some cliff, then exploded and burned. He didn't have a chance. They were also investigating the possibility he had some classified documents with him, maybe even some radioactive materials.

"It seems he stopped at a lab and picked something up before leaving. The guard thought it was suspicious, but Hollis had the clearance. Yet when they examined the wreckage, there was no trace of any radioactive substance, and if there were any documents, they were destroyed in the fire and explosion. Now tell me about Lisa and what I can do for you."

"With Hollis dead, you don't have to do anything. Of course I'll have a lot of explaining to do to the people at the lab in Los Alamos and to the D. C. police, but I can get through that. Lisa was shot in the chest by the men in the Porsche, but she's not in any danger and should be as good as new in a couple of weeks. Then we can get married."

"That's great, but there's got to be more—what aren't you telling me? On the phone you mentioned something about a new kind of weapon."

"Well, that was premature. I was talking through my hat."

"Sure you were. Now that this Hollis is dead, the weapon disappears. I could still look into it, you know."

"I know you could, Frank, but do an old fraternity brother and yourself—maybe the rest of the world—a favor. Don't. Let's just say it's a national security issue and drop it there."

"I think I know what you're saying. Because I'm a reporter, you don't trust me as a friend. Could you tell me off the record, one fraternity brother to another?"

"I don't know, Frank, maybe part of it. Believe me, there are things you're better off not knowing. But if you buy me dinner tonight, I'll tell you what I can. Then we can celebrate your big story. How is it, by the way?"

"Neatly wrapped up, but I don't think it's near as intriguing as yours. I'll let you off the hook now, but you've got to tell me something tonight. Deal?"

"Sure. Thanks for offering to help. You can take me back now. I want to be at the hospital when Lisa wakes up."

They talked about other things while Frank returned to the Pentagon lot. When the five-sided building came into view, wide and flat, Alex was once again reminded of Black Mesa, but this time how it was connected, via rock and soil, air and water, all the way across the country to the spot in the blacktop parking lot where he had burned the diary.

And the other connections between there and here, between then and now, the connections he knew existed but didn't understand. Lisa. Loyola. Henry St. Morris. Margaret and his mother. The boy in the Blue Ridge Mountains. Even Michelle and her own search for some connection to God and eternity.

Frank pulled into Lane 13 and drove by the noticeable circle of ashes. "Look at that," he said to Alex. "Probably from some demonstration. Somebody burning the flag again."

"Yeah, probably something like that."

# Chapter 43

---

Alex left the Pentagon a different man. The last clouds had been removed; Hollis was in fact dead. The diary, a blueprint to oblivion, no longer existed, burned to ashes, like Hollis and the two men in the Porsche.

Destroying the diary had been his choice, his act, and in carrying it out, Alex had rid himself of his greatest burden. Of course he would never be free of the diary's terrible secrets, but he'd eliminated the possibility that others would learn—and act on—those secrets. Equally important, the soul's vulnerability would remain a secret.

While just knowing about the Delta Effect was itself a burden, Alex could take comfort in also knowing the whole diabolical situation—the existence of G-matter and Hollis's scheme—had somehow been dealt with and resolved. How, he did not know, so while the clouds were gone, shadows remained. But the shadows, the hows, did not matter to Alex, at least not yet. For the time being, maybe for always, he would simply presume, as Doctor Bershinski did, that there was a higher presence, God, in charge of everything. Today God seemed to be in His—or, acceding to Lisa—Her heaven, and all was once again right with the world.

Best of all for Alex, Lisa was going to be fine, and their future together was bright with promise.

As the lighter, happier Alex left the Pentagon parking lot for Walter Reed, his stomach sent him a rude message: he had not eaten since lunch the day before. So instead of driving straight to the hospital, where he expected Lisa still to be sleeping anyway, where he also expected to find the *authorities* waiting to question him, he stopped at a pancake house in nearby Arlington.

Papa's Pancake House was Alex's favorite spot for breakfast when he was in the Washington area; today, Saturday, it was crowded and he had to wait to be seated. Fully relaxed, maybe even spent, he did not mind at all.

He bought a *Washington Post* from the machine outside the restaurant entrance, and he read the paper while he waited. Near the end of the front section he found a small article about Hollis. "Mysterious Accident Claims Life of Local Army Officer" the headline read. The article mentioned that Hollis was temporarily working in Los Alamos, but it did not give any details about the accident or what might have caused it. Alex could find nothing in the paper about the Porsche.

Finished with the newspaper, he passed it to another customer waiting for a table just as the hostess called his name. She escorted Alex to a small table next to the large front window and then brought him a carafe of hot coffee. After four cups of coffee and a very leisurely breakfast, Alex left the pancake house in the battered Lincoln. But not until he'd removed the metal box from his trunk and tossed it into the dumpster behind the restaurant.

Alex arrived at Walter Reed about half an hour later, once more traveling the scenic Rock Creek Parkway.

As he had expected, the authorities were waiting for him. Queued up in the corridor outside of Lisa's room were two military policemen, a District of Columbia detective, and an Army captain from the Walter Reed Administrative Services Office. Alex asked them to wait for just a minute, and before they could stop him, he sprinted through the door and into the room where Lisa was still asleep.

A nurse dressed in a white uniform stood at Lisa's bedside, her hand on Lisa's wrist. Mildly startled by Alex's entrance, she looked up from her wristwatch and lost count of Lisa's pulse.

"I'm sorry," Alex said to the young lieutenant, "I just had to see her. How's she doing?" He wondered at what she must think. The way he rushed in, his unshaven face and disheveled appearance.

The lieutenant smiled a warm smile, putting the intrusion behind her. Alex felt that she somehow understood the depth and intensity of his love for Lisa.

"She's doing just fine. She was awake a little earlier. She'll probably be waking again soon."

The MP's had filled the doorway behind Alex, blocking his exit.

"I think some people want to talk to you," the nurse told him, nodding toward the door. "Why don't you see what they want, then wait outside. I'll let you know when you can see her."

"Thanks." He pushed his way by the MP's, ready to face the assortment of officials.

The captain was the easiest to get rid of. He wanted to know how Lisa's bill would be paid. Alex explained that she was a full-time employee of Ohio State University and said that if he had to have the information immediately, he should contact the university to find out what insurance coverage she had. Somewhat satisfied, the captain left to make his phone calls.

Next, the D. C. detective in tow, the MP's escorted Alex down to the second floor and to a conference room located just off the hospital's command suite. There, after closing the door ominously but then offering Alex coffee, they asked him to explain how and why Lisa was shot.

He told them about the Porsche. A man in it—someone Alex did not know—had shot Lisa. The detective said he had heard about the Porsche's accident but had not associated it with Lisa's shooting.

The older MP asked Alex to start from the beginning, to take his time and not to leave anything out.

The story Alex chose to tell was that he and Lisa were in Washington on a short vacation. They had gone out for dinner and for some sightseeing when he noticed the Porsche following him. For no apparent reason, it tried to force his car off the road. When it could not, a car chase ensued and one of the two men inside the Porsche—the one in the passenger seat—began shooting at them. Lisa was hit, Alex played his game of chicken, and the Porsche lost. Alex said he had no idea why they did it, suggesting that it might have been a case of mistaken identity.

Before the police officers could challenge his version of what happened, Alex went on the offensive. Gesturing angrily, he said that as the Porsche was chasing him, he kept expecting, hoping to see a police car, to get some help. Even though the chase covered forty miles and took them through the heart of Washington, they did not see a single policeman.

Alex thought he'd struck a nerve in the detective, but the latter remained impassive. Then Alex told his interrogators that they should be investigating the two men who died in the Porsche; they were the criminals, not Lisa and Alex. He figured that if questioned by the police, whoever the two men worked for would muddy the water enough to take the heat off him.

Finally, Alex insisted that the three policemen follow him, and he led them to the parking garage and his car. He walked them around the Lincoln, pointing out damage caused by gunshots and the collisions, in a kind of reverse of the way a used car salesman might point out desirable automobile features.

The policemen were suitably impressed, but they still had reservations about Alex's story. The detective said he would send someone to examine the car more thoroughly, and he jotted something down in a small spiral notebook.

They returned to the conference room, where Alex was asked to repeat his story. He did, nearly word for word.

"That's everything," he lied, looking at them defiantly, leaning back in his chair with his arms folded across his chest. The ball's in your court now, he was thinking.

The two MP's went out of earshot, and after talking it over for a few minutes, they concluded that the Army had no jurisdiction, since neither the car chase nor the shooting was on military property. The senior MP, Sergeant First Class Carl Hanson, explained the situation to Alex. With a brief warning that they would return if he had lied to them, the two MP's excused themselves. Alex was left alone with the detective.

Detective Lewis Evans looked hard at Alex. He waited until the door was firmly shut again before he spoke.

"Mr. Feher, I'm going to look into the Porsche accident," he said sternly, "and I don't know what I'll find, but I don't think you're telling me the truth, at least not all of it."

Alex avoided the detective's eyes.

"You know, son," he continued in a well-practiced, softer tone, "I'm a pretty good judge of character, and I don't think you shot your woman friend. I'm also betting you haven't committed any serious crimes. So why don't you level with me and tell me what really happened?"

Alex liked the detective's gruff style. He was burly and he needed a shave. Even though Detective Evans was black, he reminded Alex of his grandfather.

Alex thought it over for a few seconds before arriving at a decision. "I'm a pretty good judge of character, too, and I think I can trust you. But first put your notebook away." Alex waited as the detective closed the pad and stuck it in his jacket pocket.

"The truth is this: The two men in the Porsche were intelligence agents of some kind, maybe CIA. They were working for somebody named Hollis, an Army colonel, who was working on his own—and purely for himself—to build a kind of nuclear weapon. I found out about it, and Hollis thought I was a danger to him, so he tried to have me killed.

"Lisa is a friend who happened to get caught in the middle. The two men followed me here, and the car chase was just as I told you before. If you examine the Porsche wreckage, you should find the gun they shot Lisa with, unless their people got to it before yours did. I imagine if you check with whoever the two men worked for, you'll get some interesting responses.

"I understand that Hollis was killed last night, trying to steal some papers from the lab at Los Alamos, New Mexico. You can check that out, too, if you don't believe me."

It was the detective's turn to mull the situation over. He scratched the stubble of his beard while he thought.

"Son," he said, "when you've worked in D. C. as long as I have, nothing surprises you anymore and you can believe almost anything. I'll check out what you've told me, and I'll be back to talk to Miss Martin."

The detective got up and offered his hand to Alex. "But if what you say is true, and I believe it is, you probably won't hear from me again.

"By the way," he added, "you'll have to file a report on the damage to your car—it was a rental, wasn't it?"

"Yes, Hertz."

"Well, I can help with that, but not until our lab guys look it over. Just call my office when you want to make your report." He handed Alex his card.

Alex thanked the detective and left for Lisa's room. He waited impatiently for the elevator to come and take him back to the fifth floor before he gave up and climbed the stairs. From the second to the fifth floor was more than three stories, because between each two floors was another floor of interstitial space, an area for plumbing and wiring and elaborate patient-care systems like robotic food carts.

Alex reached the fifth floor winded by the higher-than-expected climb, but still he sprinted the rest of the hallway to room 522. The lieutenant was just coming out, and Alex nearly bowled her over.

"Excuse me," he said, "I'm sorry."

"That's O.K.," she said. "Miss Martin's awake now, and the first thing she asked was where you were. You are Alex, aren't you?"

"Yes, I am. Can I see her?"

"Sure, but don't stay too long."

"Thanks, I won't."

Alex walked into the room and was met with bright sunlight pouring through venetian blinds. He walked over to the window and turned the plastic wand closing the blinds part way. Lisa painfully twisted her head toward him when she heard the blinds rattle.

"Hi," she said, smiling as best she could.

"Hi," he said, fetching a chair.

"I was worried about you. What happened?"

Alex pulled the chair over to the bed and sat down next to Lisa, taking her right hand in both of his. "Well, for one thing, you got shot. Did you know that?"

"Yes, the nurse told me."

"How do you feel?"

"Groggy. And sore—all over."

"Do you want me to get the nurse? Maybe they can give you something."

"No, she already did. I'll probably fall asleep in a minute. Can you stay for a while?"

"I'm not going anywhere until you're better, then we're going to leave together—that is, if you still want me."

"I still want you. Now tell me what happened. All I can remember is that two men in a black car were chasing us."

"Well, to make a long story short, after they shot you, we played a game of chicken. They lost. Their car overturned and they were killed. Then I brought you here."

"What are you going to do now? Hollis will try again. Have you talked to the police—or to Frank?"

"It's over, Lisa. Hollis is dead. He died somehow trying to escape from Los Alamos. Frank told me when I saw him this morning. But—" and Alex stopped to think about what he should tell Lisa.

"What?"

"Frank told me about Hollis this morning, but last night, while you were in surgery, Loyola told me. In a dream. She also told me you would be O.K. Then the doctor woke me up and said the same thing."

"You don't really think it was Loyola?"

"Yes, I do."

"Doesn't it make more sense that you were dreaming about her—because you miss her?"

"Then how would I have known about Hollis?"

"Maybe you have ESP you're not aware of. The dream would be a convenient way for your subconscious to surface what it knows."

"No, it was her. It wasn't just a dream. It was so real, yet so surreal. I can't explain it. But so far, everything she told me has come true."

"What else did she tell you?"

"She said not to worry about the G-matter, that it was, as she put it, 'buried forever.' She also said the G-matter files had been destroyed with Hollis.

"Then she told me Sandy was dead, but not to feel sad for him. And here's the clincher. The doctor in the emergency room last night, Dr. Emerick—he knows Sandy. Loyola passed me a message from Sandy to relay to Dr. Emerick, I guess as a way to confirm that it wasn't just a dream. You should have seen the effect it had on him. It was Loyola, all right."

"That's really weird."

"And this morning I destroyed the diary. I wasn't sure if it was the right thing to do, but I did it anyway, like I was being guided. I have the strangest feeling I was…I was part of something larger, some grand orchestration, though my part wasn't very big. I only did what I had to do—no, what I was supposed to do."

Alex stood up. "I just can't believe the last couple of weeks," he said while pacing and gesturing with his arms, "getting mixed up in something that involves the whole world. And what did I have at stake? Maybe my life, but that's nothing, nothing compared to somebody who's lost this life and the eternal one as well. And what about the millions of people who believe unwaveringly in God—a God who grants eternal life. Look what was at stake for them. And what about God Himself?"

"Herself."

"Herself. What I'm trying to say—maybe trying to understand myself—is that this wasn't my problem. It was God's problem, humanity's problem, and somehow it seems to have been fixed.

"At least it appears it has. As long as you don't think too hard about it. I mean, for God to be God, He—or She—can't have a flaw. But then God is found to have a flaw, so what happens? It gets fixed like it was never there. It's a paradox, but the way it stands right now—if I don't think about it too hard—God can still be alive and well."

"You know, Alex, I may not understand it either, but I think I'm beginning to believe it. When I'm not so drugged, I want you to tell me everything again. Then I want you to take me to Los Alamos and show me your Deer Trap Mesa and your Black Mesa."

"We'll go as soon as you're well. Then we'll talk about your moving to Blacksburg and Virginia Tech."

"You mean your moving to Columbus and Ohio State."

He laughed. "Somehow I know we'll work it out."

"I know that, too, but right now I'm going to fall asleep, before I commit to something I shouldn't while I'm…while I'm drugged."

Lisa had begun to slur her speech. The medications were taking hold, and she looked very drowsy. She closed her eyes, and a minute later Alex thought she was asleep.

"Alex?"

"I'm still here."

"The dream with Loyola. She could visit you again. Should I be jealous of her?"

"I don't think so. It's over now."

"Well," Lisa said, her eyes still closed, "I won't be jealous. I think she must have been quite a person. And I think Loyola is such a pretty name, don't you?"

"Yes, well, um," and Alex coughed uncomfortably but said nothing else, and Lisa fell asleep.

<br>

THE END